WHIPSAWED!

Five thousand dollars on the table and silence in the crowded saloon. Wild Bill Hickok edged the pasteboard toward him and looked at it: the Queen of Diamonds. The death-card that completed his flush. But the angry man across the table was having none of it.

Suddenly Hickok dove to his right, grabbing his sliphammered Navy Colt from the cross-draw holster. As he hit the floor, his opponent blew two holes through the table and the back of Hickok's empty chair. As Hickok rolled across the floor, hot lead crashed all around him. He paused long enough to pump two rounds into his enemy's chest.

Calamity Jane stepped into the vicious crossfire and fanned five slugs into two gunhands near Hickok, evening the odds some.

Wild Bill finished the job with a single bullet, sending a fourth man to his reward. Then he stood, amid the smoke and gore, and thanked Calamity Jane.

The woman smiled. "You know I'd do anything for you, Bill."

HELLBREAK COUNTRY

JACKSON CAIN

WARNER BOOKS

A Warner Communications Company

This novel is a work of fiction. Names, characters, dialogue, places, and incidents are either the product of the author's imagination or, if real, are used fictitiously.

WARNER BOOKS EDITION

Warner Books, Inc.,
666 Fifth Avenue,
New York, N.Y. 10103

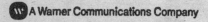 A Warner Communications Company

Printed in the United States of America

First Warner Books Printing: January, 1984

10 9 8 7 6 5 4 3 2 1

For Herb Alexander
You can ride the river with him

"[They were victims] too as we are, but victims of a different circumstance, simpler and therefore, integer for integer, larger, more heroic and the figures therefore more heroic too, not dwarfed and involved but distinct, uncomplex. . . ."

—*William Faulkner,* ABSALOM, ABSALOM!

"Me? 'Fore I met Bill, you know what I was? Just another round-heeled, hard-drinking, shanty-Irish whore, hustlin' drinks and tricks. Mostly the tricks. Leastways, then you just got to lie around on your back and your feet didn't hurt so much. That's how I started. And sure as buzzards eat carrion, that's the way I'll end up, less'n them 'Paches don't stake me out on an anthill, wrap me up in a wet, shrinkin' rawhide, leave me facedown and hairless on a bed of prickly pear. But I'll tell you one thing: for a while I'm gonna be somebody. I'm gonna be Calamity Jane Cannary, the outlaw lady. I'll sling a gun, fight them heathen savages, ride with Bill Hickok, take on Jesse James. I ain't got no pipe dreams and I ain't bound for glory. I know who I am, and what I am. I'll probably die drunk, fuckin' two-bit cowhands in some upstairs crib. Just the way I began. But for a while I'll be somebody."

—*Martha "Calamity Jane" Cannary*

"I'm forty. I spent twenty of them years, half my life, fightin' other men's wars, for other men's reasons, for other men's gain. Rate I'm goin', I'm dyin' broke and blind in a pauper's grave. Time I tried livin' a little. So this time it's gonna be for me. For myself."

—*James Butler "Wild Bill" Hickok*

The frontier is gone.
The moon is a dead rock.
Who will steal golden apples for glory?

—adapted from FALSE STARTS *by Malcolm Braly*

"I can understand how a man might wanna jump the fence. All of us figured to try it straight one time or another. I felt that way a lot of years. You think all you gotta do is straighten your hand and the deal'll turn up square. A lot of hurt and scars and heartbreak cured me of that kinda thinkin'."

—Frank James

"You know, back East they call this country the Heartland?"

—Belle Starr

PART ONE

1

First came Reynolds, a tall man on a deep-chested bay. The gelding was drenched with lather along the neck, flanks and saddle's edge. Judge Parker's posse was closing in. Reynolds did not know if the bay could make it over the rimrock and up to the ridge.

His face felt drawn and haggard. The force of the wind streaked his weathered skin with harsh white lines of alkali dust, reddening his eyes. His tan wool Stetson had blown down the back of his neck, the hat's cord taut across his throat, tearing at his windpipe.

Lonesome Charley Reynolds. He had come to the Nations as Custer's chief scout and he was leaving on the run, a wanted man. The posse's shots cracked and whined and he kicked the bay again. He lowered his head along the gelding's neck and felt his coarse black hair flatten with the wind.

Behind him, rifle and pistol shots were silenced by the sudden, heavy boom of a .50-caliber Sharps. He jerked his head over his shoulder just in time to see the big minié ball catch Sutter between the shoulder blades and exit through his chest. Lifted a full foot out of the saddle, Sutter piled clear of his horse—clear, that is, until his three-inch Texas rowels caught under the cinch, dragging Sutter facedown in the dust.

Another one down, Reynolds thought, all thanks to that kid Custer had saddled them with. A real winner. Sutter's gut-hooks gouging his horse's side, a hole in his back and chest big enough to kill him. That's the jackpot, Reynolds thought as he kicked his bay up the basin's incline.

2

He was at the top of the rimrock, his stirrup hooked over the saddlehorn, when Wilson pulled up. His roan was blowing long, rolling snorts and shaking his head, shying bites at Wilson's shoulder as he swung down out of the saddle. Ignoring the heaving mount, like Reynolds, he threw a stirrup up over the horn and began to loosen the cinch.

Then the kid rode up.

His pony was pure death. Two days before, Reynolds had caught him sharpening his big Mexican Chihuahua rowels. Now he had kicked the pinto bloody. The gut and shoulders were oozing gore.

Reynolds looked up from the spurs to the kid's shredded pantlegs. Two weeks back, when they were with Custer at Fort Lincoln, he'd told him to get some chaps, shotguns or a good pair of bullhide batwings.

"Like hell. *I* ain't no drover." Now those Union Army trousers were torn and ripped from the hard mesquite and coarse chaparral.

Reynolds glanced at the rest of the outfit. Government-issue blouse, a dirty blue cavalry cap, broad suspenders. He was sitting slumped in a McClellan saddle. Why don't you carry a bugle? Reynolds thought sourly. The captain's orderly. Reynolds fought the impulse to shoot him on the spot.

"Hey, why you two loosening them cinches?"

"Always loosen 'em before you swim 'em."

Reynolds's voice was a monotone.

The kid stood in his stirrups and stared out over the bluff. Forty feet below, a white-water cataract thundered around a bend and through the breaks of the Arkansas River. On the other bank, a half-mile down, lay the state of Kansas.

"Horse can't ford with his belly cinched tight. Can't blow the water back out his nose. He'll drown. You'll die here too, if'n you ain't got no horse."

"But—but—" the kid stammered with mounting panic.

"No sweat," Wilson went on. "Here, let me help you." He pulled the kid's boot loose from the stirrup and slipped his Henry rifle out of its saddle sheath. Reynolds was quietly removing the other boot and un-notching the cinch buckle.

"Take a long rein," said Wilson, "then stay clear of the kack. That's about it."

"Sure," Reynolds said. "You may not mind busting your balls, but we'd hate to see you break that pinto's back."

"I can't swim."

"Then I'll see you in hell, you egg-sucking sonofabitch!" Wilson yelled.

Dropping to one knee, Wilson gripped the Henry by the barrel and swung the rifle as hard as he knew how, shattering the stock in two against the pinto's rump. The pony whinnied, bucked, then tumbled over the bluff into the icy river, forty feet below. The kid was falling too, losing the reins, flailing his arms, turning head over heels, finally banging his head on the saddle fork when he hit the water.

"He brought it on himself," Wilson said tonelessly.

"And on us."

"And on Sutter."

Wilson vaulted onto his loosened saddle. Reynolds walked over to him, relieving him of the busted Henry. They were both wearing the same outfit: collarless brown shirts, faded

Levi's, frayed chaps, dirty Stetsons covered with alkali and grit.

"Wilson, we done fucked up," said Reynolds.

"Amen to that."

Again the gunfire cracked, now less than a quarter-mile away. "No," Reynolds said, nodding to the posse behind them. "Judge Parker's the man today. And his posse riding our ass. They get to say the last word."

"I be your witness there."

Wilson pulled his boots free from the bell-shaped stirrups, kicked his rowels into the roan's flanks, and with a yell, he and the horse were over the brink, rider swinging free from the saddle and clutching pommel and rein, hitting the water feet-first alongside his mount.

Reynolds's bay was now on his hocks, spinning away, but Charley kept hold of the reins with one hand, the Henry in the other. The bay was kicking, biting at him. "Fuck you, horse!" Reynolds shouted. One-handed, he spun the Henry by the lever, jacking a .44 shell into the chamber. He ducked a hoof and pulled at the reins. Wrenching at the bridle, he yanked hard on it, tearing the bit deep. He pulled the horse's head flush against his left shoulder and grabbed the pommel with the rein hand. He swung high onto his back. Still wrenching the head sideways, he yanked the bit up into the roof of his mouth, driving the horse back on his hocks, his head now flat against his leg. Then, with one motion, he kicked his rowels into the pony's sides, whipped the rifle muzzle down across the rump, simultaneously triggering a round. Then he let go the head.

Suddenly the bay was lurching, heaving, bucking. Reynolds dropped the rifle, grabbed the reins and pommel with both hands, and fought to stay aboard.

Reynolds yelled, "Jump, you sonofabitch, jump!"

In panic, the bay arched his back, put his head between his legs, bucked, and when he came down, landed on all four legs simultaneously, almost jolting Reynolds out of the kack. The hardwood stirrups were slapping up against Reynolds's face, and he was bouncing off the cantle and then off the horse's ass. Then the bay left the ground again, and Reynolds went off like a rocket. All Reynolds knew was that he was free, bracing himself for the crash against the rimrock. Only he just kept falling, both him and the bay, clear of the bluff. At the last second he remembered to drop away from the horse, not that it helped him much. Belly-flopping from forty feet up knocked him senseless.

But he made it. Puking up water, his first conscious thought was to grab the bay's tail. Floundering and thrashing, he was dragged downriver with the current.

He passed the kid, floating like deadwood, belly-down in the rapids, his head skewed at a grotesque angle. Broke his neck in the fall, Reynolds thought. Guess that saved me a bullet, or Judge Parker another hanging.

A half-mile downstream, the bay hit bottom and clambered up the shallow bank, Reynolds still clinging to the tail.

3

Now there were two of them, riding up a dry creekbed thirty miles due north of the Nations. Judge Parker's marshals hadn't followed. He and Wilson were beyond their jurisdiction. Two of the four men they had been chasing were dead, and Wilson—now shot to pieces—was close to making it three.

Wilson looked done for. The Sharps had gotten him too as he crossed the river. A Sharps would carry 1,600 yards, and that sonofabitch firing it had been good. Just as Wilson was pulling up over the bank, a slug had hit him in the side, taking out four ribs and half a lung. Wilson had pitched forward and nearly lost his seat. But Reynolds was up on the embankment by then, caught him, and forced him back into the saddle. Then, grabbing his reins, Reynolds led Wilson's roan at a high, hard lope, Wilson hanging onto his pommel with one arm. Snorting and heaving, their mounts had covered another four hundred yards in under a minute—the time it took the man with the big, breech-loading Sharps to reload and fire. By then they were out of range.

Later, when they were far beyond the river and Reynolds was sure they weren't being followed, he swung off the bay and looked to Wilson. He winced.

He lashed a leather reata around Wilson's hips, then tied it to both cantle and saddlehorn. He cross-tied his wrists and lashed them to the pommel. He slapped Wilson's face twice, trying to bring him to. But the man only groaned, still unconscious. He took the cinch up two more notches. The roan wouldn't like it, but Wilson and his Texas saddle would stay on.

Then he looked at the wound. A big hole in Wilson's side was filling his boots with blood and leaving a trail every foot of the miles they had put between them and the breaks.

Reynolds gazed hopelessly at his friend. Finally he took the red bandanna off his neck, poured some water on it from his saddle canteen, and pushed it into the hole like a plug. He lashed it tight around Wilson's chest with a length of lass rope, as tight as he could pull it, and hoped he could stop the bleeding.

If that posse found a ford, they could still be on their trail.

Reynolds remounted. He took Wilson's reins and led him off up the dry creekbed. The only things keeping Wilson in that saddle and holding in his guts were a handkerchief and rope.

4

By late afternoon the heat was stifling. The sun hung white-hot in the sky. Somehow his friend was still alive, slumped over the pommel, hands lashed crosswise to the saddlehorn, his head low on the roan's neck. Reynolds was amazed at the trail Wilson left behind him. Blood still dripped from his side, down the length of his Levi's. Reynolds never knew a man could bleed so long and live.

Vultures and hawks wheeled above them. A score of turkey buzzards floated overhead on widespread wings.

The hawks were less patient. One swooped directly in front of them. Reynolds watched as it dropped over the crest of a small hill just west of the creekbed, and then reappeared seconds later, clutching a dangling snake in its talons. It winged screaming out of sight.

A second hawk glided effortlessly above them, describing wide circles with its spread wings. Reynolds watched as it hung for the moment vivid against the blue, lucid sky. The hawk spiraled slowly upward, pierced the desert quiet with its shriek, dipped, and plunged at some unseen target beyond the rise.

Then the vultures soared overhead alone. The south Kansas land they fed off seemed poor to Reynolds—bleak and barren as an old bone. In this bitter country of dried-up brush, Wilson's remains would be a bonanza, Reynolds thought wearily. It was obvious his friend would die. He doubted he could bury him deep enough to keep the vultures off. And even if he could, even if he covered his friend with a high rock cairn, what would be the point? Instead of buzzards, maggots would feed on Wilson's remains.

They were plodding up a slope when it happened. Wilson's roan floundered on the loose black shale. The animal was sore and beat and couldn't keep his footing. He went down, and Wilson, who was strapped to the horn and cantle, was bear-caught. His mount rolled twice over Wilson, grinding the wound in the broken shale, finally landing on his thigh, breaking both his legs and most of his ribs. Reynolds watched the fall with a sideways glance, almost feeling relief.

He swung down beside his friend. His knees were wobbly. He was close to heatstroke himself. He braced himself on his own horn and cantle. When he got his legs back, he took the bay's reins and walked on down the creekbed away from Wilson. Out in the brush, he tied the horse to a mesquite bush. And since Wilson wouldn't see him, he also tied his extra bandanna over the bay's eyes.

He stumbled up to the fallen roan and the pinned rider. He bent over the animal and cut the latigo, freeing the saddle. Then he grabbed the reins, twisted his head sideways, flush against his flank. He wrenched the bit deep. The horse whinnied, kicked, and dug until he finally got a purchase on the loose sand, and then limped back up on his hocks.

Reynolds could see that the right rear leg was broken in two places, above the hock and below the pastern. The bone was splintered and bleeding.

The saddle blanket still clung to his back. Reynolds pulled it off and spread it over Wilson. His friend was barely breathing.

He led the roan a hundred feet down the creekbed. He would have taken him further but the horse was foundering now, shying at the smell of his own blood.

Reynolds's .44-40 Colt was holstered against his left hip, the butt turned out. He reached across his body with his right hand and eased it out. He'd thought of using his Winchester, but they both took the same cartridges. And when the horse was spooky, you had to get in close. Anyway, Colonel Colt advertised the .44-40 as a horse pistol.

He pulled the hammer back to full cock. The horse whinnied. He patted his neck softly, gentling him, placed the muzzle directly behind his right ear, and squeezed the trigger. The roar was deafening, and as the heavy Colt revolver jumped in his hand, the big, deep-chested mount dropped to his knees, coughed up blood, pitched forward, and died.

Reynolds replaced the spent cartridge automatically. He shoved the Colt deep in his holster and returned to Wilson.

The man was conscious now, the wet horse blanket pulled up to his jaw. His grin was tight.

Reynolds knelt beside him. "I'm gonna splint them legs, dress that wound, and put you on the bay. You're gonna ride now, so tighten up. We been in worse fixes than this. Damn, I never thought we'd make it out of that alkali flat."

"Sutter sure didn't. Neither did the kid."

"Our tobacco didn't, neither." Reynolds shrugged. "I'd roll you a smoke otherwise."

"Any grub? Some grub might do good if'n I weren't coughin' blood. Damn ribs is stove. Maybe we ought to risk a fire, cook up some coffee and a slab of bacon. Finish off them beans. You could eat somethin'. We ain't cooked in two days."

Reynolds averted his eyes and took a deep breath. A dust devil danced crazily and the mesquite looked gray-green in the early dusk. The tough branches were twisted and thorny. Some coarse clumps of grass were twisting up through the hardpan, only to be bent by the moaning wind. The mountains were vaguely visible in the west where the blood-red sun was beginning to sink, streaking the sky with brilliant shafts of light, yellow, orange, and blue. Otherwise, nothing. No houses, no rising smoke in all that sprawling emptiness.

"Lost the grub too," Reynolds finally said. He rubbed his gut uneasily.

Wilson smiled, half-grin, half-grimace. Reynolds handed his friend his canteen. Wilson only managed a sip, then coughed. Red foam frothed over his lips and dripped down his chin.

"I'll never make it," he rasped.

"You was born to be hung," Reynolds argued. "We'll just splint them legs, dress that wound some more, and you can mount up."

Wilson shook his head. "Reynolds. Just gimme your gun. I lost mine coming out of the breaks."

"Come on, Wilson. I said you'd get the horse."

"I won't make it. I hurt. I hurt bad."

"Hurt, hell. You can make it."

"I said gimme your gun. Just give it to me."

Reynolds turned his head.

"Reynolds, how the fuck do I look to you?"

Charley Reynolds let out a long sigh. "Like you was sent for and never came."

"And I'm purely wore out." He extended his open hand. "Gimme it."

Reynolds eased the pistol out of his holster. He pulled the

hammer back to full cock. Pointing the barrel away from both of them, he placed the butt in his friend's hand. He stood and walked on down the creekbed.

Afterward he returned, pried the stiff fingers off the butt, and took the muzzle out of Wilson's clenched teeth. He spread the blanket over the entire body and weighted the death shroud with the Texas saddle and some rocks. The vultures would tear it loose in seconds. Two dozen black-feathered, snake-necked carrion eaters had already half gutted the roan. Some had already had their fill and were flapping their wings, lifting a few feet from the ground, struggling to take off, but then falling back to earth, too gorged to fly. Another score were circling above his friend as well as the horse's carcass.

He threw more rocks on the blanket. It was the thought that counted.

Then he took off his battered Stetson. This wasn't his line of work, but there had to be words.

"I don't know how to put it. Wilson here was born to blood and trouble. But he stood by his friends and never backed down. You knew what he was, what his word was worth, the things that count." Reynolds glanced at the bloody breaks, and the last words rasped in his throat. "You could ride the river with him."

He put his hat back on and walked over to the bay. He took off the blindfold, swung into the saddle, and headed up the creekbed without looking back.

PART TWO

5

The Seventh Cavalry's commanding officer sat in his longjohns on the edge of his cot. He was in his white bivouac tent, contemplating his uniform. It was freshly laundered and laid out, along with his boots, on a folding camp stool. The lieutenant colonel—still known to the men by his wartime rank of brevet general—smiled at the custom-made black velveteen outfit of his own design. The padded epaulets with stars in each corner accented the breadth of his unusually wide shoulders.

The black wool campaign hat with its rawhide-edged brim was pinned up rakishly with a small U.S. coat-of-arms. This was done on the side where he swung his saber. On the opposite side an eighteen-inch ostrich plume, and under the crown hung the yellow-gold chin strap, festooned at the ends with two-inch tassels. He put on the hat, pulled open the tentflap, and stared out into the awakening camp.

It was dawn in the Black Hills. The cookfires were lit, their smoke curling into the overcast sky. A hundred other men in longjohns were milling sleepily through the long rows of tents. The only uniformed soldiers were those reporting in from night guard. They smoked quietly and circled around the fires, sipping hot black coffee from tin mess cups.

The troop was camped in the Badlands, and the morning sun rose over the eastern range of the pine-timbered Black Hills, blazing red-orange, sending shafts of yellow, red, and violet through the thick purple clouds in the early dawn. To the west lay the Wind River, where the moon shone in the still darkened sky.

Black geldings in the roped-off remuda whinnied and stamped for the wranglers to fork up the hay. The horses whinnied and bucked. Soon the great emptiness of the camp would come alive with the frenzied activities of the Seventh Cavalry and their hundreds of mounts demanding their feed.

But Custer hung back, silent, standing there by the gray canvas tentflap, glancing at his uniform on the folding stool in front of a table on which rested his campaign maps.

He had risen long before dawn, spent a full half hour ministering to his aches and pains. He'd then washed and shaved.

A striking figure with his long, flowing yellow hair, vivid blue eyes, and the heavy sword he'd taken from a dead Confederate major at the Wilderness, he appeared to be just what he was—a raw frontier specimen of cavalry manhood.

Well, he brooded, staring inside his tent at the young Indian girl slumbering on his cot, at least she thinks so. Too bad my superiors don't share that exalted opinion.

Custer looked down at his boots. Black calfskin. Their bright brass spurs with the razor-sharp rowels gleamed like mirrors. Everything seemed so right, here in the Black Hills.

He wondered where it had all gone wrong.

A general at twenty-three, the protégé of Sheridan and Sherman, his future had seemed assured. Upon his promotion to brevet general, had not Sheridan named him "the finest cavalry officer ever to serve the Union"? Had he not personally received Lee's flag of truce at Appomattox? Had not

Sheridan's wife given him the desk on which Lee had signed the papers agreeing to his unconditional surrender? And after his spectacular record of Civil War triumphs, leading charge after charge into the very jaws of Confederate hell at the Wilderness, Antietam, Cold Harbor, Gettysburg, after personally turning Lee's flank at Appomattox, after the glorious victory at the Washita over four hundred redskinned devils (later so cruelly mocked by his Washington enemies as "a needless massacre of women, children, and old people") the army let him languish for ten long years in an outpost in the dreary Dakotas, Fort Abraham Lincoln.

The implications of such neglect were too hellish to think about, but today he permitted himself the indulgence of self-pity. How could it be, he thought, shaking his head, that such a man as he—George Armstrong Custer—could wither on the vine of army ineptitude? Why? When he took his case to Washington, to Congress itself, and denounced that whiskey-drinking, bar-pounding, cigar-chewing pantaloon of a President, he was sure they'd understand. Sherman and Sheridan at least. They'd always understood. They were of a breed, all sharing the same sense of honor, love of country, pride of self. They were all men of the same stripe, all cut from the same cloth. They'd always understood his dreams. But now even Sherman and Sheridan had turned their backs on him. They'd told him in private, that night in Washington, how grievously he'd blundered.

"You attacked Grant." Sherman ground his teeth. "Before Congress, the country, the army. George, he was your supreme commander in the Rebellion. He is now your commander-in-chief. Christ, man, if he ordered a drumhead court-martial and sentenced you to be shot for treason, I could only comply. You're in a war out west with the Sioux, the Cheyenne Dog Soldiers, the Crow. To rebuke your commander in public is the grossest insubordination imaginable. When he asks for your head—and make no mistake, he will—we can only give it to him."

Give Grant my head, he thought. Not likely. Not if I get a break or two. Not if I can still pull my chestnuts out of the fire.

When Wilson, Sutter, Reynolds, and that whey-faced whelp of a kid return from the Nations, he'd see whose head got served on a plate.

6

Custer returned inside his tent and sat down on the edge of his cot. Still he contemplated his uniform: the rich texture of the wool trousers, the shine on the boots, the gleam of the brass spurs. He was eager for maneuvers and, with luck, action against the Sioux.

It was not his intention to get laid again.

For one thing, he was bone-tired. He had marched his men for thirty out of the last thirty-six hours, and contrary to popular report, Custer too needed rest.

And during the last six hours of bivouac, Yellow Flower—cousin to his translator, Monaseetah—had given him little of that.

Ever since they had bivouacked six short hours ago, she had been at him, leaching and sapping his vital energies, draining him of that inner strength he could now so ill afford to lose.

She was up again. Custer sat exhausted on his cot and watched her. She was feeding kindling into the camp stove, and he could feel rising warmth from the potbellied stove emanate through the tent.

Custer groaned.

This was her standard preamble to a morning session in bed.

He leaned his tired body back onto his cot and glared at her with a bloodshot eye. He watched as Yellow Flower scooped the Arbuckle's into the soot-blackened coffeepot, filled it with water, and set it on the stove. As she dropped chunks of bacon into the cast-iron skillet and he smelled the hickory-smoked richness of the popping, crackling fat, now mixed with the aromatic odor of the Arbuckle's, he hoped she was only cooking breakfast and prayed he was not in for it again.

This was not to be.

Custer groaned again, and as he did, his chin dropped. He fixed his eyes on the young Indian girl, on her long, blue-black hair tumbling down to her waist, and on her short linen dress, the one with the gingerbread trim he'd given her on what he had thought of as her sixteenth birthday, and which he'd discovered, to his pleasure and dismay on this long, brutal march, that she'd utterly outgrown.

Her birthday . . . Neither Custer nor Yellow Flower had the remotest idea as to when or where her actual birthday had occurred. Indians kept no calendar, and Custer had not been around at her birth. George Armstrong Custer, lieutenant colonel and sometimes brevet general in the U.S. Army's Seventh Cavalry, had found her nearly a decade ago on Thanksgiving Eve, in 1868, along the steep, icy banks of the Washita River, one bloodstained night in the Nations.

The Washita . . . For Washington and for the press, that battle was the pinnacle of Custer's ten-year war against the Indian, "a grand and glorious triumph over the Red Fiend" as a Denver paper had phrased it. But as Custer watched the newly matured body of his cook swelling the all-but-bursting confines of her thin linen frock, his thoughts were somewhat different: a bitterly subzero night of ice and snow and the stench of death, unarmed Indians shot by the hundreds at point-blank range, smoke from the guns and burning lodges so blindingly dense in the air that the eyes teared over and the throat scorched, women screaming and babies bawling as, over and over, the guns roared and the people died.

It had sickened even Custer, the carnage and the slaughter. To the point that toward the end, when he intercepted a small girl in a buffalo robe stumbling toward the river in knee-deep powdered snow, he had not shot her. Instead he had kicked his mount after her, run her down into a drift near the river's bank, and dismounted. After putting a cocked Remington .44 to her forehead, he had then unfolded her fur robe.

What he saw was a weaponless, naked child who was

staring at him coolly, her eyes neither cowed nor dismayed. A small girl of perhaps ten years, who was not awed by the great white general with his long yellow locks and bloody hands. Custer uncocked the .44 Remington and holstered it. He had had enough of this "grand and glorious triumph over the Red Fiend." Custer was many things, but contrary to much rumor and even greater false report, he was not made of stone. He lifted her up in front of him on his gelding and remounted. He ordered his bugler to sound recall, and back into the icy waters of the saddle-deep Washita, he and his men and the girl withdrew to the refrain of "Garry Owen."

Now, ten years later, he was staring at the fruits of his philanthropy. A young girl, bent over a cookstove in his field tent, her shadow flickering on the white canvas wall. And what he saw no longer bore any relation to breakfast or bivouac or Washington or the army. What he saw was a thing apart, a girl unconnected to the drabness of his surroundings. He saw a long coil of blue-black hair rolling down across the back of the thin, swelling dress. And as she bent over the cookstove, the hem of the dress was hiked all the way to her bottom, the twin globes of her behind clearly outlined through the thin cloth. Custer felt his throat tighten, his desire blaze like fire in his groin. He tried to recall some fleeting self-admonition about never squandering vital energies while on reconnaissance, but then his eyes glazed and he remembered nothing more. For at that moment she turned, the dress now low and tight against the rise and fall of her young breasts. Her wide black eyes gazed on him, eyes unreadable in their absence of expression. Her neck and the swell of her breasts were tinted red from the heat of the stove, and the rise of the longjohns above his groin was visible to all, including the girl.

Without speaking, she turned to tie the tentflap shut, and when she bent to tie the bottom thong, the dress hiked high above the thighs, the thin linen tight against her strong, firm rump.

His eyes blurred and his mind grew confused. With trembling hands, he reached to his side table for his sack of Bull

Durham. His hands fumbled the papers and pouch, and tobacco spilled on the cot's sheet.

Custer looked up and now she was standing close to him. She sat down beside him on the cot and picked up the tobacco sack and the scattered papers. She deftly rolled the quirly, twisted the ends, and putting it in her mouth, she scratched a lucifer with her thumbnail. Her mouth, illumined by the sudden flare, inhaled the smoke, and leaning toward him, she placed the quirly between his parted lips. She was close now. Her small brown hand touched the bulging underclothes, and Custer's body sagged as his breath rushed out of him in one hot groan.

She stared at him searchingly. Her eyes were now two bottomless pools, as deep as wells, as black as onyx. She said softly, her voice tremulous, eyes blinking, "Do you . . . ?"

All Custer could do was nod, speechless with his desire. Custer, the fearless Indian fighter, indomitable in battle, merciless in victory, was about to suffer conquest by his young Indian "cook," age indeterminate.

She raised her hands behind her neck and back, and released the string ties on the back of her dress. The linen frock fell from her small brown shoulders, hanging momentarily from the points of her high, upturned breasts. Then, lifting the dress with two fingers from between the swell of her breasts, she plucked it off her body and tossed it on the tent floor.

For the fourth time that night, Custer thought he would faint.

For a time he sat there speechless. Now she was pulling his longjohns off, down along the length of his thighs. Once he tried to swallow, but found he had no saliva. When he couldn't move, Yellow Flower leaned closer to him and took the quirly from between his lips. His eyes watched as she took a drag.

"Little Indian girls aren't supposed to smoke cigarettes," Custer said hoarsely.

"Little Indian girls aren't supposed to do a lot of things."

She groped the immensity of his tumescent member. Her hand slithered up the flatness of his thigh and abdomen, up over his stomach, tickling his chest hair, then returning to rest on his navel, which she tormented with a little finger.

After six hours of strenuous intercourse, she had long since discarded any pretensions to innocence. Now her eyes glinted wickedly, a small, sly smile crooked the corners of her mouth, and mischievously her gaze met his own.

"There are many things little Indian girls aren't supposed to do," she repeated with a raspy groan as she lowered her head toward his hips. "Would you like me to show you some of them?"

His face flooded with hot blood as he nodded his approval. His pupils rolled upward. Slowly, Yellow Flower was lowering herself along the edge of the cot, sliding down the length of his right leg, slipping under the sheet with him, till her hot body was spread athwart his own.

And as she took the full length of his immense member into her mouth, Custer thought he would die.

7

Breakfast had been served, and they were striking camp when Reynolds finally showed. He was riding a blaze-faced pinto and leading a big bay gelding, lathered to the hocks. Through the half-open tentflap, from his camp stool, Custer watched the exhausted scout and his wind-broke mounts. Reynolds's eyes were angry, hard lines spreading out from the corners, etched with alkali. He looked all horns and rattles.

Well, thought Custer, whatever Reynolds and his men had found in the Nations, it had gone badly. The scout was back alone—without Sutter, Wilson, and the kid. And from the caked dust on him and his mounts, it looked as though he'd seen hell with the hide off.

Custer flung open his tentflap.

Reynolds entered, straddled a folding stool, and accepted a mess cup of coffee from Quepasa.

Custer motioned for the demijohn of whiskey. Quepasa brought it, and he poured a healthy slug into Reynolds's coffee. The scout quickly drank off half of it. He took the demijohn from Custer and refilled the cup. He quietly sipped the scalding brew, his shoulders hunched.

"Was it as bad as it looks?" Custer asked.

Reynolds stared at him. Somewhere between the brim of his battered Stetson and a two-week growth of beard and dust, the red eyes smoldered.

"I can't see how it coulda gone worse."

"Sutter, Wilson, the kid?"

"Dead. All of them. Sutter got his from Parker's deps. The kid sold his saddle in the breaks, Wilson's bedded down back there in the hardpan."

Custer motioned again to Quepasa, and she filled Reynolds's tin cup halfway from the pot of Arbuckle's. He topped it with whiskey.

"And the James brothers? Any word?"

"Yeah, we spotted them and the Youngers both. Right where the kid said they'd be. Down in the Nations in that mountain hideout. 'Course, they seen us too. And gettin' back down the mountains with them on our trail was a sight. We was poundin' leather all the way. If them saddles wasn't double-cinched, we'd've bought it right there."

"You mentioned Parker's deputies?"

"Yeah, that was later. First we had the longriders on our ass a good hundred miles, halfway to the Kansas border. Only time we stopped was to uncinch and let the horses blow, grain and water them, and push on. Then just as we lose them, we pick up six of Parker's deps. The way we looked, they was gonna take us to the judge just on principle."

"You should have gone. I would have vouched for you."

"Yeah, 'cept that kid you saddled us with panicked. Threw down on them deps and killed one. Next thing I knew, we was all pullin' iron. 'Cept them deps wired ahead, and by the time we hit the breaks they had a full-scale posse in pursuit.

Some honcho with a Sharps 'Big Fifty' did for Sutter and Wilson. The kid cashed his chips in the river.''

Custer watched in silence as Reynolds fumbled a sack of Bull Durham out of his shirt pocket and built a smoke. Quepasa brought him an ember from the stove, and Reynolds lit up. He stared at Custer through the smoke, his eyes narrow with suppressed rage. It occurred to Custer that through all the years they had served together, he had never understood Reynolds. The General knew why he himself did these things, fought these wars. He understood money, power, ambition. Those were reasons for desperate deeds. But a man like Reynolds? Why?

"Is there a chance," Custer finally asked, "of getting that James-Younger gang out of the Nations?"

"Not hardly."

Custer leaned forward, his elbows resting on his knees. "Charley, I believe anything you tell me. But if that's true, you know I'm finished. Come next winter, when I'm up for review, Grant will order Sherman to have me cashiered."

"General, pardon my sayin' so, but you gotta bite the bullet on this one."

"I can't."

"Can't, hell. It's time to piss on the fire and call in the dogs. The hunt's over. You wanna take on Frank and Jesse James, them three Youngers, plus all of Parker's deps, you ain't gonna get it done. You just ain't."

"Charley—"

"No way, nohow. 'Cause even if you could ride in there and apprehend them outlaws, you'd still have Judge Parker and his deps to deal with. And if you think them robbers is bad, try Parker's deps. I just did, and look at me."

Custer motioned for Quepasa to refill his cup, but instead Reynolds lifted the demijohn and poured whiskey to the brim.

"Parker's a reasonable man. I'm sure we could work something out."

"How? The Nations is a foreign fuckin' country. Parker ain't lettin' no cavalry regiments in there. Hell, he ain't lettin' three scouts and a boy in there. And when Congress and Grant learn what you're doin', and when Parker convicts you of invadin' that country to kidnap and to kill, it's gonna be *you* he stands up on that gallows with them twelve trapdoors droppin' all at once. It'll be you swingin' on the scaffold with your neck in the noose.'' Reynolds stared intently at Custer, his face grim. ''You read my smoke?''

''Mr. Reynolds,'' said Custer, ''do I detect a failure of nerve?''

Reynolds exploded. ''General, what you *detect* is a man with a price on his head. Leastways in the Nations. They want a man fittin' my description for a capital crime down there, thanks to that last trip you sent me on.''

Custer nodded to his own coffee cup, and after Quepasa filled it, he leaned toward Reynolds and said evenly, ''Isn't there some way to bring them out of the Nations, to make them come to us?''

Reynolds shook his head emphatically. ''We can't. Them longriders are down there for the duration, holed up tighter than a gnat's snatch, than a bull's ass in fly time. You want action, pray them sun-dancin' Injun chiefs, Crazy Horse and Sitting Bull, unite the Sioux, Crow, and Cheyenne Dog Soldiers. They can give you action. All you can handle. The James-Younger boys will just get you dead.''

''Those James-Younger boys will get me permanent rank as a general officer. And don't tell me it's impossible. If we find the right kind of bait, we can do it. We can lure them out of the Nations and spring the trap. It could work.''

Reynolds was beat, done in. ''Okay, General, you win. It could be done. But not by me.''

''With the right man it could be done. A man who specialized in gunplay, infiltration, undercover operations. He could set up, say, a bank job, so lucrative it would be irresistible.''

''If frogs had wings, they wouldn't scrape their asses when they hopped.''

Quepasa cleared her throat. Reynolds and Custer turned to her.

''There is another way. What of the woman, Belle Starr? General, did you not tell me once that this outlaw, Cole

Younger, dragged both his brothers and the Jameses down to the Nations to find her, to marry her a second time?"

Custer nodded. "You mean she could make a man like Cole Younger ride a thousand miles just to win her back? That is worth considering. She must be some woman to have such a hold on a man like Cole Younger."

Reynolds nodded grudgingly. "Cole's a hard one, all right. He's ridden them high lines a good twenty years now. Sacked Lawrence with Frank James and Bill Quantrill, robbed more banks and trains 'n the South's got graves. Must have killed two hundred men. And, yeah, I know Belle. I wouldn't kick her out of my bedroll on a cold winter night. She's got a body that'd make you butt your head against a tree stump, that'd make a muleskinner pray. The face of an angel and a figure like one of them fancy St. Louis whores. I wouldn't mind a woman like that now and again."

"But not to marry?" said Quepasa.

"Naw. Women like Belle, they fuck like angels and kill like snakes. They love the smell of blood. Too many men wind up dyin' over her. Like her last husband. Some say Cole gutted him throat to balls with a bowie knife. All for Belle. Women like her ain't worth it. Not in my book."

Custer's eyes glittered. "Then we have it. First we find the right bank or train, one loaded with booty. Make it look easy."

"And if that don't work?" Reynolds asked.

"Then we kidnap Belle Starr. Cole Younger will follow her into Hades if he thinks she's in trouble. He'd drag those hellhounds, the Jameses and the Youngers too, all the way to the Medicine Line if that's what it took to bring her back."

Custer grinned. "And you said it couldn't be done."

"Just one question, General," Reynolds said. "How you gonna handle all this?"

Custer smiled. "Mr. Reynolds, it happens that there are men in this world who are quite adept at dealing with these sorts of problems. It has been my privilege to have worked with them. One served under me during the Rebellion. As a scout, sniper, sharpshooter, and spy. He's a master at penetrating enemy organizations. In the war he would actually cross their lines in Confederate gray and then gallop back to us with all their plans. Straight across no-man's-land, guns blazing at him from all sides. Ours as well as theirs. The man was a genius. Every time I went into action, I knew where the enemy was and what he was doing. I always had an inside man.''

"Must have had real balls," said Reynolds.

"Sir, he was *all* balls. During my earlier Indian campaigns, I recruited this fellow again. A marvelous scout. Same thing. Every time I joined battle with those redskinned devils, he told me where they were, what they were, how many.''

"You aren't thinking . . . ?"

"I'm sure you've guessed it, Mr. Reynolds. Who else? When Hayes and Abilene mushroomed overnight into uncontrollable cowtowns, when one million longhorns and ten thousand drunken cowhands descended on those towns, who kept the peace singlehanded?''

"Yeah, I know. Only how you gonna get him?"

"A few years back, when he shot the Abilene marshal, I helped him out of that scrape. It was murder. At least that was what the townspeople claimed. And he might well have hanged for it. Except he had a friend, a very powerful friend, a friend who had influence—with governors, senators, generals, even presidents. A friend who could intercede on his behalf and save him from the gallows.''

"You mean you were the one who saved Hickok from that hangin'?''

"Yes, in those days I was somewhat more influential than I seem to be at present. I interceded with the President and the governor. And the town fathers.''

"You mean James Butler Hickok owes you his goddamn life?''

Custer smiled. "His life—and more."

"And you think he can handle this James-Younger thing?"

"I never saw anything Wild Bill Hickok couldn't handle."

"But I heard he'd quit. Now it's just hard liquor and fast horses. And Calamity Jane. He's back in Deadwood. Makes his living dealing faro and playing poker. Five-card stud is his specialty."

"Is it true he is afraid of nothing?" asked Quepasa.

"Just about," Reynolds said. "Has a quirk about the queen of diamonds. Seems like someone dies every time he draws her. Claims the card has the mark of death on it."

"He would risk his life on such a venture?" asked Quepasa.

Custer said flatly, "Reynolds, just bring him to my headquarters in Fort Lincoln."

"I don't know, General," said Reynolds. "Last time I saw him, he'd stopped hiring out them two Navy Colts. Says he's hanging up his guns. Thinks maybe he's in love."

"Then tell him I've just ordered him out-of-love. Tell him to get that woman's face out of his lap. Tell him I have one war left for him to fight. Get to Deadwood and tell him that."

"I don't think he'll go for it."

"Tell him he owes me."

PART THREE

8

A tall, handsome woman in a gray Stetson, long black hair, and a deep tan leaned back against the bar. She lifted a boot heel, hooking it on the brass footrail. She slipped the gray Stetson to the back of her neck and let it hang there. It would be a long night.

At least she was ready for it. She was dressed in practical clothes: a gingham shirt, weathered Levi's, and well-worn riding boots. And she was heeled. Strapped to her left hip was a Colt .45, nickel-plated, with carved ebony grips. The butt was turned out. The cartridge belt gleamed with brass bullets, and since the holster was a cross-draw, she automatically kept the opposite hand free, thumb hooked in her belt.

Her left hand held a large shotglass of Double Stamp bourbon.

The woman surveyed the bar's interior. She felt edgy. Calamity Jane Cannary had drunk in hundreds of saloons inferior to the Bear's Pizzle. At least the Pizzle had a real bar of polished teak, not pine planks nailed to whiskey kegs. The liquor was actually grain spirits, not pilgrim or Indian whiskey concocted from alcohol, tobacco juice, gunpowder, red pepper, kerosene, coffin varnish, and very often buffalo chips.

She liked the Bear's Pizzle well enough. She liked its fourteen-foot-high ceilings and big cut-glass chandeliers. She liked the two dozen gambling tables and roulette wheels lining the walls. She liked the feel of the green baize, the slap of the pasteboards, the patter of the dealers—"ante's five," "dealer calls," "three little gents," "jack to the queen" —the whirring, racheting wheels, and the rattle of the dice. She liked the smells of beer and perfume and whiskey and, being an occasional cigar smoker herself, even the stogies.

The Bear's Pizzle was Calamity's kind of place. She liked the action—the miners, cowpunchers, and buff hunters at the tables or bellied up to the bar, the endless variety of "soiled doves" waving, squealing, and hooting at the crowd as they hustled their tricks up the steps to the second-story cribs. She liked the effortless efficiency of the faro dealers, dapper in stiff, boiled shirts and black silk elbow garters, who dealt all night from the boxlike "shoes." The swinging batwing doors in the cool of the night. The big drinkers, the high rollers, the money-grabbers, the hard losers. The wheelman calling, "Gentlemen pays!" "Five on the red, red and odd!" "All bets down!" She liked the piano man thundering out the chords to "Darlin' Clementine" and "Greensleeves," banging the pedal as he pounded out the refrain.

There were many things Calamity liked about the Bear's Pizzle.

But she didn't like the company at Hickok's poker table. Or the other two gunhands who wanted to kill him. She stared across the room at Hickok's table, and from the bar she heard his voice.

"Dealer folds and will sit out the next two hands." He rose from the table and crossed the bar to join her.

He was a big man. The unbuttoned doeskin jacket hid some of his bulk, but not much. Inside the open coat was the red sash in which he carried two blue-black Navy Colts with ivory grips, the butts turned out, and a white ruffled shirt, open at the neck. The tan deerskin pants were fringed on the outside and were spotlessly clean. The hand-tooled calfskin boots were imported from France. On his head he wore a soft tan Stetson hat with a rattlesnake-skin band, the rattles still on.

Wild Bill Hickok was a handsome man. Over six feet tall, his yellow hair shoulder-length. Under his flowing yellow mustache, he showed a slow, infectious smile.

Hickok stood beside Calamity. She waved down the bardog, who brought them each a drink. Dressed in the white boiled shirt, paper collar, and black elbow garters of his trade, Mac served them the whiskey. He elaborately wiped up the spot in front of them. Then he nodded over his shoulder at the two gunsels. They were kids, nineteen, tops, but wearing pulled-down Stetsons and tied-down guns.

"I know," Hickok said softly.

Mac shrugged, then turned back down the bar.

Calamity drank off half her whiskey. "How do you know?"

"Aside from the fact that they been fingerin' them gun butts and starin' at me all night? Not hard. They had a brother named Phil Coe, back in Abilene. I sorta killed him."

"Any reason?"

"I think it was over a woman."

"That weren't real bright."

"I was just a kid, wild and headstrong. Anyway, I never claimed to be bright. If I was, I wouldn't be hangin' 'round here."

Calamity ignored the barb.

Hickok finished his drink. "You spot the other yet?"

"The tinhorn in the black frock coat at your table?"

"Yeah, he's got cards stashed in the coat, and he's usin' some sort of spring-sleeve holdout to hide the leftovers. He's good too. Haven't caught him once. He's doin' it, though."

"Hideout pieces?"

"Belly gun under the table. Probably a sawed-off. Something with some kick. Also, them sleeve-extender fellas usually bring a backup man."

Calamity nodded across the room. "The sodbuster in the sheepskin coat and the low-crowned black hat," Calamity said. "The one with the beard. He's been eyeballin' the game like it was his money."

"Yeah, he's got a hard-on for something. Probably figures I fucked his wife. Damn, if I get killed, I hope it's for what I actually done."

They were quiet for a moment. Hickok turned to Calamity and smiled.

"Clem. I sure do like that name. Could stand for Calamity, you know. You like the name Clem?"

"What I don't like is you goin' back to that table."

"I don't like it much either."

"There's too many of them."

"That there be, Clem, that there be."

"I wanted somethin' different for us, not you lyin' face-down in some saloon, a bullet in your brain and blood in your mouth."

Hickok nodded and turned toward the poker table. The dude in the black frock coat was waving him over to deal the next hand.

Calamity looked at the two gunmen at the far end of the bar and remembered all the different ways Hickok had taught her to use her Colt. She remembered how they'd honed the sear and lowered the spur, oiled the action till the trigger pull was as smooth as glass, as slippery as ice, as quiet as a prayer. She remembered how they'd practiced the cross-draw, the poker-chip draw, the "border shift," both left-to-right and right-to-left.

And now she stood there with four, maybe five men ready to whipsaw her man to pieces, and she didn't know if she could even pull her gun.

She'd never killed a man.

9

Hickok was on a streak. It always went that way. When his future looked black, his luck turned hot. Like right now. He was up against a cheat, maybe the best he'd ever seen. And Hickok was still winning, because you can't cheat dumb luck. Not even with a sleeve-holdout.

Still, Hickok felt an affront. This was his private table and he was the dealer. He could not sit back and let the tinhorn bilk the other players. He had to smoke him out.

Which was why they were playing five-card stud, "Indiana style," with the first and fifth cards down. All night long. Stud was the hardest game there was. And the toughest to cheat at. In five-card stud, even bluffing was difficult. You placed your bets one card at a time, and there were no second chances to improve your hands.

With seven players sitting in, more than half the deck was on the board for all to see. So everyone knew what you were trying for. In five-card stud, attempts to fill flushes or to wire straights or fill them from the inside were obvious. When you bucked the odds, all could take note. The thousand-to-one draws, the reaching for longshots, could easily be read.

All night, Hickok had watched the tinhorn beat them with improbable hands or, more specifically, with improbable hole cards. The question was, where was he getting them?

Then it was midnight. Five of the players had quit. Something had to give. Hickok and Edwards had all the chips.

Strangely enough, it was Edwards's temper that grew short.

It had started when Hickok returned from the bar. Hickok's luck had been running with pinpoint precision. Nothing as extravagant as the tinhorn's draws, but combined with careful betting and cautious folding, he was able to take half the pots.

So by the time other players had folded, Hickok was a good $5,000 ahead, and even playing Edwards one-on-one, he continued to win. For Edwards still could not cheat Hickok's luck. He could not cheat flushes filled with the last two cards, straights filled from the inside as well as both ends, nor could he even believe, let alone steal, the pots Hickok lucked into with low pairs.

Hickok was riding the tiger.

"That can't be luck," Edwards kept saying. "I ain't seen luck like that never before."

Hickok just flicked the pasteboards across the table. Eight to the lady, queen on a case queen.

"My friend," Hickok said in a slow, easy drawl, "long as they make whiskey and cards, we'll all need luck."

"And maybe Sam Colt."

"It happen before." Hickok paused to look at the cards. "Pair's worth ten. You still in?"

Edwards kicked it ten which Hickok saw. Two pasteboards shot out across the green baize: another eight to Edwards, a deuce to himself.

"Kings still high. Possible inside straight. Very poor odds." It was time for Edwards to make a move. "Friend, you wanna jump the bet?"

"Let's do it."

Hickok thought: You also don't know about my third hole king. Or don't care. And he counted out the bills. He threw a hundred dollars in the center of the baize. Edwards matched it with a stack of double eagles.

Again the deal. "No help for the kings but a nine of clubs to our friend. Inside straight? Not very likely."

Hickok counted out the hundred-dollar gold certificates and pushed five of them into the center of the pot. Edwards matched, then kicked another five hundred. "Five hundred called, and up five."

"Two kings here against you fillin' an inside straight?" Hickok said lightly, thinking out loud. "The odds against that five hundred are a thousand to one. Call that five-hundred raise and kick it five more."

The gambler called and the pasteboards flicked out, both of them down. Edwards picked up his hole card and shielded them with his hand close to his vest. Then Hickok looked at his own draw.

He had the fourth king.

The noise in the saloon hushed. The girls, sensing the action, retreated to their cribs. The casual drinkers departed rapidly. The two gunmen stayed at the bar. The sodbuster in the sheepskin coat was sticking around. As was a group crowding a roulette wheel one table over from the poker players. Where was Edwards's backup man?

Hickok laid his cards facedown. He made a big show of reaching for a bandanna in his front pants pocket, but surreptitiously pulled a Navy Colt out of his sash and left it on his lap—a slip-hammer Colt with a tied-back trigger.

He guessed that the gambler had a cut-down .44 under the table, already cocked. If Hickok was to fire, he could ear back his slip-hammer without the telltale *click-click*.

The gambler pretended to study his cards.

"You know, Bill," he said casually, "must be nice, bein' a big-time gunny. Everywhere you go, people wanna kiss your ass. Buy the gunny a drink."

Hickok watched the gambler slip a hand under the table. He leaned back, laid his own left hand on the gun in his lap. When his hand closed on the grip, he thumbed back the hammer.

"Has its drawbacks."

"Has its points too. People wanna be your friend. 'Another drink, mister big-time gunman? Want to play cards here? Sure, your credit's good. Let me stake you to a loan if you ain't got the cash.' And some people, when they're winnin', hell, they just throw in their cards. Who wants to beat a big-time gunman? Get your head blowed off over a hand of poker? Ain't that true, Mr. Wild-fuckin'-Bill?"

"Don't know yet." And under the table Hickok raised the muzzle's angle toward the gambler's chest.

"No?"

"And we never will. Not till we bet."

With his free right hand, Hickok pushed two thousand dollars—six stacks of double eagles—across the baize. "Two kings beat a busted straight?"

Hickok knew Edwards had made his move. When his hands covered his cards and then his left went for his lap, that's when he made the switch.

Hickok also figured that Edwards was out for more than money. He wanted Hickok's life. To build a rep? Who knew? Who cared? Just forget the other men now, Hickok said to himself. Edwards comes first.

Edwards's hands were back in sight. He pushed two thousand across the table. Twenty century notes, crisp, new. Arrogantly, Edwards laid out his doctored straight.

And Hickok, placing his gun hand casually on the table, flipped the third and fourth kings.

The gambler looked on, slack-jawed, while Hickok took the pot.

"You got two grand left," Hickok observed. "Another hand of stud?"

"You're on the tiger."

Hickok dealt the cards. One down to each, then one up. Edwards showed a black ace. Hickok had two black jacks— one up, one in the hole. The ace bet five hundred. Hickok saw the five.

Hickok flipped the gambler the queen of hearts; the queen of spades to himself. No help there, and Hickok called the second five. Now Edwards was down to a thousand dollars, but still he mouthed off.

"I'm gonna bust you, Hickok, bust you down to nothin'."

"Been done before," Hickok said, and dealt.

For the fourth card the gambler drew a queen of clubs, Hickok his next jack up. The one in the hole made three. But Edwards was still cocky. He pushed five hundred across, which Hickok called.

"I'm going to raise," Hickok said softly. "The watch. Is it gold?"

Edwards nodded. "Twenty carat."

Edwards took his watch out of his vest pocket. When he opened it, Hickok saw it was a B. W. Raymond key-winder from the National Watch Company, a gold watch with a hinged lid and an eight-day movement. The winding key hung from the chain. Reading the dial upside-down, Hickok noted the old-fashioned Roman numeral IIII.

"Worth a thousand?"

Edwards unsnapped the chain from his vest. "That it be," he said. He put the Raymond in while Hickok counted out his notes.

The place was quiet. Hickok dealt Edwards one down, then hit himself with a face-down diamond queen.

Full house. Three queens—one down. Two jacks—one down.

Edwards was holding two aces up. For four of a kind, he needed two in the hole.

Edwards pulled his pasteboards to his vest. His long fingers and wide palms concealed the cards, and Hickok knew what was happening. The gambler was wearing wide French cuffs. Buckled around the bare arm within the sleeve was a clamp that Edwards would extend by bending his elbow. He would slip the card he wanted into his hand from a coat, a cuff—from wherever he hid them—then let the clamp take back the sixth card. When he straightened his arm, the device retracted by a stout elastic band.

Fairly fucking foolproof against almost anything.

Except blind luck, the tiger's ride.

Hickok watched Edwards's sleight-of-hand. A rare performance. Hickok had seen cardsharps before, of every shape and size: deck markers, phony cutters, double-shufflers, card shavers, deck stackers, hideout artists, and second-dealers. And he knew how to spot them. But this one was beautiful. He'd never seen a holdout hustler run his play so smoothly.

Edwards extended his arms. The holdout, no doubt, retracted. Whatever hand Edwards held was also, no doubt, a beauty.

Edwards leaned back and Hickok paused to ponder the situation. Here he was, Hickok thought, sitting at a large round poker table covered with green baize. He glanced briefly at the room around him. Hickok rated it as spacious, superior. The saloon was at least a hundred feet long. On all of the walls were garishly painted nudes with opulent breasts, generous loins, protuberant bottoms. They were commissioned and hung by the Deadwood madams, presumably to encourage trade. Hickok glanced at the long teak bar with its brass footrail and gleaming spittoons. Behind that bar hung an oval mirror eight feet across, with a massive frame of hand-tooled mahogany, burgeoning with bright, carved, gilded cupids.

At each end of the bar was the Pizzle's "free lunch" —quart jars of pickled eggs, wheels of strong cheese, smoked sausages and large tins of crackers.

The more Hickok thought of this world, the better he found

it. He liked the card tables, the comfortable bentwood chairs. He liked watching women of easy virtue hustling drinks and displaying their wares. He'd also like the piano man, if he were still around to bang out "Red River Valley" or "Streets of Laredo." He thought of Calamity Jane.

Then he remembered that four, maybe five men wanted to level him. He remembered that the frock-coated gent probably had a sawed-off pointed straight at him. And for the first time since that night at the Wilderness, Hickok knew fear.

The man pushed his last five hundred to the center of the table. "I also have a good horse and a hand-tooled Texas saddle. I'd place the value at a thousand."

"Sold." Hickok pushed fifteen hundred across the table and leaned back in his chair.

Edwards nonchalantly flipped over his cards. Two black aces and an ace of Hearts. A queen of clubs and a diamond queen.

The diamond queen.

Oh, shit, Hickok thought, staring at his own fifth card, his last hole card, his own queen of diamonds.

Suddenly Hickok dove to his right, grabbing the Navy Colt with the tied-back trigger. As he hit the floor, the gambler blew two holes up through the table and the back of Hickok's empty chair. The shots went off with such deafening force that the sawed-off must have been a Walker Colt, the most powerful pistol made.

As Hickok rolled, hot lead crashed all around him. Sheepskin was finding the wall behind him, and the gun off to his right must be coming from Edwards's backup man.

He stopped his roll long enough to pump two rounds into Edwards's chest, knocking him over his bentwood chair. With a lucky snapshot, he cut down Sheepskin. But while his own moves ended there, his luck held firm. From the corners of the bar, three guns blazed. Calamity fanned five slugs into the two gunmen, their return fire shattering the eight-foot mirror, knocking down one of the cut-glass chandeliers, and shattering three quarts of the Pizzle's best whiskey.

At the same time he heard a loud *thunk*. The concussion of a deflected pistol slug blew a hole in the floorboard next to his left boot. He turned. The backup man's smoking .45 had dropped from his hand. He fell to his knees and crumpled to the ground.

Edwards's partner had come up on his blind side. He would have taken Hickok's head off his shoulders from real close, except for a big man in a battered Stetson and the dirtiest collarless shirt in the world. He'd cold-cocked the backshooter with the barrel of his own handgun.

All was still. Hickok sat on the floor, his ears ringing. The dense smoke from more than twenty gunshots filled the Pizzle. The white clouds floated to the ceiling, where they whorled and curled lazily above the saloon, drifting through the charged atmosphere of the suddenly quiet room. Hickok noticed that the acrid black-powder smoke was also stinging his eyes and burning his throat. He also noticed that he needed a drink.

Still sitting on the floor, Hickok slid his Colts back into his sash, butts turned out. He looked up to see who'd just saved his life.

Lonesome Charley Reynolds.

PART FOUR

10

Hickok squatted next to a campfire, wearing worn trail clothes. He, Calamity, and Charley Reynolds were camped along the Missouri River under a stand of cottonwood trees outside of Fort Lincoln. They were still in the Dakota Territory.

Custer had joined them. His campaign hat with the pinned-up right side was pulled rakishly over one eye. The brass buttons on his dark wool blouse gleamed in the firelight. Slowly feeding branches into the dying fire, he took a deep breath and said, "Let me see if I have this straight. Bill, you say that you can't infiltrate the James-Younger gang on your own?"

"No, sir. I knew them back in Abilene, and I got on with them good enough. But they ain't gonna trust me. Not after Allan Pinkerton sent them detectives to Missouri after them. They ain't gonna trust no lawman, former or otherwise."

"That's right, General," Reynolds agreed. "Jess was so hot, he headed east and threatened Allan Pinkerton in the Chicago streets. He sure ain't gonna trust Hickok now, him being a former Yankee spy and lawman to boot."

Custer nodded. "But you say you do have one man who can get you in. An outlaw whom the brothers would trust without hesitation."

"Yes, sir," said Reynolds. "The man we're thinkin' of, why, them brothers'd follow him straight into hell."

"But you say he's doin' triple life on the rockpile in Yuma prison?"

"Yes, sir."

Custer stared at the fire and tossed in another branch. "I just don't know if I have the clout anymore. Time was, I could have gotten a presidential pardon at the drop of a hat. But I'm afraid that after my congressional testimony, Grant wouldn't get me that pardon if the man were Saint Francis of Assisi booked by mistaken identity, if he were Christ on the cross."

"Sir." Hickok cleared his throat. "We aren't askin' you to get no pardons. I'm afraid it's worse'n that. We're gonna have to bust our man out of Yuma if we want him. That's why I'm here. I'm gonna need Charley for support, plus some army supplies. Pack mules, dynamite, rations, medical supplies, considerable equipment."

Custer stared at the three of them with disbelief. "Who is this man?"

Reynolds said, "We want Outlaw Torn Slater."

Custer groaned. He lowered his head and slowly massaged his temples.

"Sir, Slater's rough around the edges, but, well, Hickok and me do know him. He pays his debts. If we get his word and then bust him out, he'll deliver. You can bank on it."

"Torn Slater?" Custer winced. "Why not talk about freeing Satan from hell? The man's wanted in thirteen states and territories. Trains, banks, murder, arson, every crime known to God and man." Custer gave each of them a searching look. "I just don't see how you can trust him."

Hickok said, "Slater was the worst outlaw I ever knew. And the best man. In a tight spot, you'd want Slater coverin' your flank."

"And there's somethin' else, General," Reynolds added. "There's a story goin' around that Cole Younger was in on that Tucson bank job where Slater got caught. Cole killed them three tellers that Slater got charged with, and when Slater caught a bullet, Cole left him to rot in that Tucson desert. Slater's got a hard-on now for at least one of the boys.''

"Cole won't be too thrilled to have Slater back," Custer observed.

"That's a fact.''

"Okay," Custer said evenly. "Tell me where and when you need the supplies. I'll arrange for it.''

"We'll have the list tomorrow. At your headquarters.''

Custer looked at Calamity. "You sure you're going along?''

"General, I wouldn't miss this one for the world.''

Custer turned to Hickok and said, "Does she have any idea what this entails?''

"I've informed her, sir.''

"Missy," Custer said, "I don't know what you think you're doing or who you think you are, whether you're looking for glory or just plain mad. But they're talking about breaking Slater out of Yuma. Through a certain mountain pass known as the Needle. They're talking Apaches, missy. Chiricahua Apaches. Lots of them.''

Calamity shrugged.

Custer turned to Hickok with exasperation. "Either of you explain 'Pache to her?''

"I did, sir," Hickok said.

"Then let me add to it," said Custer. "These 'Pache we speak of are no mortal men. They are fiends out of hell who found some way to cloak themselves in human flesh. If I live long enough, I swear before God, I shall scourge them from the earth.''

"General—" Calamity began.

"Missy," he snarled harshly, "these two men, if the 'Pache catch them, they will only torture and kill. But you? They will rape you a few hundred times, stake you out on anthills or cactus or catclaw, cut out your eyelids so you'll be forced to stare at the sun till you go blind. They'll cut out your tongue so you cannot even scream in your pain. They'll strip the skin from your hands and feet. You know why they're called Apache?"

Calamity shook her head.

"It's from the Mexican. *Apachureros de huesos*. 'Crushers of bones.' Because when the men are finished torturing you, the women, who hate white *putas* like yourself, will break every bone in your body with rocks. While you are still alive."

"She's been told," Hickok said.

"You really want her along?" Custer looked amazed.

"We need someone to contact Slater in Yuma, pass herself off as some long-lost visiting relative. Someone who can set Slater up for the break."

"You have to be kidding."

"She knows gunshot wounds. She's a good nurse," Reynolds added.

"I still don't like it."

"General, she can pull her weight. She's got the guts. It's her own choice."

Custer fixed Calamity with a look. "Yes, I've met women like you before. You've got your share of guts. And you're pretty enough to bend people to your will. Vain, arrogant, you're hard as nails. You follow men like Hickok, thinking to fly with eagles and travel the glory road." Custer's gaze grew grim. "Only eagles, like vultures, eat carrion. And the glory road is paved with rocks."

"The eagle, sir, is the symbol of our country," Calamity said with an infectious grin.

Custer removed his campaign hat. His long yellow hair was the same as Hickok's, almost as if they were brothers. Calamity watched as he slowly fingered the device holding up the side brim. The gold coat of arms was the bald eagle.

"Then I fear that our national emblem will one day be extinct," Custer said.

"General," Hickok said, "we need three for this job. She can hold her own. She's proved it. We also need a woman to parley with Slater in Yuma."

"If you say so. It's your show now." Custer stood, and the others rose to their feet. Hickok started to salute, but Custer cut him off. He reached across the fire and shook his hand, then Reynolds's. Then, slowly, Calamity's.

As Custer turned toward his horse, Reynolds said, "One more thing, General."

"Yes?"

"This may be personal, sir, and out of line, but since what we're gonna do is hazardous, I'd really like to know somethin'."

"Go on."

"Sir, I'm willin' to back Hickok and Clem here, but I'd at least like to know what's with you and Hickok. I'm gettin' paid to risk my neck. It's my job. But Hickok, this ain't his game, not no more."

Custer turned toward his mount. "You'll have to ask Bill."

Reynolds grabbed his arm, politely but firmly.

"General," he said, "I rode a lot of miles and killed some good men to help you. You owe me an answer."

Custer shook Reynolds off and swung onto his horse. Reynolds grabbed the cheek strap, and even when the horse fantailed, lunged sideways, and shied bites at Reynolds's shoulder and face, he did not let go.

Custer stared at Hickok in silence.

Finally Hickok said, "It was at the Wilderness, twelve years ago. It got pretty bad back there. The General got me out of some trouble."

"That all? Nothing to do with you pistol-whippin' his brother in Abilene? And killin' two of the General's men?"

"His brother broke the law. Them soldiers tried to kill me. No, it were what happened at the Wilderness."

Reynolds was unsatisfied. "You still ain't said what happened."

"Ain't gonna, neither."

Calamity laughed. "Hell, he don't tell me. I sleep with him, and he wakes up screaming every night. Still don't talk on it. Between that there Wilderness and them diamond queens, Bill here's got more ghosts trottin' over his grave'n Honest Abe."

"Charley," Custer said quietly, "it's no concern of anyone's anymore. That milk was spilled a long time ago. To me it's over with—blood under the bridge. If Bill here wants to call that dawn in those long-ago woods a debt of honor, I'll accept it. I'm grateful too. At the moment I need all the help I can get.''

Custer wheeled his mount and trotted back to his escort, waiting for him by their horses some two hundred yards up the river.

Calamity pinned Hickok with a hard stare. "I'm still with Reynolds. I'm gonna learn what happened that night before this is over, or it's gonna be your ass."

"Not likely," Hickok said.

He kicked dirt on the fire, then headed downstream toward his horse.

PART FIVE

11

Five days by train, five more by Butterfield-Overland stage, and they reached Fort Grant in the Arizona Territory. A small, dusty town, it lay in the middle of the Southwest Desert, a good day's ride from the San Simon River. Their gear had been delivered by Custer's quartermaster to a small ranch near the river rather than to the nearby fort, for reasons of "military hygiene."

"I don't think the General wants to be associated with us," said Calamity.

"You mean with us robbers, murderers, and jailbreakers," Hickok added.

"Yeah," Reynolds said. "I don't like that company much myself."

They climbed down off the stage. As they walked toward the square adobe relay station, they were met by a tall *mestizo* named Chucho.

"Chucho in Mex is short for Jesus," said Hickok to Clem.

"Uh-huh. And *He*'s now wearin' sombreros, sidearms and four-inch rowels."

He was the *caporal,* the foreman of the ranch.

Chucho was something to look at. Calamity took in his outfit: the white muslin shirt, the *charro*-style black pants, tapered and tight above the knees, the bottoms shoved into high black riding boots. She was impressed by the straw sombrero with its small crown and foot-wide brim turned up in front. When Chucho turned to lead them to their horses, his big wheel-spoke spurs with their four-inch rowels clanked along the jetty with every step.

Hickok had also noted Chucho's getup.

"This desert's gonna be a scorcher. I figured some of them muslin shirts and straw sombreros might help. Though, damn, I hate takin' off this felt one."

"Yeah," said Calamity with a snort, "it'd take years to grow that much mold on a new one."

They walked down a dusty road beside a stream, past willows, rushes, and clumps of bluestem. It was late spring, and Calamity noted that the water was still high in its banks. By a stand of salt cedars, Chucho's men were waiting with their animals—a paint, a blaze-faced bay, and a line-backed roan.

"These will do for now, boss," Chucho said. "At the remuda you can pick your own horses. And pack mules. And other things too."

They swung onto their mounts, and rode at a lope downstream along the dusty road.

12

Calamity had never been south of Abilene, and the ride into the desert was a new experience. She had thought deserts were flat, arid and dead. Like Kansas during a summer drought. But this close to the San Simon River, there was water, and water meant birds, animal life, trees, and chaparral. Deer and jackrabbits shot through the distant mesquite.

Spotted coyotes and wolves and ground squirrels scurried into the bushes as they rode past. Birds, seemingly by the hundreds, constantly darted from cactus to thorn trees to pinyon bushes.

And as the narrow trail—now just a dry arroyo—wound among the boulders and between the deadfall, Calamity became especially aware of the cactus. The desert was a virtual forest of these thorny bushes: flat-paddled prickly pear, the spiny ocotillo, the squat round barrel with its big curved spines, and the imposing saguaro, rising to over eighty feet, its many arms arching out and up, high overhead.

Scattered among the cactus were aloe vera, with their bright yellow-orange blossoms, as well as pinyon bushes, Spanish bayonet, fan palms, and huge century plants, just sprouting their vivid yellow blooms.

They passed under the overhanging bough of a desert jackpine, and a large long-billed wren perched on the bough glared down at them, guarding her nest. To the left Calamity saw a striped Gila woodpecker picking a hole high up in a saguaro, nearly thirty feet overhead. A roadrunner darted off the trail and vanished into the chaparral.

An owl hooted somewhere in the brush, and Hickok said, "Damn, I hate them desert owls."

"Yeah?" Calamity said, leaning toward him on her pommel.

"The 'Pache say the owl has the gift of prophecy, and when he hoots your name, you die. And them desert owls is always callin' *Bill! Bill! Bill!*"

"Sounds like this time you got reason to read the omens."

They moved behind Chucho single file into a wide wash with a creek running along the bottom. Chucho signaled to dismount, and they loosened the cinches and let the horses drink.

"Five more miles to the ranch. We have supper. You get your stuff. Then, I think, you be gone in the morning. *Es verdad, Señor?*"

"*Verdad, amigo.*"

They pushed on. The horses picked their way among a jumble of rocks strewn along the streambed. Occasionally they passed under a cottonwood or alongside boulders, some as big as freight wagons. On both sides of the wash, the rock gullies and rolling slopes were covered with cactus: pincushion, pencil-thin cholla, prickly pear.

Twice Chucho stopped, scaled the side of the wash, mounted a boulder, and studied their backtrail.

Another three miles down the arroyo, the Mexican led them out of the creek where the nearby farmers watered their stock. Calamity watched their own tracks disappear into the heavily traveled slope.

Below the next rise, Calamity saw the Mexican's homestead. The spread consisted of five huts made of sod, clay, and interwoven maguey stalks. The roofs were also of sod, packed on a mesh of maguey and mesquite. Through the valley threaded a good stream, on both sides of which were large patches of corn, beans, and maguey. A barefoot peasant in a small straw hat and white muslin shirt guided a span of mules. Calamity watched a funnel-shaped cloud of dust rise behind him as he plowed, then settle and disappear. Chucho motioned them on. Leaning on their pommels, they started down the steep grade into the valley where their gear was waiting.

13

They ate early, squatting on their haunches around a campfire—tomatoes and jerked beef fried with hot red chilis till the skins split, and frijoles. It was served in bowls and they sipped Arbuckle's coffee from tin mess cups and brushed away the droning flies.

After the meal, Chucho took them into a small, cool shed two hundred yards from the other buildings. It leaned against cottonwoods and was well shaded. Inside was a water barrel, and two crates of explosive.

Straight dynamite, it had been packed in wet sawdust and

carefully bundled in canvas tarpaulins. Each stick was individually wrapped. Reynolds dug one out of the sawdust, removed its muslin wrapping, and showed the dynamite to Calamity and Hickok.

"We won't need fuses for these," he said. "They're leaking so much, all you'll have to do is throw one. They'll go off like grenades."

"That's why we got to cool them off, stop the sweating. The liquid nitro will blow us up before we get to the Needle."

He poured water from a two-gallon bag over the dynamite. Then they left to pick out their mules and saddle horses.

The stock was penned in a makeshift corral of mesquite, maguey stalks, and dried mud. Two of the mules were staked out some distance apart, and Chucho explained, "These mules are *dos machos*, boss. They kept jumping the horses and the *señorita* mules."

"You ain't givin' us no mares," Hickok said, eyeing the Mexican suspiciously. " 'Specially with that dynamite."

"No boss, *dos machos* are mine. What you got is in the corral."

Calamity looked over the stock. Eight horses and four mules. The horses were compact animals, fourteen to fifteen hands, with powerful shoulders and hindquarters, short legs. Lots of strength and balance, good for the rocky desert country they would be covering. A roan, two sorrels, a deep-chested bay, a good-looking paint, a mustang, a big gray, and a black, wall-eyed gelding. The mules were jacks, all gelded.

Reynolds stared at them with narrowed eyes. He said to Chucho, "Missouri mules?"

"No boss. Mexican."

Reynolds nodded. "Good. I requisitioned them. Mex mules can feel their way over rocks, through swamps, 'round rattlesnakes. They're more surefooted. With this kinda freight they'd better be."

Chucho led them toward the largest of the five sheds. On the way, Reynolds offered, "You know what they say about stud mules?"

"No," said Calamity.

Hickok grinned and Reynolds continued, "A stud mule'll walk around for a year with a hard-on stout enough to drive rail spikes with. Won't bother nothin'. Then one day he spots a mare, any kinda mare. And suddenly he's on her. Then there's nothin'll get him off. Not bullwhips not prod poles nor blastin' powder. Blow his head off and he still don't quit. He'll keep right on fuckin'. And he don't stop till he comes."

Another hut of sun-baked sod, mesquite, and maguey. The big Mexican pulled the peg from the hasp and let them in. The only light filtered dimly through windows partially screened by mesquite branches. Chucho lit a coal-oil lamp fastened to a wall bracket.

Along the sides of the hut were the stacked crates of supplies. Hickok took the eighteen-inch "Arkansas toothpick" out of his back sheath and pried the tops off each of the four-by-four crates. He sorted through the supplies and finally found what he was looking for.

Four quarts of Jack Daniel's Sour-Mash Whiskey.

Reynolds opened one and took a deep pull. Life glowed in his weary eyes. He passed the bottle to Calamity. She took a drink and passed it to Hickok. He held on to the bottle.

"I'd suggest we assemble the sawbuck mule packs outside, load them up, then ride the mules to them in the morning. Same with the saddle packs. We'll keep four of the eight packs light. Those we'll put on the extra horses. We'll want them fresh, since we'll be ridin' them out. Questions?"

"Yeah," Calamity said. "What's the Needle like? Will we have trouble gettin' through?"

"Shouldn't have. There ain't a drop of moisture for fifty miles either end of that pass. Any man goes in there's gonna have to haul a week's worth of water. We should have the Needle to ourselves goin' in."

"How 'bout gettin' back out?"

"That's a problem. On the other side of that canyon, about a hundred miles to the south, is a 'Pache reservation. Chiricahua. Meanin' the worst kind. And they got a special deal worked out with Yuma. Any escaped prisoners got a hundred-dollar bounty on them. Per head. The 'Pache just bring back the head. Hell, the guards don't even chase the escapees. 'Fraid the 'Pache'll mistake 'em for convicts.''

"You expect trouble comin' back?"

Hickok nodded. "There's only one way out of Yuma. Through the Needle. The others lead straight into the Sonoran Desert, which gets you nothin' except death by dehydration.''

"So them 'Pache'll know where to find us?"

"They'd know anyway," Hickok said. "They're the best trackers in the world.''

Reynolds looked confused. "I thought you told Custer Calamity knew all this.''

"She knew there'd be Apaches, and she'd heard they were bad. I figured, Clem, you'd say 'yeah, uh-huh,' then be afraid to back out later on when you saw what it was really like. Well, now it's later on, and it's here, and it's for real. And if we don't make it, it's gonna be the last thing we ever do. That canyon's the devil's own frying pan. To escape them savages, we're gonna have to blow up half that pass behind us. If the heat and the 'Pache don't get us, that flyin' rock will.''

"And that's assumin' we can get Slater off the rockpile in the first place," Reynolds put in.

"Which is assumin' he's even alive," Hickok said. "Knowin' that bastard, he was planted the day he got there, and Warden Stark just ain't got 'round to tellin' the world.''

"It'd be just our luck," said Calamity.

"Our good luck," Hickok said. "If we pull him off that pile, our bad luck begins.''

Calamity grimaced.

"If they catch up with you," said Hickok, "keep one round in the chamber. For yourself. They ain't honor-bound to bring you back in one piece. All Warden Stark wants is a recognizable head.''

"Who invented this plan for catchin' convicts?"

"Stark. He's run prisons for twenty years. Claims no one's ever escaped from one of his and lived. Swears the day it happens he'll resign.''

Calamity glanced over at Reynolds and saw him eyeing her fixedly. "You still plan on goin'?" he asked.

"Reckon so," said Calamity with a shrug.

"You 'spect to protect us from them heathen 'Pache?" Hickok said, grinning.

"I was more concerned about Torn Slater."

"As I recall, you knew him once. In a manner of speaking."

"There weren't much manners, and there weren't much speakin'." Then Clem said softly to Hickok, "But it weren't no big deal."

"I wonder if he's still alive," said Hickok.

"I 'spect so," Reynolds said. "He's part 'Pache himself. He must like this desert fine."

Hickok nodded. "He got snake blood in his veins."

"And venom in his dick," said Reynolds, grinning at Calamity.

Then Reynolds pulled a pack saddle out of a crate and they went back to work.

PART SIX

14

A tall, heavily muscled man stood on the northern rim of the Yuma Prison rock quarry. He was wearing a striped, collarless prison shirt. The man was yelling at a guard crossing the quarry floor a hundred yards below him.

"Takin' it off here, boss!"

The sergeant, slowly trudging across the quarry in a faded Union Army uniform, waved up the slope to no one in particular.

"Takin' it off there, Slater."

Slater slipped out of the prisoner's shirt.

He was big: blocklike shoulders, large, heavily veined biceps, and a massive neck. He had a shock of thick black hair and a surprisingly narrow waist. Torso bared, other oddities appeared. A long, deep knife scar ran diagonally from abdomen to shoulder. A puckered bullet hole entered above the collarbone, and reappeared in a small white sunburst pattern just above the shoulder blades. That was where the fragmented minié ball had exited. The scar tissue, long since healed over, was bone white against the red-brown of his tan. On his naked back, Slater wore the wide white stripes of Yuma Prison.

He paused to look into the pit below. The quarry was a good three hundred yards across and a hundred deep. The sides sloped gradually. The men, most of them still in striped shirts, worked the sloping sides and bottom, swinging sixteen-pound sledgehammers. Just breaking rock.

The prisoners wore hightop shoes. Some had one or two sets of leg irons over the hightops. For each attempt to escape from Yuma, or for each assault on a guard, a convict got a new set of leg irons.

Slater stared down into the quarry—"the cauldron" as it was known to the men who worked the Yuma pile. As he watched, two hundred hammers rose and fell, and the quarry echoed with the ringing of steel on rock. Slater leaned on his sledge and took off a red bandanna. How many days had he spent in the hotbox that last time? In that four-by-four-foot corrugated steel shed, the iron dog collar on his neck short-chained a mere two feet from his ankles? A week? A month? Two months? How many years in the deep granite hole *under* Yuma? Time came and went in the hotbox and the hole, and the only way to survive was to ignore the hours, days, years. Fight the battle against the heat and sweat and pain and—worst of all—the isolation, minutes at a time till they opened the door, dragged you out, and threw you back on the pile, till even the pile itself seemed a relief.

A crooked, wolfish grin angled up the side of Slater's face. He stroked the sweaty handle of his sledge and briefly recalled what had won him that last trip to Stark's hotbox. The warden's chief flunky and apprentice torturer, Sergeant Thomas T. Stryker, had chivvied him one too many times with that pick-axe handle, which each of the bulls carried as both a walking stick and a truncheon. During the past three years, Slater had been flogged and boxed and buried in the hole six different times for abusing Stryker.

Three of those six times, Slater had been punished for verbal abuse in the guise of insults to Stryker's mother. That fat bastard was obsessively sensitive about the sainted old lady, and when Slater could no longer tolerate him, he'd describe in detail one of the more elaborate unnatural acts that Slater claimed the old hag had performed in order to conceive a bastard as twisted, stupid, and mortally ugly as her brain-damaged son. Slater would send Stryker into towering frenzies that culminated in the red-faced sergeant swinging two-handed blows at Slater's head with the pick handle. Slater would then, despite the leg and wrist shackles, disarm Stryker and either break his pick handle over his knee or batter Stryker's face. Lately Slater had become more careful. Eight months ago he'd landed a right cross with a little too much on it, and broken Stryker's jaw in six places.

He was sure that time the guards—at Warden Stark's behest—would kill him. Afterward, he was told by the convict doctor he'd done six months in that granite hole. A prison record. The misadventure had also won him his third set of shackles.

To this day he had not worked the kinks out of his back and shoulders. For, each time he was sent to the hole, Warden Stark short-chained him. An inch-thick iron collar was riveted around Slater's neck and from the collar loop a one-foot chain, eighteen links in all, clamped to the center link of Slater's leg irons. Slater had a total mobility of less than two feet.

Compared to the short chain, the hole's sixteen cubic feet seemed like freedom forever.

Slater turned his back to the pile and began attacking a granite boulder on the quarry's rim. And while hammering at that barn-size boulder was agony, it did for a time supply Slater with a glimpse of what appeared to be the free world. For beyond that rock was Freedom Point, and beyond the Point was a sheer dropoff of one hundred and twenty feet—straight into the fork of the Gila and Colorado rivers. That particular piece of cliff was named after the countless convicts who, after deciding that death was preferable to a life on the rockpile, opted for the last act of free choice allowed them. Weighted with thirty pounds of leg irons, they went over the edge. When they landed, they sank like dead weight.

The hammers sang now, an echoing, ringing clang of steel

on rock. Occasionally Slater pulled the red bandanna out of his pocket and shouted, "Wipin' it up here, boss!"

And the walking bull in the faded uniform shouted back, "Wipin' it off there, Slater."

Then he'd swab his forehead and neck, and his eyes would wander over the perimeter of the pit and across the scorching plains of the Great Sonoran Desert, the hellish frying pan that was now his life. Overhead the sun burned in the harsh, blue, utterly cloudless sky with an intensity unequaled in North America. Here the skies yielded less than four inches of rain a year. The winter temperatures topped one hundred degrees, and the summer heat soared over one-forty. Here the buzzard, the sidewinder, and the Gila monster died of dehydration. Here was desert hotter and drier than Death Valley, the Kalahari, the Sahara.

Here was Slater's life.

He stared down into the Cauldron. As the sun approached zenith, the quarry had become a sun-blistered inferno. Beyond it was only desert. Beyond that, the Mogollon Mountains and the Apaches.

Beyond that—*nada*.

15

As Slater methodically worked the north slope, he eyed Stryker making his afternoon rounds along the quarry rim. *I've broken his jaw in six places. I've knocked out three of his teeth. I've told him his mother fucks donkey dorks. Why doesn't he give up?* And then Slater thought wryly, almost— but not quite—with sympathy: *Maybe he's too much like me.*

A half hour later, as the sun began to set, Slater was working the big boulder overlooking Freedom Point, pounding fist-size chunks out of its base. Visible through the fog of rock dust, he could see Stryker approach. Pretending not to notice, he continued swinging his sledge. Stryker's raucous voice preceded him as he came up the slope.

"If it isn't my old buddy Slater, fresh as a daisy from how many months in the hole? How's it feel to stand up straight for a change?"

"How's it feel not to suck your supper through a straw?"

With a loud, echoing *crack*, Stryker brought the pick handle across Slater's kidneys. Longer and stouter than an ax handle, it could shatter a man's back. With his six-foot, 260-pound bulk, Stryker could deliver a formidable blow.

"What's that, punk?" Stryker said. "Wouldn't care to repeat it for the old sergeant, would you?"

"Just askin' how you felt, Sarge, that's all. Haven't jawed with you for a spell."

"Feelin' good, Slater, feelin' very good." Stryker leaned against the rock while Slater continued hammering at the side. "Really, though, I'm more concerned about you, Torn. How a boy of your breedin' and upbringin' ends up on the long road, doin' hard time."

"It happens, Sarge. It sometimes do," said Slater as the sledge rose and fell.

"Well, I'm here to change all that. See, Torn, I got me a new attitude now. I don't see myself no more as just bein' another hard-rock guard, bustin' balls and breakin' heads. I see myself as a preacher among the heathen, on a mission from God."

"You know, Sarge," Slater said, "that broken jaw must've cracked your brains."

The pick handle sang through the air and landed with an angry *whack*. A second livid welt striped Slater's back. He grimaced, but quickly turned it into a crooked grin.

"Yeah, Slater, Warden Stark and I was havin' a nice long talk about you just the other day. We was discussin' what Stark called 'the relative merits of keepin' you alive.' We was discussin' your long history of robbin' trains and banks, of stealin', of murder and assault. We was talkin' of your evil friends—the late William Fuckin' Quantrill, Frank and Jess, Cole Younger. Stark says he's just about come 'round to my way of thinkin'. Says 'specially after that last episode, he can't see much reason for lettin' you stay around.''

"I got a reason for you, Sarge."

"I'd like to hear it."

Slater stopped swinging his hammer, turned, and faced Stryker head on. Stryker backed off three feet and gripped the pick handle with both hands.

"Where else would you find enough blood to suck?"

Stryker's face twisted with rage. He tapped Slater on the chest with the tip of the pick handle, not too gently. "Don't press your luck. You're on thin ice."

Slater shrugged, picked up the hammer with one hand, and drove it hard into the granite boulder. Then he took it in both hands and drove it harder still, knocking out a big chunk that fell two inches from Stryker's foot.

"Watch your step, Stryker. This quarry's one evil place for some men. Lots of mean people on this hard-rock pile."

"I know this—you've had it," Styker returned in a soft, hoarse voice. "I know we're tearing you apart like a plucked chicken. One of these nights the boys and me, we're payin' a call to your cell. And when we're done, there won't be nothin' left but a grease spot."

Slater continued driving the heavy sledge into the boulder without missing a beat.

"I'm shakin', Stryker."

Stryker was so enraged he forgot to put a third stripe across Slater's bare back.

"You're all horns and rattles out here on the rockpile, with your friends to pull me off you. See how tough you are when me and the boys get you out of your cell. Stark's approvin' that action. Just for you. Says you're a special case."

"Stryker, get in the wind."

"A real haired-over hombre, huh? Well, I seen hillbilly scum like you and them Quantrill boys you done rode with. And I seen what yellow-bellied egg-suckers you all turned out to be when a couple of real men got you alone."

Slater stopped, faced Stryker, and let the hammerhead rest on the ground.

"Stryker, were you really in Kansas?"

Stryker's voice was trembling with rage. "You heard what I said 'bout the likes of trash like you, scum what rode with Bloody Bill and William Quantrill."

Slater grinned. "Well, I'll be. All these years we been feudin', I wondered why. You Jayhawkin', Red-Leggin', bluebelly sonofabitch. Was it Jim Lane or Jennison?"

"Both, you fuckin' asshole."

"Straight deal?"

"I worked for both. I jailed all kinds of trash."

"Where?"

"Lawrence, Kansas."

Suddenly Slater wasn't grinning. Memories flooded back. The Lawrence jail had been the main torture chamber for Jennison's Red-Legs and Jim Lane's Jayhawkers. Slater scratched his head. And sonofabitch, the chief jailer had been named Stryker. He'd never connected the two. But Stryker was still talking.

"And believe me, I know what it's like to get some redneck sonofabitch on the end of a rope, watch him screamin' for air, legs kickin'. Then cut him down when he passes out and start all over. I know what it's like to ax-handle some white-trash punk till he's screamin' for mercy. I know Southern scum like you and Quantrill and Bloody Bill for the whinin', egg-suckin', snivelin'—"

Slater had had enough. He picked up the hammer, and when Stryker jumped back in shock he began driving it into the granite again, blow after blow, slowly and precisely. And hard.

Now that Slater had the hammer in his hands, Stryker was quiet. Slater could see from a corner of his eye that he was struggling to regain his nerve.

Then Stryker was at him again.

"Hey, Slater, a big honcho like you ought to be able to stand that hotbox another month. What do you think? Rid me of lookin' at your ugly face. Or maybe you'd like out of this hard-rock cunt? Horizontally, in a pine box? 'Cause that's the only way you're leavin'. You know that? Cemetery Hill, that's the only place you're goin'. No livin' to a ripe old age for you, Honcho. No children playin' 'round your feet. No wife to mourn your passin'. The only land you're gonna own is that six-foot hole we plant you in. No one to care for you, no one to pull the grass up over your head when we lower you into the ground. Honcho, you'll be all alone."

Slater slowly put his hammer down. He stared at the guard. "Stryker, is it true what they say about your camp-followin', rebel-suckin' old ma?"

Stryker raised the pick-axe handle with both hands. "I was wonderin' when you'd start."

Then it was quiet.

Two hundred prisoners on the rockpile put down their hammers and stared.

"You know the penalty for insulting a guard, Slater. Is it worth it?" Stryker tightened his two-handed grip on the handle.

"Just repeatin' simple facts, Stryker, from people who knew her well."

Stryker's sneer was demented, the left side of his face twitching uncontrollably. He was already dipping to one knee for a better swing.

"What's that, trash?"

The quarry was dead silent. When Slater spoke, his words echoed eerily through the heat, rock dust, and sudden silence, reverberating off the quarry walls.

"That the bitch scraped you off a reservation whorehouse wall, then hatched you out on a hot rock? No truth to that, is there, Stryker?"

Stryker swung the pick handle as hard as he knew how, directly at Slater's kidneys. Slater caught it in his left hand, and in one fluid motion, feet planted, he pivoted, bringing a roundhouse right across his body, putting his back into it, feeling every ounce of his two hundred pounds behind it. He drove the punch straight into Stryker's mouth, feeling the teeth pop and the bones crunch against his fist, watching Stryker's eyes dilate in stone horror and then grow dim as he passed out cold.

Then Slater felt himself slamming the back of Stryker's head on the granite boulder. Five prisoners pulled him off. Two of them were holding an arm and the third had a forearm pressed against his windpipe. The other two had his legs. But by now Slater was actually feeling good. In fact, he felt comfortable, relieved.

Two more cons were bending over the guard, staring at the bloody mess that had been his mouth. One of them was saying, "That Stryker must be crazy, fuckin' with Slater like that. He's the hardest drill in this here factory."

"Jesus, you see Stryker's eyes? They ain't even human. They belong on a dead carp."

"Man's nothin' but death—death with a little skin stretched over it."

"Never shoulda fucked with Slater. Stryker only works here. Slater *lives* here."

By now the armed guards were jogging over to the fallen sergeant, their Henry repeating rifles at full cock. One of the prisoners was yelling, "You ought to see Stryker. Looks like Slater killed him this time."

16

Already stripped to the waist, Slater was strung up by the wrists to the top of the flogging post. He hung there into the evening, his toes dangling inches above the ground.

After mess, Warden Stark ordered the entire 257-man population into the yard. The gun bulls were manning the high adobe walls and catwalks, with their repeating rifles cocked.

After a fifteen-minute wait, Warden Stark, a tall, distinguished-looking man in a black frock coat, muttonchop whiskers, and steel-rimmed spectacles, appeared. Standing before the men, he pointed to Slater and shouted, "This here is not an exercise in savagery but a lesson. The point of this lesson is not pain for pain's sake, misery for the sake of misery, this here lesson has a point. We intend to prove to you prisoners that life outside the walls is easier than life inside. The best way to prove it is to make life inside as disagreeable as possible. Some people argue," Stark shouted, his words echoing eerily through the twilit yard, "some people feel such lessons are wasted on men like Slater. Floggings, rock quarries, hotboxes aren't enough, they say. Men like Slater only understand three things—a dropping trap door, a taut noose, and may God have mercy on your soul. Some people around here wish Slater had been caught and convicted in the Nations, then hanged by Judge Parker. Parker, they say, knows how to deal with men like Slater. He'd hang Slater twice if he could. That's how some men look at it. I feel otherwise. A little chastism is good for the soul, sayeth the Lord. I feel it is our Christian duty to convert misguided souls such as Slater. And I feel that one day he will see that Light. For in this prison the way of the wicked is strait and narrow. And hard. As you shall all see."

His speech ended. He stripped off his frock coat, his brocade vest, and his black tie. A guard crossed the yard and handed him a fifteen-foot black Durado bullwhip, coiled, rosined at the end. Stark stood by Slater a moment, then whispered, "Okay, let's see what you're made of."

He paced off twelve steps from the post, then turned to face the exposed back. Only the last two feet of the whip would strike Slater's back.

Gripping the stock with both hands, Stark laid on fifty lashes.

Three times Slater passed out. And each time Stark ordered him revived with buckets of water.

Still Slater took it, tight-lipped, mute, the only sound in the yard the ear-cracking blasts of the pizzle.

One of the prisoners, a former cellmate of Slater's, whispered to a friend, "He's one hard rock."

"Hardest on this pile," said the other.

Then the guards cut Slater down, rubbed brine into his back to shrink the livid slashes, and dragged him over to one of the hotboxes in the middle of the yard. Halfway there he pulled his arms free and stumbled into the hotbox under his own power.

Made of corrugated tin, it was four feet on a side. Slater was short-chained by a guard. A honeybucket was thrown in after him.

PART SEVEN

17

They crossed the fifty miles of living desert in two days, and if that desert was living, Calamity had no desire to see the dying variety. Not only had it been an unbearable inferno, the ride itself was rough.

Furthermore, Calamity could not get over the feeling that they had stuck her with the shit detail. She did not appreciate hazing the three pack mules and the extra horses. She recognized the dangers in handling the dynamite mule, which was Hickok's and Reynolds's job. Yet she did not go along with having two grown men baby one goddamn mule just because he was hauling four kyacks of dynamite packed in wet sawdust.

But that was what they were doing. At three o'clock that morning, Bill had rousted her out of her bedroll. He'd then made her grain and water the stock while he fixed a meal of hardtack, jerky, coffee, and canned tomatoes. Afterward they loaded the panniers onto the kicking, braying mules. She watched irritably as Hickok and Reynolds talked soothingly, gentling them, meticulously flattening out even the tiniest wrinkles in the saddle pads, then balancing and rebalancing the loads over and over. When they were finally pleased with themselves for the inspired job they'd done, she watched with dismay as Reynolds tried to throw a one-man diamond hitch. It took him at least a dozen attempts on the first two animals. Most of the time the hitch simply collapsed when he tried to pull the lash tight, and he ended up with the fifty-foot rope on the ground.

Hickok kept saying, "I was packin' mules up and down the Sante Fe Trail, Calamity, while you were still in diapers."

To which she just snorted, "Tell it to them jugheads."

Eventually Hickok and Reynolds reconstructed the forgotten skills of muleteering. And when it was time to hitch the dynamite pack, even Calamity could no longer feign indifference. Reynolds, prepared to throw the one-man diamond, hauled on the lash rope. She watched nervously as the load wrenched and jerked and strained, as the kyacks and panniers and crossed wooden sawbucks creaked and groaned, till he finally pulled the load together, threw the hitch, and tied it off.

When the hitch held, they managed to seem casual about it.

They saddled their mounts—a big sorrel for Reynolds, the roan for Hickok, and a spirited, white-stockinged gray for Calamity. They said their goodbyes to Chucho and started off. Calamity and her jerk-line string were far out in front, while Reynolds, Hickok, and the dynamite trailed slowly behind.

It was not a pleasant ride. Calamity hazed her string from the rear. She dodged their flops, cursed at the flies. She watered and grained them, adjusted and rebalanced their packs, flung stones at their rumps when they balked, cursed and kicked them when the rocks didn't work, and lay her wrist quirt across their flanks when all else failed.

Hickok and Reynolds sweet-talked their mule.

But Calamity wasn't impressed. She still cursed Hickok and Reynolds. Half the time her back and rear end were so sore from that damned McClellan and the irregular gait of her snuffy gray that she found it easier to follow the mules on foot and lead her horse by the *mecate*.

On and on she trudged and cursed and rode. And the farther they traveled from the San Simon River, the more barren the land became. Stands of prickly pear, yucca, and saguaro, lush fields of blossoming maguey and bushy mesquite with rich ripe berries gave way gradually to wind-bent sagebrush, coarse, stunted saltbushes and tumbling balls of weed, bleached as white as bone by the desert sun. The sand changed in texture. As they approached the Mogollon Mountains—those southernmost cliffs of the Rocky Mountain chain—the desert lost the feeling of fertility. The soil itself seemed to die. As they pounded out the hard, hot miles, the desert floor changed to hardpan and the flora turned gaunt and gray.

Calamity drove and hazed the mules. The sun, rising over her back, became a hammerblow by noon. The air within her sombrero's low crown grew steamy. She kept soaking her red bandanna and tying it around her forehead till Hickok caught her at it, rode up, and ordered her to go easy on the water.

She yelled, "Go fuck yourself!"

For the first time ever, she saw Bill become genuinely angry. His eyes flattened.

"I catch you wastin' water again, I'll whack you black and blue with a knotted packline. In case you haven't figured it out yet, this is for real, Clem, for keeps."

She began at last to understand how much trouble they were in for.

On and on they rode. They hammered out the miles on shank's mare and ironshod hoofs. As they moved closer to the eastern face of the Mogollon Rim, the cliff wall bulked huge against the darkening western sky like a black, blank wall two thousand feet high. For the last hour of their pilgrimage, they rode under its shadow. Calamity unpacked a serape—that all-purpose Mexican maguey blanket, poncho, ground cloth, and tarpaulin—and rode with it pulled tightly around her shoulders. Her eyes searched the maze of cliffs for the pass that would lead them through the mountains. Once when Hickok rode up to unload more water for the dynamite, she'd asked him about the canyon.

"The Needle ain't no gorge nor no canyon nor no pass,"

he said. "It's a whole string of gorges, canyons, and passes, each one leadin' into the next. And it's the only route through them mountains."

"Hope you ain't suggestin' we could get lost in that maze an' die of thirst?"

"No way. I led mule trains through there as a boy. That sorta thing you never forget."

"Like throwin' the one-man diamond hitch?"

Hickok allowed himself a small smile. "That too." Slipping the three-gallon waterbag over the McClellan's modified horn, he reined the big, deep-chested roan around and headed back to the dynamite mule at an easy lope.

18

They camped along the hot eastern face of the cliff. And that night after the campfire died, Hickok came to Calamity's bedroll.

"'Bout time, cowboy," she said, reaching over to unbuckle his pants.

"Who says that's why I'm here?"

"Why else you come by my soogans, 'steada sawin' wood? You seekin' my wise counsel and advice?"

"Maybe." Hickok was lying alongside Calamity. Inside her bedroll, she was naked. He reached his hand in and casually stroked a silken thigh.

The deliciousness of his touch shot through her like the sharp shock of a bee sting. A pleasurable bee sting. She moaned involuntarily and said, "Speakin' of wise counsel and advice, what are your recommendations for threadin' the Needle and springin' Slater?"

Suddenly his middle finger was probing her vulva; his thumb and middle finger were expertly kneading her tingling clitoris.

"Oh!" Her eyes were shut tight, squinting against the half-pain, half-pleasure of his intrusive touch. "Oh!"

"Maybe we should reconsider the weaponry. Springfields have better range than the Winchester but not as much firepower. Of course, they do jam less often. What do you think?"

"Oh!"

Her groans were grating in the back of her throat, and now she was seizing Hickok's hand and grinding it hard against the soft inner folds of her cunt as he continued kneading, squeezing, and tormenting the hard little button.

"Oh! Oh!"

With her free left arm she pulled Hickok toward her and kissed him frankly on the lips, pushing her tongue deep into his mouth. She held the panting embrace for a seeming eternity, all the while massaging his right hand against her crotch as tiny pre-orgasms shot through her cunt like short electrical jolts.

Hickok broke free. He grinned wickedly and his eyes flashed with mean merriment.

"Love me just a little?"

He removed the offending digits and propped himself up over her on both hands.

"Uh-huh," she said thickly through clenched teeth. "Sure I do, you bastard. But you don't get it free. You earn it. It costs you something. Now."

Slipping her hands behind the back of his head, she gripped his long yellow hair with both fists, and putting every ounce of back and arm muscle behind her next move, she slammed his face into her bushy cunt just as hard as she knew how. Simultaneously locking her legs around the back of his head, she ground his face into her vulva with a vengeance, rubbing his mouth, teeth, tongue, nose, and eyes into her warm, juicy snatch.

She gritted her teeth, violently bit off her yelps of pleasure, choked off her delicious shrieks as a torrent of tiny spasms tore out of her. Over and over the shocks and jolts of her ecstasy shot through her. Her head was bobbing up and down excitedly, and her jaw was slack with adrenaline exhaustion.

With her last aching orgasm, her arching back collapsed, and her breath whooshed out of her in a long desperate gasp. She lay there inert. Her head was skewed at a grotesque angle.

She looked as though she'd been killed, not brought to sensual fulfillment.

It was only when she felt Hickok's hand under her ass, gently lifting it off her bedroll, and saw the ominous specter of his tremendously erect cock hovering over her crotch, that she again became alert.

"No, please," she moaned.

She rolled Hickok over onto his back and climbed on top. She lay prone upon his supine bulk. Lazily she kissed his cheek. Now she was drained from the torturous ordeal of her multiple orgasms. She was falling asleep.

"Why not?" he asked.

"Please, Billy. My cuntie's sore. You wore it out. It needs a rest. I need a rest." She lay on top of him, buried her face in his neck, drifted casually toward the long abyss of sleep.

"You cuntie's sore?" Hickok whispered, his voice a high-pitched mockery of her urgent plea. "Well, that's easy to fix."

"Uh-huh," she said pleasantly, and kissed his cheek and laid her face back into his neck.

"We can fix that right now."

Calamity felt his body sliding away from her, her face bouncing softly against his chest, the stout ridges of his muscular stomach, the hard flatness of his abdomen.

"Uh-huh," she murmured sleepily.

"This will give your cuntie just the rest it needs."

She felt her head being gently elevated by his knees and his hands.

"Will this give it a rest?"

She opened her eyes dreamily.

She was staring down at Hickok's enormous cock, inches from her face.

It was swollen with lust, its head the size of a small, delicious apple, pearling with passion.

"Will this let your cuntie cool off?"

She looked up at Hickok. His eyes glinted, unable to repress the smile that was spreading across his face.

She lowered her gaze, and with wary resignation took his massive member fully in her mouth. She began sucking him off with precision and affection. Over and over his orgasms were pumping out of him, so fast and furious that she could not contain them in her mouth.

She released his prick and took the rest of his orgasm in the face. She stared up at him, her cheeks and hair covered with his lust. She pulled him down to her and kissed him frankly on the mouth.

"Hope that satisfies you, cowboy. We had a hard day today, and we got a harder one tomorrow."

"And a hard one tonight."

"Hold it there, cowboy. I still ain't ready."

"You was born ready."

Hickok began inserting his still erect cock into the inner folds of her cunt. Again he massaged the hard marble of her clitoris. A small yelp ripped out of her throat.

To her delight, the startled yelp did not discourage him.

"Didn't hurt you none, did I?" Hickok said, continuing the insertion.

"You sure did, cowboy."

"What you 'spect to do about it?"

"Ask for an apology."

"Then what?"

"Then I'm givin' you till first light to stop."

Hickok whooped, grabbed her hips, and they began the long, amorous ride home.

19

At first light they went into the mountains.

The entrance to the Needle began modestly enough. It was

more a crack in the cliff face than a canyon. Hundreds of feet high and fifty feet across. After a few miles it slanted athwart a larger fissure, which then broadened into a typical pass.

Chilled and shadowy in the early dawn, they threaded their way. Now Hickok changed the order of march. He rode out through the twisting canyons with two large grain bags slung over each side of his saddlehorn. They were filled with sawdust, straight dynamite, and crimping pliers. In a saddle-bag Hickok carried a small sack of dynamite caps, each one packed in heavy muslin and wood shavings. Tied to a saddle ring he had both a knotted climbing rope and two long coils of fuse. Calamity watched him packing crampons for the shoes, as well as climbing spikes and field glasses.

Before he took off, over coffee they had discussed the retreat from Yuma. Hickok explained, "When we come galloping through this pass, them 'Pache are gonna be on us like stink on shit. They're gonna have more and better mounts, they're gonna know their way in and out of this maze. They'll run 'round us like we was infantry and they was horse soldiers."

"Now you tell us," said Calamity.

"What we got to use is firepower and diversion. We'll have half this goddamn pass wired to blow. It'll surprise the hell outta them. Second, we're gonna have caches of water and ammunition stashed at the beginning, middle, and end of the pass. Them 'Pache'll be better mounted but they'll still be weighted down, 'especially with water bags. Our horses'll only be carryin' us. Third, we got grenades. They ain't much. Brass tubing, black powder, and shrapnel. But I doubt that them 'Pache've ever seen one. Hell, they'll think they're fuckin' cannonballs. Any questions?"

Reynolds looked puzzled. "Hope the General 'preciates all this."

"Since there ain't no questions," Hickok continued, "I'll offer one small observation. Them 'Pache know this pass better'n us. They may have shortcuts. They may not only nail us from the rear, they may surprise us from the front. So keep an eye out for secondary passes. Comin' back, look for possible ambushes.

"Now I'm gonna head up front. We shouldn't find no travelers. This here pass is too dry, and no one wants to pack all that water for no good reason. Which means, if we do encounter strangers, they're up to no goddamn good. Be prepared to shoot first. Some kill-crazed bandidos or renegade Mescaleros put a bullet into Charley's dynamite mule, leave your soul to Jesus and kiss your ass goodbye. Better to risk killin' a stranger needlessly than risk all of us gettin' blowed up. Ain't no good reason for any man to be travelin' these canyons. Remember that and shoot first."

"You gonna take a pocket mirror with you?"

"Right. It's an old 'Pache trick. If any bandits catch our signals, they'll think we're Injuns. Two flashes means trouble. You signal back once to acknowledge. Then send Charley ahead to reconnoiter."

"That about it?"

"Watch where you plant them charges. That there's sympathetics detonation' could set off the nearby charges."

"Yeah, same goes for throwin' these makeshift grenades. Remember, the shock could set off the dynamite."

Calamity stood up. "Like you said, this is for real."

Hickok turned and swung onto his roan. He stroked the horse's neck, then patted his two bags of caps and dynamite.

"This may be the last real thing we ever do."

20

Now it was Calamity's turn to haze both the jerk-line string *and* the dynamite mule. She was scared. Not only did she fear the explosives might blow, she felt hemmed in. On each side of her the cliff walls loomed above fifteen hundred feet, and the canyon's floor was less than a hundred across. It had been carved out of the sandstone cliffs by an ancient river, but since that time that once lush land had been desert, the canyon empty and unimaginably dry.

Calamity kept the dynamite mule a dozen steps behind her and led him by his *mecate*. She hazed the jerk-line string from the rear. She kept the string up front as a kind of scout for poor footing and sidewinders. If any mule spooked at a rattler, reared back on his hocks, and shook off his sawbucks, she wanted that jack to be packing water and gear, not dynamite sweating nitro.

With the sandstone cliffs towering above her on each side, she felt like an insect crawling along the canyon floor. Hickok continued ahead, traversing the cliff faces and wiring charges. Reynolds scouted the trail in front and behind them. Clem just stared at a mule's ass and prayed that a falling rock didn't hit the one in back of her.

PART EIGHT

21

During Slater's three-year stay in Yuma, he had gotten to
know the prison doctor well. Repeated floggings from Warden
Stark and gang-stompings from Stryker and his men had
resulted in frequent visits to the prison dispensary.

Doc Harper, an elderly, balding gentleman, now pushing
seventy, had been sent to Yuma on an abortion conviction.
But when the warden discovered that Harper knew his stuff,
he immediately gave the old man a private cottage and
complete run of the prison. Since no free doctor had ever
been rash enough to accept a position at Yuma, Stark was
happy to have a physician—and a competent one at that—
who could look after the ailments of both the prisoners and
the staff.

As for Slater, he had initially dismissed Harper as a
tiresome old quack. The doc had been too painstaking in
treating Slater's injuries, too friendly a conversationalist, and
much too interested in Slater's earlier life. The old man was
endlessly curious about Slater's years with the Apaches,

action he'd seen during the Rebellion, his years with Quantrill, Frank and Jess, and the Youngers.

Such curiosity was suspect, but Slater grudgingly gave the old doc his due. Harper had kept him alive. Slater did not place any special value on this. In most respects, life on the Yuma rockpile was worse than no life at all. But still the doc—through constant care and treatment of Slater's ills—had made survival possible.

There was that time when Stark decided that a year's isolation in a basement cell beneath the main blockhouse would do Slater some good. At his own peril, Harper had slipped Slater books and occasionally some food.

And from time to time, old man Harper had dropped in on him. These visits were supposedly for medical reasons, but in fact he came to talk, to supply human contact—something strictly forbidden in the hole.

Slater would explain to Harper that he liked the food packages, but that the books were a waste. Slater couldn't get over the fact that fictional books such as *Don Quixote* and *Tom Jones* were untrue.

"Who wants to read a lotta lies made up by some man who weren't even there to tell you what never happened in the first place?"

Harper had no answer.

However, when he introduced Slater to Homer, Slater quickly understood what those stories were about.

"Yeah, Homer weren't too bad," Slater had explained to the old doc. "That Trojan Horse Odysseus give Troy, that gift were real clever. The way he blinded that big one-eyed fucker, yeah, that got it done all right. But, hell, you say that war stuff may be true. Bet it be. That'd explain why I liked it. It ain't like Homer's shittin' us."

Harper allowed that since an archeologist had unearthed Troy, there was some basis for the story.

"It all be true," Slater said, nodding his head for emphasis. "That *Odyssey* stuff too. I could tell. It sounded real."

22

The morning the guard opened the door to the hotbox and Slater stepped out into the blinding sunlight, he found that after the short chain was removed, he had trouble straightening. He was surprised, however, to discover that the bulk of his discomfort came from his back's ferocious itching, a sure sign that the whip scars were healing.

He knew that he owed this to Doc Harper. The night he was flogged, Harper had had him hauled out of the hotbox and laid belly-down on an infirmary cot. The bone-deep lacerations that were too wide to heal, he stitched. The smaller ones he cauterized, and in the following days he saw that Slater had daily dressings.

Harper was there the morning Slater came out of the box. He looked at Slater's back and said, "The lacerations shouldn't reopen." He turned to the guards. "Drop him off at the infirmary after breakfast. I'll give him some clean grease to put on those scars. The sun's going to shrink them out on that pile, and he'll have to stay lubricated."

Slater was still blinded by the light, and he had a thirty-day growth of beard. He faced the direction of Harper's voice.

"Why all the bother, old man?"

"You mean, why keep you alive?"

"Yeah, you bust your nuts gettin' me into shape so Stark can bust me down again. Seems kinda inefficient, you ask me."

"Son," the old man said to the convict with a look of real sadness, "you may not understand this now, but one day I believe you will. Human life, even in this hellhole, is a gift, a rare gift."

Still squinting, Slater grinned. Harper winced at the crooked curling of the pulled-back lips, the feral savagery of the wolfishly bared teeth. Slater said, "Maybe, doc, though I don't see what's so rare 'bout life in Yuma. Maybe them gods of yours've dealt me one of them Trojan Horses. Maybe this gift of life is hidden away, locked inside somethin'. Wherever it be, I sure can't find it."

"You will. When your war ends."

"What happens then?"

The doc gave Slater a gentle smile. "The odyssey begins."

"Doc, I just don't see no voyages takin' place 'round here. I don't see no boats nor no seas. Only sand, mesquite, and sidewinders."

"No one-eyed giants who eat men whole?"

Slater was still squinting, though not from the sun. He was peering at the doc with narrowed eyes. The guards were starting to pull him toward his cell block. He shook them off.

"Maybe one or two of them cyclopses. I see a few of them."

"Then your odyssey's begun."

23

Slater worked the whole day on the quarry rim. Under his striped prison shirt, his back was covered with the doc's grease.

All day he swung his hammer and sweated. And wondered about the doc's statement. "War's end, odyssey's beginning." As he worked, he stared down into the great bowl of the Yuma quarry—a dust-choked, demon-driven inferno, filled with strange, inhuman men, men like himself, men with flat reptilian eyes and crooked grins. He saw no odysseys there. Staring over the Sonoran Desert at the distant, arid mountains, he saw no hope of escape.

All he had left was his private war with Stryker and Stark,

no "progress of the spirit" or "search for the soul," the sort of thing Doc Harper talked of.

And yet he felt somehow, some way, that old man was right.

24

That night he lay on his stomach on his cot. The Yuma cells were little more than holes carved into a sheer sandstone cliff, long tiers of tiny caves big enough to sleep only one or two men. The openings were covered with iron latticework and connected to each other in front by long iron catwalks. These caves had been chiseled into the sandstone cliffs years ago by the prisoners. Men lived in them like animals, often chained to the stone floor.

Slater tried to ignore his itching back and his aching muscles. Doc Harper had left a book for him: that dog-eared copy of *The Odyssey*, which Slater had read the year before in the hole. He knew now why Harper had lent it to him. In Odysseus's return from the wars, Slater felt, he could see similarities to his own life. His years with the Apache, then Shiloh, then Quantrill, then Jess and the Youngers, a whole decade spent on the owlhoot trail. But this was Yuma, not the Aegean. And yet . . .

That night he got a visit. The turnkey had his cell door unlocked and handed him the ducat. Slater was dumbfounded. He'd never had a visitor. Why should he? His outlaw friends weren't about to walk through those prison gates, his women weren't the kind to visit hell for a chat. His kin were long dead.

The cell door opened and he walked out the door, down the iron catwalk, his leg irons clanking. He descended the three-story steel ladder into the moonlit yard. The stars were out by the thousands, bright, unblinking. And the constellations: the

Bear, the Big Dipper, Orion the Hunter. And then there was Polaris. It occurred to Slater that he hadn't seen these stars in three long years.

Visitation was in the main blockhouse, a square adobe building two stories high. He followed the guard through the open door and into the lobby with its Spanish furniture and gloomy portraits of Lincoln, Washington, and Grant. On the second floor, the room had two doors. Visitors went in the first entrance, prisoners the second.

It was invariably vacant. Yuma was the end of the line, and in the prisoners' minds the ever-empty visitation room served only to remind them of their doom. Yuma prisoners were the country's refuse, forgotten men. Slater wondered absently if this so-called visit wasn't one of Stryker's jokes.

Then he saw her. A young woman dressed in widow's weeds—a long black dress and a black bonnet. What is this, Slater thought, a schoolmarm in mourning?

He walked to the far side of the room and sat down across from her. They were separated by a wire screen. He looked through the mesh.

Calamity Jane Cannary was grinning at him from under the hood of her bonnet, an index finger at her lips, motioning him to be silent.

"Brother Torn," she said loudly, "the family's so worried about you. I've come a far piece to see you, all the way from the old Virginia homestead."

Slater grimaced. The closest he'd ever come to Virginia were the desolate fields and thickets around Shiloh Church.

Which was in Tennessee.

And all he'd ever seen there were the rifles and bayonets of those twenty thousand dug-in bluebellies in front of that country church, a long blue line of shooting, screaming Yankees that cut the rebel regiments to pieces. And sent General "Fightin' Al" Johnston to an early grave.

"Thankee kindly," he mumbled to Clem.

"Brother Torn, I got some very bad news. Pa passed away just after the fall tobacco harvest. We buried him under the old chinaberry tree out in the North Forty. We thought it best you hear it from your blood."

Slater stared at her. His real pa was murdered by Jayhawkers when he was eleven. He'd never seen his ma. Years later, down in Mexico, Cochise had told him that she had been part 'Pache.

"Pa—you know how religious Pa was—he always prayed that you was gettin' enough of the Bible here. On his deathbed he begged me to come out here and talk to the warden. Pa fretted on it steady. Pleaded with me to get out here and talk to the warden 'bout Sunday meetin', hymn singin', and such. Pa wanted to make sure you had a Bible of your own. Warden Stark—such a lovely man!—said I could give you one. I left it with him for you. He said that a certain Sergeant Stryker—was that the name?—would be so pleased to give it to you."

"Thankee."

By now the guard, sitting by the door, had gotten up and walked into the hall and was conversing with a second screw. Calamity quickly whispered the plan.

"Okay, Bill and me got a way to break you out."

"Can't be done."

"Sure it can. You go over Freedom Point."

"Not likely, Clem. Even if I survived the hundred-and-twenty-foot fall, which ain't likely, I'd drown with all this weight. I'm sportin' triple leg irons."

"True, that fall might kill you. I can't make no promises there. But as to drownin', Bill'll be in the water waitin' for you with a lass rope tied under his arms. And an extra one for you. I'll be on the other side with a span of horses. The two ropes'll be hitched to them. I'm pullin' you two across the fork of them rivers."

"That's the Gila and the Colorado. They ain't no creeks. They be rough and muddy."

"They be muddy, all right."

"Yeah, I know. 'Too thick to drink and too thin to plow.' Bill ain't gonna see much if'n he expects to go divin' for me."

"You got a better idea?"

"I ain't sure, Clem. Don't sound possible."

"Torn, you gotta weigh possible freedom against definite prison. Triple life in that Yuma Cauldron is the definite."

Slater's eyes narrowed. "Why you doin' it?"

"Does it matter?"

He shrugged. "No, guess not. Though I'd still like to know."

"Remember them 'iron enemies of bankers and railroad barons' you rode with up in Kansas and Missouri after you and Quantrill and Bloody Bill busted up?"

"You mean Frank and Jess and Cole?"

"Hickok wants you to help bring 'em in."

"Ain't exactly my line of work. I admit I got it in for Cole, leavin' me shot to pieces out there in the desert arroyo. But I ain't never lawed." He shook his head vigorously.

"Maybe breakin' rocks suits you better. It's only for life."

"When do I make this jump?"

"Tomorrow mornin'. When you see the horses hitched on the other bank of the river and me alongside them."

"Hope I don't land on Bill," he muttered. "It's gonna make one hellacious splash." He stood up to leave, then said softly, "Say, Clem, man told me today I was goin' on an odyssey. That's some sort of long trip. 'Pears he was right."

"That got somethin to do with water?"

"Did once."

"Then that's you."

"Sonofabitch."

The guard waved to him then. He headed back to his cell.

25

The next morning Slater knew he had to take the plunge. When he caught mess, and the quarry chain, he knew this was his day. He was busting out if he had to grow wings.

He wanted to tell Harper, tell him and thank him. Somehow he felt he owed him. In ways he still could not describe.

He clinked up to the quarry rim. By now it was 6:00 A.M., and on the far side of the river, he saw two people ride up on horseback. The man kicked off his boots, then dove into the water. Seemed innocent enough. No one was even watching. Except Torn.

He swung fiercely at a granite boulder, his hammer singing across the quarry with a hard, steady *kkk-ling kkk-ling kkk-ling*. For the first time in three years he almost enjoyed his work, because, yes, he finally had his chance. And hell, if the jump worked, why, the guards wouldn't even follow. They left the dog-work for the 'Pache. And Hickok must have an answer to that. Probably a deal with Geronimo.

He was swinging full tilt, flushed with dreams of freedom, when he heard the faint, whistling hiss of the pick handle and felt the sickening *whack!* across his kidneys. He turned, his back and side erupting with pain.

And there was Stryker with most of his teeth missing.

"Remember me?"

"Yeah, you're Father Christmas."

Again, the whistling hiss and the *whack!*, this one exploding across the shoulders.

"Try again, punk."

"Florence Nightingale, Yuma Nurse?"

Again, the whistling hiss, this *whack!* driving hard into Slater's right shoulder. Slater pretended to glance at it, so he could check Hickok's position in the water. Hickok was swimming hard, but he needed two minutes. Just two minutes.

Stryker spat on his hands one at a time. He gripped the end of the pick handle with both hands and said, "Okay, asshole, you and me. Down in the Cauldron. You're enjoying this big bad boulder too fuckin' much. Me and the boys want you down in the pit with the dogfaces." Slater glanced at the gun bulls above the rim, with their repeating Henrys. They were all watching him, rifles at the ready. "You got it," Stryker said. "They're all primed. One wrong look, one false move, and they're blowin' you off this pile."

Slater was still staring at the gun bulls when the third

whack! hit. It caught him across the shins totally by surprise. Both his legs gave and he was rolling down the slope.

When he got to his knees, he was covered from head to foot with rock dust. He was now a hundred feet from Freedom Point, most of the distance up a steep slope. Stryker threw his hammer at him. It bounced off his back with a *thud!*

"Now get up and break some rock."

Slater grabbed the hammer and stood. Stryker caught him with another *whack!* across his left shoulder. By now rage had flooded his brain, and he was hardly aware of any damage Stryker was doing. Finally he had a real shot at freedom, and this baboon was blowing it for him. He glared at Stryker, his upper lip curling uncontrollably, his eyes narrowing. The hammers in the quarry were silent, all heads turned to the two of them. Stryker was shouting about "Southern scum" and "Confederate trash," but Slater wasn't listening to the words. And only when Stryker stopped shouting long enough to catch the look in Slater's eyes did he realize he was in trouble.

Stryker had a dozen gun bulls covering him on the rim.

He was armed with a club against a shackled, beaten man.

And yet Stryker was in trouble.

"You know," Slater said quietly, "there's been times you got me pissed, but no more."

Stryker gripped the pick handle with both hands. "Yeah?"

"You're about the sorriest sonofabitch I ever met."

"That so, Honcho?" Stryker backed up a half-step.

"Other men pull their time, get off this quarry, and go home. But not you. This is your home. You're gonna swing your dick on this hard-rock pile forever. You're gonna die right here in this heat and dust. You're the biggest lifer in this jail."

"You know the penalty for insulting a guard," Stryker said, studying Slater carefully. Slater was holding the hammer loosely, the head resting on the slope.

"Stryker, I considered doin' you a favor and puttin' you out of your misery. But that'd be too kind. I like you on this hard-rock pile. Only I don't want you swingin' that pick handle. Or your mouth. Or your dick."

"What do you want me swingin'? That bullwhip tonight? Maybe Stark'll let me strip the hide off your back."

"The only thing you'll be swingin' tonight is crutches."

"Then come and get your time."

Stryker stepped toward Slater and swung the handle at his temple.

Slater ducked, and the momentum of the miss made Stryker lose his balance.

Quickly, Slater broke both of Stryker's kneecaps with his sledgehammer. By then, bullets were kicking up rock fragments all around him. Slater groined Stryker with the big sledge, shattering pelvis and testicles.

Then he dropped the hammer and made his break up the slope. With thirty pounds of iron on his ankles and shins, that hobbling run up the crushed rock was the hardest thing he ever did. Repeating Henrys were peppering the slope from every angle—in front of him, behind him, to each side. Rock fragments stung and cut him, explosions of dust blinded him so badly he couldn't even see the rim when he finally reached the top. All he could think was, Freedom! Freedom!

He went over the cliff's edge without even seeing it. All he knew was water rushed at him with incredible speed and his weighted legs straightened him up till he was almost vertical.

Then he hit the water.

His knees slammed into his chest so hard he thought he'd somehow landed on rock. But then he couldn't breathe and he sensed he was choking on water.

He knew he was sinking like a stone. Then he passed out and he knew no more.

26

Hickok looked up. Slater was no longer visible. Then he heard the shots and guessed what was wrong. A guard had obviously moved Slater off, and Slater was now making his break for the cliff's edge.

Even in the river, where Hickok treaded water and fought the current, the gunfire was impressive. Hickok could not believe a man could survive it. Fifty shots? Sixty? It sounded like the Wilderness up there.

But then he looked up and saw Slater fall.

Feet first, and straight at him.

Hickok dived till he thought his ears would burst. Slater's landing was explosive, deafening under the river. Then something heavy glanced off his shoulder. He blocked it with his knee, then encircled it with an arm. He swung the other arm around, and he thought he had Slater by the waist and the leg. He grabbed on tight, and when he had a grip, he got his legs underneath him and kicked toward the top. He kicked again and again and again.

Then he realized they were still sinking. In another few seconds he would black out.

His strength was deserting him. Slater's body was sliding down his own till they were face to face under the water. Slater's eyes had rolled back, showing nothing but whites. For all he knew, Slater was dead.

Pull, Calamity, pull! was his last coherent thought.

He clung to the sinking man and fought against oblivion.

27

Calamity stood on the opposite bank. Earlier, she'd dallied each of the two ropes around the modified saddlehorns. She had double-cinched the saddles and lashed extra latigos around the chest harnesses. If those saddles didn't hold the two ropes after all that, they could kiss Slater goodbye.

She had not liked Hickok's plan back in Deadwood, and she'd liked it less after she'd seen the fork in the two rivers.

True, Hickok had somehow made it across on his own, but she knew she would have to tow him back.

When she first saw the setup, she'd yelled at Bill, "How the hell you expect to find and pull him outta there? You can't see nothin' in all that mud. Hell, you even got him jumpin' into two rivers, not one. The Colorado and the Gila *both*."

Hickok was terse. "Ain't no other way."

Now, as she heard a fusilade from inside the quarry, she could only shudder. That damned Slater couldn't even drag his ass over that cliff without bringing the whole U.S. Army down on him.

Then she saw him jump—jump, tumble, drop, fall, whatever it was. He managed to hit the water upright—thanks, no doubt, to those heavy leg irons. Unfortunately, he was also landing directly on Hickok. Only seconds before Slater hit, Bill spotted Slater and dived.

Then the river above him exploded like someone had fired a mortar.

How long she stood there she could not say. Did Bill have him? Should she flog the horses? Only when she saw the prison gun bulls lining up on the rimrock, firing their rifles at the concentric waves fanning out below, did she know it was now or never. Bill and Slater were not coming up on their own.

She had no other choice. She laid her wrist quirt across the horses' rumps as hard as she knew how. The big gray and the line-backed roan shot forward, the loose ropes swaying over the bank, drifting down into the water. Calamity, screaming obscenities at the horses, laid on the quirt again and again.

The slack paid out, and the ropes snapped taut. Both saddles jerked violently, chest harnesses and cinches digging into the rearing team. The horses slowed with the sudden weight, and Calamity lashed them harder, cursing herself for not having four fucking mules to haul them out.

But the horses dug. Frightened by the hellbent harpy behind them screaming and whipping their flanks, they got back on their hocks and heaved. Twenty, fifty, a hundred yards. Calamity looked back at the lines. One was loose.

So Hickok was on the rope, and Slater never got lashed up.

Ignoring the mount with the loose, flopping line, she bent her efforts on the snuffy roan, the only one now hauling weight. She laid on the quirt. She didn't look back, but drove him on and on. Hickok would make it or drown or get shot dead in the water. She'd pull him up alive or dead. One-fifty, one-eighty, two hundred yards.

Then the horn snapped off the saddle fork and went flying past her head like a bullet. The snorting roan, freed of the weight, broke loose and shot away from the banshee flogging him.

Calamity, exhausted and sobbing, fell to her knees.

She looked back and saw no one. She'd come up empty!

She pulled herself to her knees and ran down the gray. She snubbed the reins around the horn and hung there for a moment, clutching at the pommel and cantle, struggling to get her breath and her legs. She knew what she'd have to do. Round up the horses, get back to Reynolds, then ride like hell through the Needle. No way to set off the charges with Hickok gone . . .

"Goddamn you, gimme a hand!"

She turned her head. Hickok was clambering over the edge of the embankment, one arm clutching the rimrock, the other hanging on to the legs of Torn Slater, slung belly-down over his shoulder.

Then she heard the dull rattle of Henrys and saw the bullets whining off the rocks all around Hickok and Slater.

"Gimme a hand. No, just get them fuckin' horses. Jesus, Calamity, they're runnin' clear back to the Needle."

She laughed in spite of herself, tears blurring her eyes. She vaulted the gray, then rode down the roan. She tossed a loop over his head, reined around, and raced the two hundred yards back to the embankment. As she came within range of the gunfire, she dropped low across the gray's neck, leading the roan behind her.

"Damn, am I glad to see you," said Hickok.

"It's mutual."

She swung off, and looping the gray's reins in her belt to keep him from bolting, she grabbed Slater's free arm.

"Use the roan," she muttered to Hickok. "The horn's broke off."

They threw Slater belly-down over the roan, where he slowly, reflexively began to vomit down the horse's side. Calamity followed the reins, still looped in her belt, till they led her to the gray. Grabbing the horn she blindly, wearily swung on. She pointed to the empty stirrup and held out an arm. Hickok swung on behind. Wildly, the bullets kicked up dirt behind them. Somehow none of them struck home.

Keeping the roan between them and the gunfire, they headed into the Sonoran Desert, toward their two extra mounts, hobbled in the mesquite. Past saguaro and creosote and wind-bent sage.

Far in the east, where the sun rose slowly, Clem could already feel its blistering heat.

28

Within a mile of the river's edge, the cactus died. And a mile after that the yucca vanished. They were in a desert so scorching and barren and arid that the sagebrush withered and bleached out white.

Eighty miles of desert. Eighty miles till they reached the Needle. Eighty miles of choking heat.

Calamity had expected this. She and Bill had crossed it at night and, knowing they would be back in the day, had cached their water cans at forty-mile intervals, hoping to take some weight off the horses.

But nothing would help the roan. The struggle at the breaks where he had pulled both Hickok and Slater across the river had broken him. Ten miles from the first cache, he dropped to his knees.

He was finished. Slater was still belly-down on the hornless saddle. Hickok dragged him off, so the horse wouldn't fall on him. He then cut the latigo and pulled off the saddle.

Hickok patted the fallen roan's neck to quiet him. He then took the Colt out of his holster, and pressing the muzzle tight between the roan's eyes, he pulled the trigger.

Slater was semiconscious, lying on his back. They propped his head up and Hickok got out a 'scope from his saddlebag. The desert was flat and hard and the air clear. Nearby was a decent-sized dune from which Hickok could almost see to Yuma with the 'scope.

He climbed the sandhill and studied the backtrail. When he came back, he said to Calamity, "They ain't comin' from there," and pointed toward Yuma. "Why cross a desert when you can send them 'Pache? Best goddamn trackers, soldiers, killers in the whole fuckin' world."

"Will they be waitin' at the pass?"

"Naw, we'll beat them there, and if Reynolds sets them last two charges right, we'll delay them even more after they get there. But it's a two-day ride through them canyons and gorges. They'll have time to catch up."

"I hope he's worth it," Calamity said, staring at the half-conscious Slater.

"He was once. He may be again. But for now you best sit him up. I'll water and grain the stock. We got more water and another rest at the cache. It ain't too far."

"Let's forget about restin' at the cache. I don't wanna meet no hostiles at the pass. I'd as soon we keep pushin'."

"Then grain and water them horses; rub them down too." He pointed to the fallen roan. "We ain't doin' too well far as livestock goes. They need a lot of rest. Maybe we better conserve."

Calamity had to agree. "Hope Reynolds is doin' better with them charges."

"Better be somethin' special, extra special."

29

Reynolds thought he was doing something special.

Ten hours ago on the desert floor, he'd 'scoped the long, thin lines of a geological fault. The seams appeared to slant diagonally through the cliff wall, eight hundred feet above the canyon's mouth. If he was correct and if he could work the last of his charges into the largest of the fault lines, he could close the canyon's western mouth and blow those Apaches to high hell.

That's what he'd thought ten hours before. It had been early morning then. He'd stood in the shade of the western face, where he'd been safe and comfortable. Now that it was afternoon and he was dangling from a rope six hundred feet above the desert floor, the sun was baking his brains. Reynolds wasn't so sure.

For one thing, he didn't know how much longer he could hang from that knotted rope. The end of it, one hundred feet above him, was lashed to a spike hammered into a ledge high above the canyon's mouth. He had spent eight hours of hand-over-hand, foothold-to-foothold climbing just to get that spike in. Reynolds had had to squeeze his way up a long vertical fissure. He'd braced his back on one side of the crack, his feet on the other, and spent five full hours, knees against chest, squirming up the chimney. He'd spasmed his legs with the effort. He'd scraped his back raw and bleeding. Once he had slipped and dropped six feet down the shaft, braking himself to a grinding halt with his shoulders and his feet.

And it was from there—four hundred feet above the desert floor—that he'd worked his way into the long, slanting crack.

It stretched diagonally along the canyon wall, some two

hundred feet to the lined fault. The problem was the tightness of the fit. A foot deep and eighteen inches wide at the base, it had taken Reynolds two full hours to get there.

Twice he got stuck. Once he panicked, convinced he could not get his breath, and almost rolled out of the crack and over the cliff's edge.

Two-thirds of the way up, a big, hairy tarantula rounded a corner and faced him eyeball-to-eyeball, just standing there as if waiting for him to move. He knew from experience that tarantulas could jump as much as two feet, and he did not want to risk swatting it. So, slipping the hammer thong off his Colt, he eased it out of the holster, and ever so slowly, after working the pistol in front of his face, he pointed the muzzle at the bug and shot the spider to pieces.

Inside that slanting crack, six hundred feet above the desert floor, he thought he would go deaf.

Then he reached the end of the line. The ledge was a dozen feet beyond the crack. Lying on his stomach, staring out across the canyon's wall, he could not believe he had run out of footing. He'd misread his sights.

Well, there was no way he was backing up.

He found a handhold, secured a purchase, eased his body out of the crack.

And swung out over the abyss.

How long he hung there he could not guess. It seemed forever, and only when he felt his muscles cramping and realized he was losing his grip could he force himself to move.

But he found foot- and handholds and made it to the three-by-six-foot ledge. Down into the ledge he then drove the spike with the steel butt of his Colt. He tied the climbing rope and went over the side.

Here he was, six hundred feet above the canyon floor, pressed against a sheer cliff of pale sandstone, facing the fault.

He looped the end of his knotted climbing rope around his chest and tied it off. To his belt he had lashed a grain sack of dynamite packed in wet sawdust. He opened the bag. The fault line was a black seam two hundred yards long and two inches wide. Plenty of room in which to wedge his last six sticks of dynamite.

He took a roll of white medical tape from the bag. Using the entire length, he made a huge X over the black cliff face and the charge. Each slanting line was three feet long and a foot wide.

He wanted it visible from a long, long way off, up those twisting desert canyons.

He rested awhile in front of the charge. Slowly he eased himself another dozen feet down the canyon wall. He tied himself off a second time and took a piton from the grain sack. Then, carefully, praying that he would not disturb the sensitive, impacted dynamite, he drove it into the rock.

He tied one end of the second climbing rope coiled around his chest to the spike. Grabbing the knotted rope tightly, he worked his way down the cliff, paying out the coiled slack as he went. Fifty feet down he found his exit. Earlier that morning he had 'scoped a second slanting crack, which would get him back to the vertical chimney, which would then take him to the canyon's floor.

He hoped his legs and back could stand the descent.

30

Hickok was right.

By sundown their mounts were wrung out. He called a halt, and they made camp three miles from the Needle.

While they grained and watered the stock, Calamity looked around. Dried mesquite spread out over an endless expanse. There was little in the way of wildlife. A paisano bird fluttered in the stunted brush, and overhead a turkey buzzard wheeled in the dusk, keeping lonely vigil.

What the buzzard hoped to find, Calamity could scarcely imagine. Besides themselves, the only living things she had seen were rattlers, Gila monsters, scrawny desert birds, scorpions, and foot-long centipedes. She wondered if they themselves could be the buzzard's prospective dinner. Perhaps it knew something they did not. She looked to the south and wondered if the buzzard was waiting for a distant war party of Apaches.

By the time the Arbuckle's was brewing, Charley Reynolds rode into camp, leading the jerk-line string of mules. Bacon and pan bread were on the fire, along with a three-quart pot of beans. Clem was pouring second cups of coffee. Hickok had removed a canteen of Jack Daniel's from the pack on the extra horse and was lacing both his and Slater's coffee. Calamity put down the fire-blackened coffeepot.

Reynolds dismounted. Still holding the packline and his horse's reins, he waved to Slater.

"Torn, welcome back to the land of the free."

Slater looked around him at the sparse chaparral. "Ain't exactly like I remembered it."

"This ain't nothin' like nobody remembered it."

"You get them charges planted?" Calamity asked, tossing Charley the whiskey canteen.

"Reckon so. Lost half my hide doin' it. But if we hit it right, them charges should bring down half the mountain. I found a long black seam right over the mouth. Should go five hundred feet down."

"And that's where you planted it?"

"Yep. We can detonate her with the 'Big Fifty' from a half-mile or so up the pass. An old sharpshooter like Hickok here could, that is."

"Hope so," said Hickok. "We're gonna need every break we can get."

"And the first break should be rest, grub, and an early start at sunup," said Reynolds. "So lemme unpack, picket, and grain these here ani-mules. Then I'll eat and have a snort. Ain't et since first light." He tossed the whiskey canteen back to Clem.

"Us neither," Clem said.

31

They ate a big meal—bully beef, beans, pan bread, and canned peaches. Sitting around the fire on their McClellans and bedrolls, they drank Arbuckle's, sipped whiskey.

To the west the sun blazed blood red, sinking slowly toward the distant rimrock. Calamity watched it for a long while. Then she turned south where the immense desert curved over the distant line of the horizon and died away in a haze. She glanced to the purpling east above the black cliffs, and the sky soon to be filled with wheeling constellations. Then she turned west again, to where the sun was now setting. When it vanished, that part of the sky darkened, and the western stars appeared with surprising swiftness.

The fire died down. Hickok pushed sand over it casually with a boot.

"Across a night desert, a 'Pache can spot a fire a good fifty miles," Hickok said.

"Wouldn't build me no quirlies neither," Reynolds offered.

"That's a fact," Hickok concurred.

Slater nodded his agreement.

Clem sipped her whiskey and shrugged.

Nobody did much talking for a while. Judging from the way Charley's hands shook, he had had a rough day. Calamity could guess that climbing that canyon wall had been hell uncorked. She'd seen the cliff face when they rode out of the pass, and it had gone straight up. Over supper, while Charley was bedding down the mules, she'd asked Bill how Charley scaled that sheer rock wall.

"The hard way."

"Torn," Reynolds was saying over the cooling ashes, "you lived with the 'Pache, didn't you?"

Slater nodded. "I was raised by them as a kid."

"Never told me that," Calamity said, looking at him sideways.

"Ain't nothin to brag on. Most people would look on that as a misspent youth."

"Maybe it was," Calamity said. "Considerin' how you turned out."

"'Pears that way," Slater said. Calamity watched his smile. He had many wide, good-looking teeth. She felt a small stirring, and then she remembered that long ago—before Bill, before Deadwood—she had liked Slater very much.

"So how does it look to you?" Reynolds asked Slater. "Our escape plans through the Needle and such?"

"All right on paper," said Slater. Hickok tossed him the whiskey canteen and Slater refilled his mess cup. "Guess we find out tomorrow when them 'Pache come ridin' up our ass."

"How you judge our chances?" Calamity asked. "Havin' lived with them heathen redbellies and all?"

"Oh, I ain't judgin' nothin' and I sure ain't complainin'. Hell, we all gonna die someday. I'd just as soon die out here, fightin' 'Pache, as in some damn jail. I will say your plan ain't perfect, though, not against no 'Pache, leastways."

"How you figure?" Calamity asked, leaning on an elbow.

"Well, your plan is scary, I'll give you that. That first explosion, the way Hickok describes it, that alone'd turn anyone back across this desert to wherever he come from."

"But not the 'Pache?" Calamity said.

"No, not your 'Pache. He ain't no mortal man. He ain't scared by firepower. Hell, the army tried usin' howitzers on them a few years back in one of them New Mexico canyons, and they still kept comin'. So a little noise and a few rockslides ain't gonna run them off. The 'Pache'll know from our tracks there's only four of us. When they see all them pack-mule tracks, they'll think we got booty." Slater sipped his whiskey from his mess cup. "And they won't worry none about gettin' ambushed in the pass. Ambush is a 'Pache specialty, and the Needle is the 'Pache's canyon. They'll know every nook and cranny, every in and out. Once we go into that Needle, it's their play."

"We'll slow them down a bit," Hickok said. He refilled his mess cup from the whiskey canteen and passed it to Reynolds.

"Yeah, and we'll ride the hocks right off'n them horses, headin' through," Reynolds said.

Slater shrugged.

"Think we won't?" Calamity asked Slater.

"Sure we will, if them nags got the bottom. But them animals have been ten days hard travelin' through the desert. They're beat. That 'Pache pony herd'll only have a day's ride on it. Also, you three load a horse down with grain, water, saddles, rations, and the like. A 'Pache travels different. 'Pache carries a little water, maybe."

"How do their horses feed?"

"On mesquite and prickly pear. Then the 'Pache eats the horse. Hell, if we make forty miles a day, a 'Pache'll make a hundred. When all their horses give out, that 'Pache'll make seventy a day afoot."

"So you expect action?" said Reynolds.

"Yeah, that canyon's gonna be a ball-buster." He upended the canteen. "Damn, that's mighty mild liquor. Or have I just been in jail too long?"

"Both, I 'spect," Hickok said. "The whiskey's a present from Custer. Somethin' called Jack Daniel's Sour Mash. Company sprung up after the War, back there in Tennessee. The General said it were expensive."

"It's good, I'll give him that," Reynolds said. "This stuff died painless with me."

"After all the Injun whiskey you've drunk, rattlesnake poison'd die painless with you," said Hickok.

"What's Injun whiskey?" Calamity asked, taking the canteen from Slater.

"Little of everything. Grain alcohol, cayenne, blood, gunpowder, India ink, sagebrush, lye soap, throw in some buffalo chips, you got it."

"Buffalo chips?" Calamity repeated incredulously.

"An Injun don't get a three-day hangover, he don't believe

he was drunk," Reynolds explained. "The buffalo chips guarantee he'll be *mucho* sick."

"Charley," Hickok said, "that Injun whiskey'll go down hard after gettin' spoiled on sour mash."

"Yeah, I'll probably have to give up drinkin'."

"Sure. 'Bout the time you give up eatin'; breathin', and chokin' your chicken."

"Maybe."

Hickok yawned. "Torn, why don't you put your bedroll south of here and take first watch. Clem'll go second, I'll go third, Charley fourth. Watch should face south, though a man can circle on you. Don't 'spect trouble yet, but you never know. Spread the bedrolls far apart. No point in bunchin' up. Just makes an easy target."

Hickok rolled up his bedroll, stood, and walked off into the brush. Reynolds drifted east. When Slater headed south, Calamity stayed put.

For a long time she waited, her head resting against the fork of her McClellan. Overhead, she watched the constellations wheel imperceptibly around the Pole Star like the minute hand on a watch. The Mexicans called them *El Reloj de los Indios*, the Indians' clock. And Hickok claimed you could actually tell the time by their movement.

She followed Bill to his bedroll, but by then he was asleep.

32

It didn't take Calamity long to find Slater. He was a hundred yards south of the camp and sitting on his saddle blanket, his head against his McClellan. He seemed more interested in watching the stars than in looking for Apaches.

"You never told me you was raised by no 'Paches," said Calamity.

"It ain't nothin' to brag on."

"Yeah, but that sure do explain a lot about you. Outlaw Torn Slater! No wonder you rode them high lines. Stands to reason the scariest outlaw alive should be trained by the 'Pache.''

"Yeah, 'spect so.'' He turned his head sideways on the saddle and stared up at Clem. "You know, you still ain't explained why you're here.''

"I told you the reason before you come.''

"Naw, that's Custer's reason. I mean *your* reason. Ain't no reason worth what you're goin' through. What any of you are goin' through.''

"I ain't so sure 'bout it anymore, neither. Oh, we all claim we got our reasons. Charley, he says he's strong on Custer, the army, and what he calls duty. Says it's what he does, what he gets paid for. Bill claims he's got this thing that happened back at the Wilderness, in the War, something between him and Custer.''

"Custer saved his life. So what? That was war and a dozen years back. Lotta men saved your life. And you saved theirs. But that ain't no reason to go crossin' this barren desert and takin' on half the 'Pache nation.''

"Tell it to Bill. He claims it's more'n that.''

"What could be more?''

"Bill won't say. All I know is, it must be somethin' to make Bill Hickok go through this. He is one cold dude.''

"You must love him a lot to go through all this yourself.''

"I really ain't so sure. I was more sure when we started out. But I don't know. That damn Custer, he got me thinkin'. Know what he said, Torn? He claimed I was in this for the glory.''

"I don't see much of that.''

"Yeah, but that's what the bastard said. And he told me I'd learn that 'the hard way.' He said that 'eagles eat carrion' and that 'the glory road is paved with rocks.' Well, he weren't far from wrong.''

"So why do it?''

"You wouldn't understand.'' Clem averted her eyes. "It's different with you and Bill and Charley. You three, you always been somebody.''

"You be somebody.''

"Me? 'Fore I met Bill, I was just a round-heeled, hard-drinking, shanty-Irish whore, hustlin' drinks and tricks in cowtown dives. Mostly the tricks."

"So I recall."

"Well, leastways then you just got to lie around on your back and didn't hurt your feet so much. That's how I started out. And sure as buzzards eat carrion, that's the way I'll end up. 'Less'n them 'Pache stake you out on an anthill, wrap you up in a wet, shrinkin' rawhide, or leave me facedown and hairless on a bed of prickly pear. Maybe. But I'll tell you one thing. For a while I'm gonna be somebody. I'm gonna be Calamity Jane Cannary, the outlaw lady. I'll sling a gun, fight them savages, ride with Bill Hickok, take on Jesse James. I ain't got no pipe dreams, and I ain't bound for glory. I know who I am and what I am. I'll probably die drunk, fuckin' two-bit cowhands in some up-stairs crib. Just the way I began. But for a while I'll be somebody."

"And all this time I thought you was doin' this for love of Bill."

"Oh, I love him all right, but you know, Bill ain't the kind to get too close to."

"He never was what you'd call sentimental."

"Naw, he always said that when a man was a ballsy, two-fisted, rawhide-tough sort of man—you know, a man like you or him—a woman feared him for it, then hated him. Then the man hated the woman."

"Does he hate you?"

"Naw, he said it were different with him and me. He said it was like we was cut off the same piece of cloth."

"You believe that?"

"I believe this—I believe you and him, you're real men." Calamity was sitting down on the ground beside Slater now, her eyes wide and expressive. "Torn, you been without a woman three years now, and we all may die tomorrow. You need a woman." Calamity was sitting next to Slater on the blanket. His head was still propped on his saddle, but his eyes were watching her intently.

"Yeah, well, I ain't about to fuck around with Bill Hickok's girl, not after he dragged me out of the Gila."

"The horse dragged you out. I flogged that roan till the pommel busted off."

"Till the roan died."

"Just like you might die tomorrow when them 'Pache catch up with us."

"So might you."

"Which proves my point."

Calamity reached over and gently touched his member, rising under his gray canvas prison pants.

"Whoa, now," Slater said. "You didn't hear me, woman. I done a lot of hard things. I killed and I robbed and I made war. But I don't fuck a friend's girl. I got some rules."

"And I said Bill don't care. All he thinks of anymore is dyin'. Has nightmares all the time. That thing back at the Wilderness with Custer. He has nightmares 'bout that one a lot. Then there's this other one, 'bout a poker game. Draws the queen of diamonds and gets killed. In fact, claims now every time he draws the card, someone dies. Got to the point he's scared shitless of it."

"When I knew Bill, he weren't scared of nothin'."

"He's scared now. He's cat-eyed scared. Can't sit noplace 'cept back to the wall, the gunfighter's chair. Always hearin' footsteps, checkin' his backtrail. He ain't got time for jealousy. He's too scared of that diamond queen."

"I still ain't fuckin' with his girl."

"You fucked with me before. As I recall, you liked it."

"You wasn't his girl then, so that made it all right. And anyway, I paid."

"And I said Bill don't give it no mind. All he cares about is ghosts."

"Ghosts?"

"Says he's got premonitions. Says someone's walkin' over his grave."

With a sudden thrust, Calamity grabbed Slater by the crotch. She giggled when she felt through the pants his tremendous erection. It was so big that through the canvas her fingers could grip less than half its circumference.

She slipped her left arm around his neck, and as she kissed him open-mouthed, she released his throbbing organ. Quickly, dexterously, she unbuttoned his fly.

"I said I got a code."

By now she had fished his huge member out of his fly. She was straddling him, vigorously shaking her hips as she slipped adroitly out of her Levi's. And when she unbuttoned her muslin shirt and her breasts flopped out in front of Slater's face, she could see his doubt disappear.

"I don't swing no wide loop. I don't fuck no friend's girl," he said hoarsely.

Now she was ready, glorious in her nakedness. Hickok had once described her as "a magnificent bitch, a rogue lioness of the gender," and she'd always thought that a compliment. Above all, she prided herself on her body, on her high breasts, which had always seemed to ache for a man's touch, on her slender torso, on her long white legs and dense pubic bush, black and rich.

She lowered her cunt down onto the head of his sperm-slick cock, and slowly gyrating her hips, she enclosed and massaged his member's tip.

"But—I—"

"Don't worry, honey," Calamity grinned, descending further down the great length of his achingly long, massively thick cock. Slowly, forcefully she increased the pace, pressure, and heat of her stroke, squeezing his prick for all it was worth, quickly, professionally bringing him to the moment of orgasm.

"But—I—I—"

As the come was rushing out of him, Clem had her way. In mid-orgasm, she flipped him over. And as his body flopped onto hers, Calamity's own desires mounted. The touch of his body heat, the smell of his rut commingled with her own, all merged with her own wants and needs. Her breasts were full and high, bigger than they should have been. She groaned and pushed Torn up away from her. She shoved her nipples, now taut and hard, up into Torn's face.

"How long has it been?" she said, her voice soft and raspy.

"Forever."

He was on top, and he took full advantage of it. He pulled out his member till only the tip was in her. It caressed the inside of her labia, feeling, searching, luxuriating in the inner folds of her cunt. Then he pulled the head out, and stroking the lips of her vulva, he slowly circled her clitoris, roughly, forcefully massaging the sensitive button harder and harder, till the charge built and built over and over, more and more. A jolting, almost painful electric shock ripped through her, head to crotch to foot.

She knew it was going to be good now, so she wanted to slow it down, prolong the pleasure. She began playfully unbuttoning his shirt, casually exploring his body. And when the last button came undone, she closed her eyes and rubbed the bottom of his belly, blindly feeling for the essence of the man.

She started with the pubes, and after roughly massaging those hard, bristly hairs, she began caressing the firm curve of his abdomen. She worked her way up till she came to a tough line of flesh, a long welt of scar tissue running the entire width of his lower belly, hipbone to hipbone.

She had asked him once where he'd gotten it. Slater had said nothing, but later Hickok had told her that a Comanche warrior had tried to disembowel Slater with a lance. Torn had parried the thrust, deflected the tip, though not the lance's edge. He'd blocked further thrusts with his own weapon, an eighteen-inch bowie, and he'd left the Comanche scalped, castrated, and decapitated in the bloody Texas sand.

Calamity's hands moved up the stomach. She paused over his navel, then worked up the hard, flat ridges of his stomach. The belly too was a collection of knotted contusions. The longest was a two-foot welt of dense tissue traversing his entire torso diagonally from left hip to right shoulder, a mean red bitch of a scar, gouged deep into his flesh by the turned-away, overhanded thrust of a Yankee bayonet. That was at Shiloh. He'd blunted the attack with an elbow, and put a knee to the Yankee's crotch. Then, after breaking his wrist and knocking aside the empty rifle, he'd forced the bluebelly facedown in the Shiloh mud, shoved a knee into his back, and grabbing the soldier by the throat and chin, had wrenched the head back till audible above the din of cannons and musket, had heard the dull *crack!* of the breaking neck. Then he crawled back through the mud and muck and bursting shells to his own rebel trench, leaving the dead Yankee lying in a pool of Slater's own blood.

Calamity's touch moved upward. She felt the puckered bullet hole just above the clavicle and reached around the neck, then straight down till she found the exit hole just above the shoulder blades, an inch to the right of the spinal cord. A new one. She'd ask about that.

She rubbed laterally across the broad back, and felt a tingling thrill of excitement. These were new. The wide white stripes of Yuma Prison. Yes, this was something special. She licked her lips and pulled him down to her, inserting her wet tongue into the puckered bullet hole below the clavicle, stroking the wide back scars and gyrating her hips while his prick continued to massage the outside of her crotch, rubbing over and over the raw sensitive button of her clitoris. She shut her eyes and softly, inaudibly groaned.

Slater slipped a hand under her ass and pulled her hips up toward him. He increased the pressure on her clitoris, and now she was avid. Pulling him harder onto her, she dug her fingers deep into his back and raked the Yuma scars cross-ways with her nails, gouging, tearing, as if to expunge them forever from his memory.

"Give it to me," she whispered, throwing her head back, shoving her hips up toward his. "Give it to me hard."

One hand clutching her ass, he raised his hips high above her, then drove down angrily with his prick. Now they were both crotch to crotch, his balls pressed against the cleavage of her ass. She was stabbed to the base of her spine by his tremendous member. Her neck arched in the air. Now her head was rolling back and forth on the ground, the tongue lolling out of her mouth. She was oblivious to everything but her own intense needs. Her hips ground desperately against his, the breath caught in her throat, and she wanted him so badly she thought she would die. She was groaning for more, and without thinking she lifted her knees, clamped her legs over his shoulders, and lifting her ass up off the ground, she pumped powerfully, as hard as she knew how, at Slater's plunging cock. She was inventive, expert, and inexhaustible. She was drunk with the secret desires of this dark liaison. Slater was mad with the pent-up lust of three long years, and that excited her too. Calamity was burning up with the thrill of having two lovers now, delirious over the sheer enormity of Slater's member, the awful inner knowledge that this might be the last fuck she would ever know.

He plunged into her over and over. Her nipples, swollen and hard, dug into his chest. He cupped a hand over a breast, rudely squeezed a stiff nipple, and she barely managed to swallow her yelp. So she then grabbed him around the back of his neck and pulled his mouth down onto hers, probed her tongue deep, and suppressed her groans with frantic kisses.

Through the night their crotches plunged and circled. She rode Torn in his frenzy, courted and teased him. He rutted at her as she grew bold, smashed at her when she bucked and fought, and when they came, the orgasms pumped out of them hard and fast, from so deep a well that they hurt for more.

And when they reached for that last, long, hard, grinding climax, Calamity believed that tomorrow would be beyond harm.

She'd already died tonight.

PART NINE

33

Calamity awoke smiling. She murmured incoherently and then felt someone shaking her arm. Bill was dressed, his hat pulled down over his eyes. In the dim light of dawn, he was pointing west across the flat, arid plains. She rubbed her eyes, sat up, and looked. Reynolds was standing off to her left and also staring south, through a rifle scope. She squinted and saw a cloud of dust on the horizon.

"What is it?" she asked, confused.

" 'Pache. What else'd stir up that much desert?"

"They after us?"

"Who else would be comin' that hard?" Slater was saying from where he stood behind her. "Not them fat-assed screws from Yuma. That's for sure."

Reynolds was walking toward the remuda, wasting no time. "Whatever it is, let's mount up. We're packin' nothin' but guns and bullets, food and water. None of Calamity's bustles or pantaloons. We gotta ride."

"But we had a day's head start on them," she said

unbelieving, while already pulling up pants, throwing off blankets, and pulling on boots. "How could they know?"

"Maybe they didn't know. Maybe this is just a 'Pache war party on a border raid from Mexico. Maybe they ran into that horde of vultures circling the dead roan, then picked up our tracks and are movin' in for the kill. One thing's for sure, nobody but a 'Pache'd rattle his horse's hocks across a desert like that. They know the trail's fresh, and after finding that dead roan, they'd know our mounts is old. They're closin' in for the kill."

Calamity squatted on her haunches and rolled up her bedroll. Her friends were already going through saddlebags and kyacks, keeping what they needed, puncturing and discarding the empty water cans.

Reynolds was graining and watering the stock. By the time they'd saddled the four best horses and Calamity had helped Hickok and Slater rub them down with linament, Reynolds was already working on the mules, throwing pads on their backs. While Calamity smoothed out the wrinkles, Hickok and Slater heaved on the loaded, tied-down packsaddles. They threw their diamonds, tightened the double-rig cinches and chest harnesses, then tied the jerk-line to the lead mule. Slater quickly vaulted his mount and put his hand out for the pack line. Charley threw away a grain bag, punctured the next-to-the-last water can, and mounted. Hickok and Calamity each swung onto their horses.

"Slater," Hickok said, "Calamity and Charley here know where the water, grain, and ammunition are cached. So stay with them. You'll need them supplies, gettin' through that Needle."

"Where'll you be?" Slater asked.

"Once you enter the Needle, I'll be covering your back porch, settin' off rock charges. Don't wait up. Just pound leather as fast as you know how."

Calamity leaned back on her cantle and raked Hickok with a hard, over-the-shoulder stare.

"Don't know as I like that, pard, you havin' all the fun."

"Ain't no other way. You three couldn't find the charges." He smiled gently at Calamity. "This here's a one-man job."

"End of discussion," Reynolds said.

Then he reined his horse around and headed for the Needle. Hickok and Slater turned and followed, and grudgingly Calamity kicked her horse after them, thinking to herself: Damn you, Hickok, it ain't supposed to be this way. Damn you to hell, west and crossways!

34

For a half hour they cantered dead east into the long, dark shadow of the Mogollon Rim. The black volcanic mountain chain loomed almost as one large mass. The cliff face jutted straight up out of the desert floor. The huge presence blocked passage out of the desert for two hundred miles in any direction. Their only egress was through the Needle.

Unlike the Needle's entrance, the rock-strewn mouth was big—fifty yards across and a thousand feet high, the straight rectangular passage framed by talus and black volcanic cliffs. Careful to watch for broken ground, Calamity entered the pass at a dead run, whipping her horse with the *mecate*, passing Slater and his jerk-line string. She cornered the first bend in the canyon at a high lope, entering the maze of twisting draws and winding gorges that would be their death or deliverance.

The sun burned white-hot overhead. She felt her mount heave, and she knew their horses could not stand the pace. Six days in the hot sun had worn them down, while the 'Pache pony herd would be pounding through the pass with tallow to spare. Their own stock no longer had the bottom.

Hickok and Reynolds were up ahead. Around the next bend she saw Reynolds stand in his stirrups and point out the first charge. He'd marked it right on the canyon wall with a white *X*. Somehow he'd scaled the talus, climbed over five hundred feet up the black cliff, planted the charge, then marked it. It made her dizzy even to think of the climb.

A half-mile up the canyon, she rounded a bend. Reynolds's dust continued up the pass, but Hickok was standing at the canyon wall. His horse was tied to a piece of mesquite growing out of the talus, and Hickok was screwing a scope over the sights of a Sharps "Big Fifty." Calamity reined up alongside him.

"You ain't hittin' that X with no rifle. You can't see it through them canyon walls."

"Got me a perch a few hundred feet up."

"Yeah? You still can't hit that X a half-mile away."

"A half-mile ain't shit. A buff hunter at Adobe Walls killed a Comanch a mile off with one of these. Smoked him smack through the head."

"You ain't no buff hunter."

"I was a sharpshooter in the War."

"That was 'fore your eyes give out."

"Then I'll smoke 'em by smell." He gave her a bright grin, slung the rifle diagonally across his back, and started up the talus toward his crag.

Slater came peeling around the bend, the jerk-line string close behind, and charged on up the pass. Reynolds was already long gone, and Hickok had his back to her.

Damn him, she thought. Hickok never left her any choice, never. As usual, he was leaving her behind. She wheeled her mount around and kicked it hard up the pass into Slater's dust.

Two miles up the canyon, she rounded a bend and found Slater and Reynolds standing by their horses. Here the canyon broadened to a width of over two hundred yards, and the talus sloped gradually. Reynolds motioned her down and pointed toward a scarp several miles distant. She could see the white X on the black cliff face where Reynolds had planted the charge.

"Get down, grab the *mecate* and part of that jerk-line string. He hits that charge, half this pass might come down."

She wrapped the *mecate* twice around her wrist, and just as Slater shouted to her, "No!" she saw the distant cliff erupt in a red-orange ball of fire. The crack of the rifle and the dynamite's *ka-whumppp!* echoed, slapping and booming off the canyon walls like rolling thunder. The shock waves hit the cliffs and rocks around them, gravel flew in all directions, large rocks dropped off the talus. Charley suddenly screamed, "Middle of the pass!"

But now the horses were bucking and rearing. The jerk-line mule string, too spooked and snuffy to be led, was braying, kicking savagely. The lead animal, the white gelding, bolted, the string close behind. Reynolds yelled, "Let them go. We'll catch them later."

Calamity clung to the bucking dun and struggled to pull him from the falling rock, but she still watched the distant cliff face as though hypnotized. The upper half hung suspended, hovering above the canyon wall for a seeming eternity, then slowly cracked loose in a colossal burst of flame, crashing to the canyon floor with a *boom!* that knocked Calamity to her knees.

But now the dun was exploding, and she was snared by the *mecate* twisted around her wrist. The dun lunged, his hooves slashing all around her. She was being whipped and thrashed and dragged along the canyon floor. A hoof cracked against her shoulder. Her arm flooded with searing pain, then went numb. She was dragged and spun along the rock-strewn footing.

Suddenly she stopped spinning. Slater had the dun by the cheek strap. He was yanking his head sideways, twisting violently, driving the curb bit deep into his snorting mouth. With his other hand he wrenched the dun's ear. When he let go, it was only to grab his pistol by the barrel and hammer the dun between his walled eyes with the butt.

"Get loose of the line!" he yelled.

Calamity untwisted herself from the *mecate*, and then Slater grabbed the reins and jerked the dun's head all the way back flush against his flank. Slater grabbed the apple and swung up high onto the dun's back. She heard hooves pounding and turned to see Reynolds kicking up the pass toward the cache. She turned back the other way, and now Slater had reined her dun around and was booting him down the draw, against the dun's will, toward Hickok and the rumbling rock walls.

She had no choice but to continue afoot.

A mile up the pass, Charley returned with Slater's sorrel. The horse was rank, but Reynolds held him and she was able to swing on.

"Where's the mules?" she asked.

"I staked them by the first cache," he said, and turned on up the pass.

Their supplies were behind a boulder in the loose talus. There they dismounted, loosened their cinches, and rested. Reynolds watered the stock. Afterward they rubbed the animals down with old grain sacks, filled their canteens, and waited.

Finally, ironshod hooves echoed up the pass. Hickok and Slater rounded the bend, riding double. Slater halted the dun by the cache and Hickok slid off the rump.

"How'd it go?" Reynolds asked.

"You done good," Hickok said. "We buried half of them damn 'Pache."

"Did it close up the pass?"

"Not quite. There's still a gap big enough for a man to walk a horse through. Which they're already doin'."

"Did you get a look at the whole war party?"

"Yeah. Renegades, up from Mexico. There was seventy-five or a hundred, before the slide. We still got thirty or forty on our backtrail. And they ain't stoppin' to bury no dead."

Hickok loosened his cinch buckle to let the dun blow. Reynolds was filling his Stetson from one of the water cans, and the dun finally stopped long enough for a drink.

"Where's your horse, Bill?"

"Under the talus."

"Well, let's cut a mule loose," Reynolds said grimly. "Slater, you still know how to ride 'Pache?"

"Reckon so."

"Take the line-backed jack. He's almost as fast as the dead gray. Hickok, take my pinto. He's the most rested. You're gonna need him. I'll pull packline from here on out."

The dun finished drinking and Calamity cinched him up. She vaulted his back and turned to head out. But then Hickok spoke.

"Okay, Charley, fine. But we already give it our best shot.

And it ain't been enough. From now on, it's switchback fighting. In and out, back and forth, shoot at a 'Pache, toss a grenade. It's a cut-and-run, rear-guard action."

"No other way."

"It's a one-man show."

Reynolds said nothing.

"Look," Hickok went on, "we got a small lead. If we push it, ride these here oatburners into the ground, then hump out of here on muleback, we can just about make it." He unholstered a Colt and broke open the loading gate. He put a sixth bullet into the wheel under the hammer and shoved the Colt back into his holster crossways. "But that's a job for one man." He loaded the hammer cylinder of his second Colt, then crossed over to a pack mule and pulled an extra Winchester and three boxes of .44-40 shells out of a kyack. He also took out an extra saddlebag. "This one's got some grenades and three more sticks of dynamite. From now on I want you three poundin' leather straight out of this pass. No waitin' up for me. If my horse goes down and I can't get one off a 'Pache, your comin' back won't help me none. I'll be too damn close to them savages. You three just keep goin'. This is my job. If I do it right, we'll all come out okay. If I don't, we won't. I just don't want no short-horn heroes gettin' in my way."

He vaulted the pinto's back, reined him around, and headed toward the 'Pache. Anger welling in Calamity's throat, she started to mount the sorrel, but Slater grabbed her arm, stopping her short.

"You ain't goin' noplace, Jane, and that's a lock cinch. You'll just confuse him, maybe get him killed. His best chance is on his own, alone. It's what he does best. It's the only chance any of us have, him included."

But Calamity was hot. "Like hell I'm leavin' him out there alone. No heathen 'Pache is stakin' him out on no anthills nor catclaw. I'll—"

Her head exploded as Slater slapped her across the side of her face and temple, a long, ringing, roundhouse right. Her eyes were instantly aflame, her nose running, and the entire left side of her body felt numb.

She was sobbing, "You scum-suckin' sonofabitch!"

But Reynolds was saying, "You move it now, Clem."

And Slater was shaking her by the elbow. "I'll whack your ass with a knotted packline and tie you to your goddamn saddle."

Then he threw her onto her mount, and vaulted his own. He lashed the horse with the mule's *mecate* and charged hard into her dust.

She thought: Damn you, Hickok. You'll die and leave me here alone. Like I always knew you would, you cat-eyed sonofabitch.

35

Hickok had picked his spot well. Here the high canyon walls narrowed and made three right-angle turns. There were also plenty of boulders along the canyon walls for cover.

He tied his pinto to a mesquite bush. The horse was out of sight just around the first of the sharp bends. Then, with a Winchester in each hand and the saddlebag over his shoulder, he dog-trotted down to the second bend. There, behind a wagon-size boulder, he propped the loaded Winchester, barrel up. Alongside it he placed a grenade and several packets of Lucifers, each packet bound with tape.

Trotting down the pass, he stopped sixty yards before the next turn and scaled the talus slope till he came to a sizable crack. In it, twenty feet above the canyon floor, he shoved a stick of dynamite. He climbed down and jogged on to the third turn. In the middle of the bend, a jumble of boulders blocked part of it. They afforded him some cover, so he squeezed in between them and waited for the 'Pache.

He heard the ponies' hooves, and when they rounded the corner he knew he was in trouble. It was a small band, which meant that the war party had divided in case of ambush.

Hickok had no choice now. The Apaches trotted past him—twenty mahogany-brown warriors in breechclouts, riding spotted ponies. As the last one rounded the bend, Hickok jumped out behind him with his Winchester cocked. He shouldered the rifle, aimed for the wall charge, and squeezed.

He threw himself back behind the clump of boulders while, simultaneously, the canyon wall erupted into flame, black smoke, and flying rock. Hickok jumped back into the pass and levered his Winchester into the choking cloud of debris, firing at everything that moved, man or animal.

He crossed to the opposite side of the pass and trotted along the canyon wall through the dead, the dying, and the settling dust. Fifty yards up the pass he scaled the talus and jammed a dynamite stick into a crack fifteen feet high. He could already hear the approaching hooves as he headed back across the canyon to another jumble of rocks behind the next turn, jamming bullets into the rifle's breech as he ran.

Two braves with smoke-blackened faces met him as he reached the boulders, and he shot them dead as he ran, levering the Winchester as fast as he knew how. The rifle was heating up and the hoofbeats were loud, very loud. He turned, and the party was around the last bend, almost on top of him.

He fired a snapshot at the wall charge, and again the canyon erupted in flame and rock fragments.

Without looking back, Hickok jogged on up the pass, into the settling dust of the explosion. Slinging his rifle across his back, he pulled out both Colts. He entered the rock dust with both guns blazing.

36

Turning the next bend, he grabbed the propped-up Winchester. Bracing his back against the curving wall, he paused to catch his breath. He then stuck his head around the sharp turn.

Three bullets smashed into the talus.

Jumping out into the pass, belly-down, he levered four rounds into the swirling dust and saw two Apaches fall.

Rolling back behind cover, he stood up, his legs trembling, back against the wall. Riderless horses from the first explosion were now galloping past him by the score. Gripping his rifle barrel with both hands, he waited till one of them was close enough, then swinging the Winchester he laid the stock right between the pony's eyes.

Temporarily stunned, the trotting paint rocked back on his hocks. Hickok grabbed him by the mane and, dropping the empty rifle, swung onto his back. One hand on the mane, he grabbed an ear with the other, and gripping with his knees, drove his rowels into the paint's gut. The paint reared on his hind legs like a jackrabbit, then shot off up the canyon, Hickok pressing his head low against the paint's neck, bullets singing past his ears and cracking and whining off the canyon walls.

He might have made it, but when he rounded the far turn, an Apache bullet caught the paint just below the right ear and instantly the horse went down, skidding across the canyon floor, then crashing onto Hickok's locked right knee, pinning it under its flank.

His guns were empty, the saddlebag falling away from him, out of reach. His only thought was: Don't be taken alive. This pain is nothing compared to what they will do. He reached for the Arkansas toothpick in his belt sheath, intending to cut his own throat, but the haft was jammed under his left side. He could not even kill himself.

And rounding the turn came three braves on horseback.

Then he heard the rapid cocking and firing of a Winchester behind him. He saw the three 'Pache horsemen fall, and suddenly three riderless ponies were rounding the curve and pounding up the pass over the bloody head of the dead paint.

Calamity dropped his saddlebag on his stomach and said, "Better find somethin' in this bag of tricks. I hear more horses."

He dug out a grenade and a taped packet of Lucifers. He handed them to Calamity. She put down her rifle and lit the fuse, and as six braves on horseback loped around the turn, she lobbed the pipe bomb above their heads while she and Hickok crouched behind the paint.

The pass shook with the explosion, and when the 'Pache ponies vaulted over them, they were riderless.

Then Calamity was up again, levering her Winchester into the backs of two 'Paches who were trying to escape on foot. When the second one fell, Calamity sat back, jamming bullets into her rifle.

"You better have somethin' good left in them saddlebags, Hickok, somethin' goddamned good."

He reached into the bag and pulled out one dynamite stick. And one loose cap.

"That cap's come off, and I ain't got no pliers with me."

Horses' hooves were drumming nearer.

"So what do I do?"

"Throw it down the canyon and shoot at it with the rifle," Hickok said. "It'll go."

"I ain't no trick shot. What about the cap?"

"Get the cap on, and you could throw it at the wall just around this turn. Hit the wall cap first, it'll go. But we ain't got no pliers to cap it off."

"Fuck the pliers."

Calamity took the cap in her mouth, placed it over the blasting nub, and crimped it on with her front teeth. She grinned as Hickok turned his head and pressed his hands to his face, waiting for the charge to blow in her mouth.

Now the hoofbeats were loud, very loud.

Calamity stood up, rounded the bend, and facing the oncoming Apaches, hurled the cap-end of the dynamite stick at the far canyon wall directly alongside the braves.

The wall burst into flame and she was blown back over the fallen paint and onto Hickok. Rock showered all around them, burying them in dust and debris.

She rolled off Hickok and dizzily pulled herself to her feet. She stumbled around the turn and levered her last three rounds into the swirling dust cloud. She pulled out her Colt and emptied that too.

Squinting, she stared down the pass. For a hundred yards, all she could see were several score of dead horses and

Indians shrouded by choking smoke, their heads and limbs skewed at grotesque angles, eyes staring sightlessly into the sky, their blood staining the canyon floor.

Six smoke-blackened Apaches in breechclouts and warpaint remained standing, and came up the pass afoot. She dived around the turn, back behind the fallen pony. Leaning against the paint's head, she jammed slugs into the Colt's wheel, the hot metal blistering her hands. As she pushed the third round into the cylinder, the braves came around the turn. Spinning belly-down over the paint's head, she aimed the cocked, half-empty Colt at the nearest 'Pache, now standing directly in front of her, only to have him kick it from her hands.

The paint-streaked, soot-blackened 'Pache over her was grabbing her hair and putting his long, curved scalping knife to her forehead. As her screams pumped out of her, over and over again, a volley echoed from down the canyon, barely audible to Calamity's deafened ears.

The 'Pache .dropped the scalping knife, then fell face-down, a bloody hole in his forehead.

The five braves behind him were cut down by the fusillade, their faces frozen in stunned surprise, their bodies riddled with bloody holes.

Stepping over Calamity, rounding the rest of the bend, came Torn Slater and Charley Reynolds, their Winchesters smoking.

37

When they rode out of the Needle, it was night. Hickok sat his mule hipshot, favoring a gimpy left leg and a sprained knee. Calamity's head ached and her ears rang from the blast that had gone off only a dozen feet from her and Bill. She was clutching the pommel, barely able to stay on her worn-out gray. Reynolds and Slater were feeling the toll of a hundred aches and abrasions. At rest, their mounts—a mule for Charley, a bareback mustang for Slater—stood spraddle-legged and trembling.

Still they rode that night and morning, slept only in the afternoon. At a small ranch near the river, Charley bargained for horses, mules, food, and supplies, while the others forded the river on foot, downstream and out of sight.

They were now high-line drifters, on the run.

That night they made camp on the far side of a ridge, remote enough from the ranch to risk a fire. Squatting around the coffee, beans, jerky, and pan bread, Reynolds said, "After tonight, you're on your own. Custer wants me up north, and there's a price on me in the Nations. Judge Parker nails me there, he'll hang me higher than the gallows. Bill, you still got that telegraph key?"

"Yeah, it's in that there kyack."

"Then signal Custer back at Fort Lincoln. Let him know what you're doin'."

"All right. You can also remind him not to be inside Fort Smith when we lead them outlaws to that bank. Them boys'll reconnoiter, and a few hundred bluebellies might just scare them off."

Reynolds nodded and glanced at Calamity. "Clem, you looked good comin' through that pass. You looked real good."

She said nothing, but nodded wearily.

"Torn," Charley said, "I hope you find what you're lookin' for. And don't feel too bad about Coleman Younger. He left you to rot in that desert arroyo. He's just gettin' what's comin'."

"That's what we all get, Charley. What's comin'."

"Reckon so." Reynolds fixed Hickok with a sideways glance. "Sure wish I knew what you and Custer went through at the Wilderness. Musta been a pisser, whatever it was. You're payin' a mighty high price for it."

"You're payin' some kinda price too."

"Nope," Charley said, yawning. "They're payin' me. One-twenty-five a month. U.S. Yankee dollars." He yawned again. "Damn, I could use some more of that Jack Daniel's. Pilgrim whiskey'll never taste the same."

Then they were all rolling over and groaning, " 'Night." Calamity turned on her side, pulled the soogans tightly around her, and drifted off into a sleep without dreams.

PART TEN

38

They rode.

Calamity suggested that maybe they ought to take the Overland Stage or get a train at some remote rail spur. Hickok smiled his small, crooked smile and reminded her they were now outlaws. They might just as well submit to federal authority as take public conveyance.

Torn said, "No, for us three it's gotta be them ridges. Ain't no other way."

Clem stared at Slater irritably and said, "You always been an outlaw?"

"No. I was a baby once."

They rode.

Every dawn they rode into what Calamity called "some special hell for outlaws." East into the sun rising over the rimrock, sending out long shafts of blue and orange and yellow light that spread all across the sky. Here was a landscape of tortuous canyons, grotesque rock sculptures, dried-up gorges, as though they had somehow wandered onto the moon. Here was a silent ocean of mesas and buttes rolling in all directions to all horizons. Here was a land that heard no voice save the dry moan of its winds, witnessed no vision save the glare of its blindingly bright sun in its ever-cloudless skies. Once they entered its sweeping emptiness, with its towering saguaros and scorched plains, it was as though no man had trespassed here before.

They no longer measured time in dawns or days or nights, nor did they count the meals they ate. They measured time in things like the horses they rode and traded for, the streams and canyons they crossed, the terrain they covered.

They especially noted the horses. They went through every size, shape, temperament, and color. Every kind of mount. They rode grullas lighter than seven hundred pounds and once got a hammerhead gray sixteen hands high, so big Calamity could not get a bridle on him. Wiry cow ponies, big line-backed roans, deep-chested, blaze-faced bays, snuffy colts, a splay-footed mare so feisty it took Torn and Hickok a full half hour every morning to top her off. They got two Appaloosas so beautiful that Calamity cried when they traded them. Raw-boned sorrels, platter-footed braying mules. Sabina mares and tough northern broncs. Sometimes they rode dray horses, and once Hickok got a black thoroughbred stallion with three white stockings, which at another time he would have kept to race. All of the horses whinnying and nickering, while they tightened the cinches, shoved their feet deep into the stirrups, straightened in the creaking saddles, and rode.

They forded hock-high streams, floundered in stirrup-deep creeks and saddle-high rivers. They half-drowned in rapids and once went over a falls.

They crossed deserts so hot and dry the dust rose lazily and hung in the air. They pulled wet bandannas over their mouths and noses, but still the dust filled their teeth and lips. Their lips cracked and bled and the blood clotted with dust and streaked the deeply etched lines in the corners of their squinting eyes.

Each sundown they curried and grained their mounts and hobbled or staked them near grass. Each dawn they rode east out of the dry, barren bottomlands of the Sonora, out of the hills and foothills and black slate cliffs of the southern

Rockies. They rode through gray-green mesquite and chaparral, the land gaunt and bare, a land of wind witches whirling crazily across the arid plains, a land of heat waves and mirages shimmering across the scorching steppes, making the horizon dance. They rode into the low hills dotted with prickly pear and creosote and palo verde and tall saguaro with twisting branching columns, eighty feet high and more. On the slopes they rode through yucca, agave, and ocotillo, through buzzing insects, darting ground squirrels and rabbits, through the sudden flashing of the bright-colored birds.

They learned the wrath of the sun at its zenith, when its rays struck with an almost physical force, like hammer blows to the neck. On the barren sands the mesquite turned pale yellow, the creosote bushes wilted and parched, the curved, dried-out ribs of a fallen saguaro lay bleaching in the dust.

When occasionally a sidewinder coiled, buzzed, and spooked a horse, when a tarantula jumped or a Gila monster skittered in front of them, those moments only served to relieve the monotony. Otherwise there was nothing—save the sun, which burned their skin as dark as animal hide, steamed the air in a sombrero's crown, lathered the horses, baked the brain.

They no longer counted the dawns. They no longer tried to ride by night and sleep by day. The sun was too hot for sleeping. It was easier to change horses more often, drowse in the saddle, and not count the rising suns.

They rode.

39

In the Staked Plains of Texas, they stopped in a town. It was time for new horses, decent whiskey, maybe a bath. They were only five days' ride from the mountain hideout, no more.

The place they picked was just a scattering of adobe

buildings. A general store with a backroom bar, a restaurant with rooms upstairs, a stable with a blacksmith's forge and an adjacent horse corral. A church that doubled as a town hall. A school. Two houses. The town was called Sweetwater after its one good stream.

When the three of them rode down the street, they were something to look at. They'd changed their clothes in the event that the dodgers on them contained descriptions of dress, but after weeks on the trail, the new outfits looked threadbare. Hickok's tan plainsman's hat, like the dirt-streaked lines around his eyes and mouth, was caked with dust, as was his shoulder-length blond hair. His red bandanna still covered his nose and mouth, and his eyes were shielded by wire-rimmed eyeglasses with smoked, circular lenses. The white cotton shirt with the thin blue lines was filthy, its right sleeve tattered. He still wore his bullhide chaps because his Levi's looked so bad. His tired buckskin was stone-bruised and wormy. Hickok also needed a drink.

Slater looked better. His Stetson did not show the dirt as badly as Hickok's, nor did his collarless brown shirt or his gray twill pants. He'd escaped from Yuma wearing hightops, so his present boots were new, black, hand-tooled, with four-inch heels. He rode straight-legged, deep in the tree of his McClellan saddle. He took a long rein on his big, deep-chested gray. On his left hip he wore his Colt, butt turned out. In a belt sheath he packed a good bowie with a ten-and-a-half-inch blade. He was smiling. He was heeled. He was back in business.

Calamity looked the best of the lot. The night before, while the men slept, she'd bathed in a stream and washed out her clothes. Her Levi's and yellow muslin blouse were clean. Her knee-high black boots were freshly rubbed with saddle soap, and she'd beaten the dust out of her Stetson. Like Hickok's, her horse—a dun-colored Texas cowpony—was through. He was old when they traded for him, and listening to him wheeze, she feared he would not grow any older.

Behind them trudged their pack animals, two jacks with cross-buck packsaddles, covered with tarpaulins and tied off with lash ropes. Hickok held the packline loosely in his left hand.

They rode to the livery stable–blacksmith shop at the end of the street and tied up at the hitch rack. They gave the horses and pack mules enough slack to drink from the long wooden water trough in front of the rack. Automatically they hooked a stirrup over the horn and loosened their cinches before going to the farrier's.

The shop was in a large building. At the far end was the stable, with a hayloft overhead. The floors of the open stalls were covered with straw and reeked of manure. At their end of the barn stood the blacksmith's forge, its bed of charcoal glowing. Propped around it were the soot-blackened tools of his trade—hammers, tongs, clamps, chisels, and hook-bladed knives.

The farrier was a big, balding man with a red nose. He wore a long leather apron and heavy canvas gloves. His name was Evans.

He was tonging a red-hot horseshoe off the brazier. He stood it on the anvil and tightened his grip on the tongs. Five ringing bangs with the hammer narrowed the big curve at the shoe's base—the so-called frog—and the farrier tossed it, steaming and sizzling, into a bucket of water.

"Yeah?" the farrier said without looking up.

"Got five animals outside. Like to trade for fresh mounts."

"Got some horses in the 'dobe corral. Look 'em over." He pulled another shoe out of a keg and laid it on the forge. He pumped the overhead bellows, and the coals in the hearth crackled and glowed a bright crimson.

They crossed the livery and studied the remuda of saddlehorses and gelded jacks. Hickok roped out a buckskin, a blaze-faced gray, a big roan, and a hammerhead mule for the pack animal. He added a wiry paint and a big dun for the extras and tied them to the corral fence.

The farrier came out and examined both sets of animals, then took the trade plus fifty dollars. Hickok peeled the bills out of his oiled silk money belt.

Standing by the hitch rack, he asked Evans where they could get a bath, a drink, and a good piece of beef.

The big farrier folded his arms. "Can't. Leastways not around here. A couple of miles yonder," he said, pointing down the dirt road, "we got this travelin' show. Big circus-type tents, they say. Sent this here circular out six months back, advertisin'. Tiger tamers, a Wild West show, and the like. Whole town bought tickets."

"Town does seem empty," Hickok observed. "Why ain't you goin'?"

"I got too many horses to shoe and look after. Big cattle drive comin' up in a week or so. Also, Ortega Ruiz, in the next county, got himself the liquor concession. Be a lot of drink and carryin' on. Don't hold with drink. 'Specially that Mex piss Ruiz mixes up. If'n you're lookin' for a drink, I'd look elsewhere."

"They serve food at this tent show?" Slater asked, rubbing his gut.

"You hungry?" the farrier asked.

"I could eat the ass out of a rag doll."

"Well, you won't find nothin' 'round here. Hell, it's only a few miles. Can't hurt you too much. Just watch out for the coffin varnish."

"That bad?" Calamity asked.

"It could grow horns on a muley cow."

Calamity resaddled the mounts. Hickok and Slater packed the mule's cross-buck onto the new jack. They checked the balance and the cinches and swung onto the fresh horses. They headed for the tent show. It was on the way, and there might be some fun.

40

Two miles up the road, at the top of a rise, they stared down at the tent show. Or rather, they stared at a tent. There was one big top about a hundred feet across, a couple of food-and-drink stands, and a lot of buckboards and horses.

There were people too, mostly women and children. They were streaming out of the tent and heading toward their wagons as fast as they knew how. Many of them were already pulling out.

"What's the rush?" Calamity wondered.

"I don't know," Slater said. "Don't rightly care, neither. Let's get down 'fore they close."

Hickok looked dubious. "Ain't much of a show, you ask me."

"It ain't exactly Bill Cody's Wild West Super Extravaganza," Calamity agreed. She kneed her horse down the rise.

They hitched their mounts and walked over to the food stand. What was left was displayed on tiers of long boards braced by Arbuckle's boxes. A woman in a blue calico dress and a bright yellow bonnet was hurriedly trying to pack. She was not unattractive, but the Texas sun had aged her prematurely. At thirty she looked bitter, grim, hatchet-faced. And nervous. She was now struggling frantically to jam wheels of cheese, cans of sardines, ham and beef roasts, loaves of bread, numerous pies and cakes, and a two-gallon coffeepot of freshly-brewed Arbuckle's into the crates. They weren't going to fit.

"What's the hurry, ma'am?" Hickok asked.

"I'm closin' up," she half-snorted.

"Well, we just got here," Slater said, "and we brung our appetites."

"Well, you can un-bring them, 'cause the show's over."

"Can't we at least take some of that grub off your hands?"

She stopped packing and said, "It'll have to be fast."

"Well," Slater said, licking his lips, "half a ham, two loaves of bread, a dried-apple pie, and about half a wheel of that there yellow cheese'd do just fine. If you're so all-fired anxious to get out, maybe you could fill two of these canteens with that Arbuckle's."

The long boards laid out on nail kegs served as a counter. Shoving a long fork into the ham, she quickly divided it in two with a crosscut saw. The wheel of cheese she halved with the same homely tool.

She packed cheese and ham into an Arbuckle's box, placed the pie on top, filled Slater's canteens with coffee, and said, "Two dollars and fifty cents." As Hickok counted out the money she added, "Now, I'd take that grub and skedaddle, if you know what's good."

"We was hoping to get ourselves a drink, maybe a jug."

"Advice still holds."

By now all the women and children were putting leather to their teams. The wagons and buckboards were rocking forward on their axles and pulling out.

" 'Pears that you have a point," Hickok said. "Still would like that drink, though."

"Well, if them drovers in that tent don't kill you, the liquor will."

"Is it bad?" Calamity asked.

The woman looked her up and down, then fixed her with a hard stare. "It'd raise blood blisters on a rawhide boot."

"Thankee kindly, ma'am," Hickok said, tipping his hat. Lifting the Arbuckle's box under one arm, he turned and headed toward the tent flap, Slater and Calamity in tow.

Inside, it was dark, hot, and boozy.

In the rear they saw a bar consisting of two large hogsheads of whiskey.

Calamity stared at the barrels and licked her lips. "We been dry a spell."

"I be your witness there," said Hickok.

Slater produced a canteen. "We can always get more water." He turned it upside-down and emptied it on the hard-packed dirt floor.

"Think the whiskey's as bad as they say?" said Calamity.

"Smells worse," Hickok said.

The vendor was a Mexican with a drooping mustache. He wore a white muslin shirt, black *charro* pants, boots, and no hat. He had a brace of tied-down .44 Remingtons and double cartridge belts. As they approached the stand, he gave them a grin. Slater handed him the two-quart canteen and asked for three shotglasses. The Mexican laid them out on the raw pine plank and filled them from a bottle which he described as "fresh from the barrel, boss." He grinned again as he pointed to the tapped keg.

A drink in her hand, Calamity turned to stare at the ruckus. Eighty or ninety cowhands with sidearms, shotguns, and rifles, and two with lynch ropes, were crowded around a man and a woman in a buggy.

The woman was of late middle age and built like one of the whiskey barrels. She wore a gray Stetson pulled down over her forehead, the cord tight under her double chin. A red, richly embroidered blouse, a long black skirt and boots, and a pearl-handled, nickel-plated Colt strapped to her hip completed the outfit.

The man wore a black frock coat, a black vest, a bow tie, and a white boiled shirt. He had jet-black hair and angry, flashing eyes. He was in his mid-thirties, Calamity guessed. He would have been kind of cute, she thought, if he hadn't looked so mad.

A middle-aged farmer in bib overalls walked up to Ruiz with a quart mason jar. He handed Ruiz six bits and belched. Ruiz filled up the jar.

"This is lynchin' or a shotgun weddin'?" Calamity asked the farmer.

"A little of both. Seems a handbill was sent out promisin' a real Wild West show with Buffalo Bill, Kit Carson, Wild Bill Hickok, and the like. Lotta people sent in money for the tickets. Then this dude from back East rolls in with the show, and it ain't nothin'. Some cages full of wild animals, some local people sellin' food, Ruiz peddlin' his pilgrim whiskey, and this Eastern dude readin' poems. And he ain't got no money for a refund on account of the show ain't what the circular promised."

From the far end of the tent, a wagon drawn by two horses pulled up. The crowd cheered, and the drovers started firing their Colts into the canvas overhead. A barrel of hot black tar and four gunnysacks of chicken feathers sat in back of the dray.

"What's the shorthorn got to say for himself?" said Calamity.

"Claims he ain't responsible."

"Maybe he ain't," she said.

"Aw, hell, the boys got to blame somebody. That tenderfoot up there recitin' poems, singin' drippy songs, strummin' that fuckin' lute ain't no fun. And he sure ain't no Wild West show."

"Seems to me that if he swindled anybody, he wouldn't've come 'round lookin' to get caught."

"Aw, the boys are startin' on a big drive next week, clear to Montana. They got to let off a little steam."

Calamity looked at Bill. "That ain't no little steam," she said, pointing to the vat. "That tar'll skin him to the bone."

Suddenly Slater spat a large mouthful of pilgrim whiskey across the tent floor.

"Goddamn!" he screamed. "I'll tell you what's responsible." He wheeled around, leaned across the bar, and grabbed Ruiz by the front of his white shirt. "You goddamn skunk-suckin' sonofabitch! What did you put in this shit?"

Hickok laughed. "My friend here got his taste spoiled a few weeks back. He ain't used to real whiskey." Hickok took a bite from his shotglass. His face paled.

Calamity gave hers a ladylike sniff, then sipped it.

"Holy shit!" she howled. "I been poisoned! This tastes like buffalo bile!"

But Slater, who'd tossed back a four-ounce glassful, was the one who was hot. His face working with rage, he screamed, "You Mexican motherfucker! I'm seeing what you put in that keg."

Some of the cowhands began drifting over to the stand for a better look at the commotion, and Calamity couldn't help grinning as Slater began to give them a show. Dragging the Mexican over the counter by his shirtfront, Slater vaulted the boards and changed places with the barkeep. Turning to the keg, he pulled out his Colt, grabbed it by the barrel, and hammered the top of the barrel with the pistol's butt. With the third blow it shattered. Slater fished out loose fragments and stared inside in horror.

Turning to his audience of drovers, Slater yelled, "You want to see what you've been drinkin? Look!"

He tipped the barrel on end. Whiskey slopped and sloshed

over the side. The cowhands groaned at the waste. Then strange objects began tumbling out onto the ground.

Two dozen rattlesnakes lay at his feet.

"Sidewinder whiskey," said Calamity.

Ruiz looked at her, puzzled. "Gringos go for it, no?"

In seconds the drovers had Ruiz up over their heads and were carrying him to the buggy where the poet was being held. They were shouting, "Lynch him! Lynch him!" Calamity followed behind. Slater and Hickok remained by the bar. When Calamity glanced back over her shoulder and nodded to them to come with her, Hickok was laughing.

Slater was turning green.

Ruiz had been stripped of his guns and was up on the cart alongside the shorthorn. A cowboy shouted, "Well, Ma, do we lynch 'em both?"

The heavy woman in the gray Stetson raised her hands to quiet the men.

"Now, boys," she said, "you know me a long time. Hell, most of you punched beef on my spread one time or another. Half of you is takin' the Bar B-L herd up to Montana next week. You know I like to see you have a little fun. But this is goin' too far. Ruiz, he lives here. He didn't know no better'n to put them rattlers in your liquor. Thought you liked it that way. He'll give you your money back, you don't like his whiskey. And he'll throw in that spare keg free for those who do. Won't you, Ruiz?" Ruiz nodded gratefully. "But the shorthorn here, the Professor, he or his people or someone he represents took your money under false pretenses. Meaning they robbed us. He says he don't know nothin' 'bout it. Well, fine. But somebody's got to pay. So you want to raise some hell. Here's Shorthorn, there's the tar and feathers. Let's take a little hide off the Professor."

The crowd hurrahed, and when Calamity couldn't make herself heard, she skinned her Colt and fired three shots overhead. She pushed through the crowd, her face red with rage, and shouted, "Now wait a minute. Stands to reason the Professor didn't steal no money from you. He wouldn't be here if he done it. Hell, he'd be long gone in the tall corn. The people who sent him out here stole your cash. Fine. Take this here tent on account. Must be worth a good two hundred, three hundred bucks. Buy yourselves some real whiskey.''

"And I say take the tent, then tar and feather the Professor too!'' the old lady yelled in return.

The mob was in a howling frenzy. The old lady grabbed Calamity by the arm, dragged her aside, and said in her ear, "Listen, my boys got a thousand-mile drive ahead of them. I'm givin' them one last sendoff to remember me by, all them days and nights on the trail. They're takin' a herd from the Staked Plains to the Medicine Line, and they're gonna have one hellacious time 'fore they go. They're gonna get drunk, then tar and feather this shorthorn, and then get more drunk.''

The crowd was howling, "Give us the shorthorn!'' When Calamity looked for Bill and Jake, she saw that they'd left.

She turned to the Professor and said grimly, "Looks like they're gonna do it.''

He stared in disbelief at the steaming black tar. "Are they boiling me in oil?''

"No. In tar.''

"I take it,'' the Professor said evenly, his voice a rich baritone, "they did not like my poetry.'' He seemed saddened at the thought.

"They was expectin' somethin' else.''

"That makes a difference,'' he said, his spirits somewhat improved.

Calamity thought, Damn, you got stones for a fuckin' shorthorn.

Two of the boys started grabbing at his black frock coat. One of them yelled, "Ride them 'round on a rail awhile, then dump him in the tar.''

"We ain't got no rail!''

"Then give him the tar!''

Calamity looked out into the sea of snarling faces. Mean, vicious, drunk, armed to the teeth with .45s, shotguns, and repeating rifles, no one could back down this mob.

The Professor caught Clem's eye. "Perhaps if I recited another poem?''

"William-fuckin'-Shakespeare couldn't help you now.''

"No, I don't believe so. These sons of the sagebrush have

no taste," he yelled back to her as the mob started dragging him out of the buggy.

Suddenly a dozen shots rang out and the loose tentflaps were pulled back from the outside.

Then it happened. Two roaring, full-grown lions, three snarling, purple-assed orangutans, a Bengal tiger, and a soaring bald eagle were piling into the tent.

Instantly the howling mob released the Professor and raced for the open air. Just as quickly, Calamity seized the Professor's arm and yelled, "This way!"

Her gun cocked, she dragged him back to the rear of the tent and out by the cages. She found Hickok among a row of empty animal wagons—empty, that is, save one, which he had entered. He was standing inside the open cage of a huge North American grizzly.

The bear was lying on his side, face turned upward, jaws open, snoring raucously.

"You lazy sonofabitch!" Hickok was screaming. "I said wake up! I killed one of you with a knife when I was just a boy. And I'm about to do it again!" He started banging on the bars with his canteen full of snakehead whiskey. "Wake up, you ugly bastard!"

But now Slater was peeling around the corner of the tent on his gray, leading the five other horses. He halted the mounts alongside the grizzly's cage, and Calamity dragged the Professor over to the roan. She vaulted onto its back and left a stirrup empty so the Professor could swing up behind her.

She turned her head, and Hickok was suddenly upending the two-quart canteen full of sidewinder whiskey into the grizzly's open, snoring mouth.

"Drink, you bastard!" he howled.

A quart of whiskey gurgled out of the canteen and into the grizzly. And then he was on his feet and roaring like the legions of hell were in him, fighting to get out. The mule and five horses were spooked and lunging sideways. Slater's gray was dancing across the hardpan, while Slater was trying to control the jerk-line of bucking, kicking animals. Calamity was fighting the roan, and the Professor was hanging on to his savior for dear life. Hickok leaped out of the grizzly's cage and raced after them afoot. Catching up with the buckskin, which Slater had kept from bolting, Hickok grabbed the apple and at a rolling gait, kicked off twice and swung on, vaulting onto his horse at a dead run. The four of them were headed right for the Nations.

Meanwhile, Slater had managed not only to handle the jerk-line but to hang on to the Arbuckle's box full of grub. As they charged across the plain, he gave the rebel war whoop.

Calamity glanced over her shoulder, and to her dismay she saw the whiskey-crazed grizzly bear charging straight into the crowd of drovers. With an ear-cracking roar, the grizzly scattered the mounts and their would-be riders all through the fairgrounds.

Calamity galloped up alongside Slater, the Professor hanging on behind her.

"They're gonna track us down for sure," she said.

"Not likely," Hickok said. "Them drovers got three lions, a Bengal tiger, three crazed apes, a bald eagle, and a drunken grizzly out stalkin' their herds of beef. They won't get one wink of sleep till they're clean into Kansas."

"You know it!" Slater yelled, still clinging to the food box. "Now let 'em try to tar and feather that grizzly."

41

The Professor got the extra dun, and again Slater had to go bareback.

Then they rode.

They rode that night, then all the next day, resting for only a few hours in the morning. The following evening they came to a stream near the base of the Nueces Mountain. At sunrise they would start up the trail toward the hideout.

While Slater grained the stock, and the Professor tried and failed dismally to start a fire, Calamity and Hickok found a

nearby telegraph line. Hickok took out his sharpened crampons, which Reynolds had used in the canyon, as well as the
transmitter telegraph key and cable.

When they returned to camp a half hour later, Slater got
Hickok and Clem away from the Professor and said, "What's
the word?"

Hickok threw down a scrap of paper. It read, *"We're on
the way. GAC."*

"That stands for George," said Hickok.

"He must have a lotta confidence in us," Slater said.

"In you," Calamity said flatly. "After we get to that
hideout, it's your show."

42

Calamity fried the ham, then simmered it with the beans.
She served it with pan bread and the half-wheel of cheese,
and for dessert she warmed up the dried-apple pie. Afterward
they leaned back around the fire on their McClellans and
bedrolls, sipped Arbuckle's, and smoked Bull Durham.

"Professor," Calamity asked, her eyes half shut, "you
never did tell us what you did. Besides swindle them cowhands."

"Madam, I am a poet. I travel, lecture, and recite my
verse. Perhaps you've heard of me. My name is J. P.
Paxton."

"Sonofabitch," Calamity said. "So you be a poet? What
sort do you write?"

"The only ones Calamity knows," Hickok interjected.
"Rhyme with Nantucket."

"I'm not familiar with any works about Nantucket,"
Paxton said. "No, I may hail from New York, but my poetry
is not about the decadent East. I write instead of the Golden
Land, madam, that country west of the Big Muddy and east
of the Blue Pacific, that magical place which, in one of my

more recent poems, I called 'the final fortress of the Lord Himself, His Last Bastion of Justice, Truth and Right'."

"You ain't talkin' 'bout the Staked Plains, that place where them drovers was fixin' to do you in, are you?" said Hickok.

"No, my good man. That tawdry episode was a singular disappointment in my pilgrimage."

"I don't know, Professor," Calamity said, leaning her head back against her saddle. "I don't know as this trip of yours is such a good idea. Takes a special breed out here. You just don't look the type. Me and my friends—Jim there, and Jay"—she winked slyly at Hickok and Slater—"hell, we be used to the West's rough ways. We've drifted and saddle-bummed these plains, like goddamn dust devils, from hell to west to crossways. We be used to the bumps and hard knocks. But a man of your breedin' and education? Hell—"

"No need to fret, my dear," the Professor observed good-naturedly. "Yes, I realize I may receive my share of 'bumps and hard knocks' on this journey, just as you say, but this is something I really must do. If I am to continue my work. If I am to write honestly."

"I got to side with the others," Slade said. "Seems like you got a good life in New York. Decent food, a nice house, a peace officer on every corner to keep you safe. It ain't like that out here. Things get rough, real rough."

"Sir, I'm afraid I have no other choice. There comes a time when a man has to be frank with himself. Candidly, sir, my whole career and reputation—my life itself—has been one protracted hypocrisy. My poems and stories and lectures and books are second-hand fabrications lifted from libraries and newspapers. The acclaim I've received has been given to me falsely. The emoluments should never have been mine."

"Emoluments?" Calamity looked puzzled. "That got something to do with money?"

"Yes. And it's money I've taken under false pretenses."

"You mean you even get *paid* for talkin'?" Calamity said, grinning cheerfully. "Hell, Professor, at least you ain't done nothin' dishonest. Sounds like you got it made. It were me, I'd just forget this dumb expedition, get my ass back to New York, and collect some more of them there ' 'moluments under false pretenses.' Stack them double eagles like they was flapjacks. Beats workin'.''

"No, my mind is clear. I'm going to face my destiny. Then I shall return and write my poetry from the heart, my *furor poeticus* forged in the crucible of experience, a new and different art imbued with hard-won authenticity.''

"Sounds like bad medicine to me, pilgrim," said Calamity. "Suppose you face up to your country and you don't like what you see? Or worse, like them drovers, your country don't like you? Hell, it could turn that poetry of yours ranker'n that rattlesnake whiskey.''

Hickok nodded sympathetically. "Got to agree with the lady, Doc. You got yourself a damn clever dodge with that there poetry stuff. Lots of them emoluments, no work to speak of. Why risk messin' it up?''

"Sir, my work is inauthentic. I've already 'messed it up.' My only hope now is to face the frontier, write my poems truthfully, and let the readers judge their worth.''

Calamity gave the man a tired grin. "Professor, you think you'd recognize your West if you saw it? Suppose you stumbled over some real-life gunnies and desperadoes—men like Bill Hickok, Torn Slater, Jesse James?''

"Oh, I'd know them. Count on it. I've been thorough in my research of the West. And I shall be thorough in my pilgrimage. I shall leave no stone unturned. I shall persevere—''

"Per-sev-eer. Professor, you got me there," Calamity said, yawning. "If it weren't past my bedtime, I'd say run that by me again." She glanced sideways and gave Paxton a hard stare. "But the next time you start turnin' over stones, just watch what crawls out. Some of them got sidewinders underneath. Kick over the wrong rock, it'll be the last 'authentic thing' you ever do.''

She rolled into her soogans. Hickok was already snoring. In the distance a coyote barked. Soon Calamity was asleep.

J. P. Paxton, poet and lecturer, stared into the dying embers and wondered who these strange people were.

43

The next day was a scorcher. By midmorning they'd gotten the Professor only as far as the North Fork of the Red River and were in bad need of a rest. Under a stand of cottonwoods at the river's edge, they unsaddled their horses and pulled off the sweat-soaked blankets. They watered the stock from cylindrical canvas morrals, then began rubbing them down with handfuls of grass. They staked the horses under the trees for fear they'd hobble to the river and bloat.

Over the next rise was a trail. It would take them to the James-Younger hideout in the mountains. Upriver about two miles was a relay station for the Overland Stage Company.

"Yeah, Professor," Calamity was saying as she leaned back lazily against the roots of a cottonwood, "catch that stage and head back East. The Nations ain't no fit place for a well-bred man."

"I don't know. The West, they say, is where we find ourselves."

"Yeah? Well, too bad for them Injuns, then." Calamity's eyes sparkled.

"You three will be all right?" the Professor said. "There are not only renegade Comanches, but I understand that the James-Younger gang is hiding out somewhere in these mountains. They're notorious desperadoes. Do you know of them?"

Smiling at Slater, Calamity said, "You knew some men who rode with them boys. With Quantrill too. Didn't you?" She sucked on a piece of bear grass.

"Yeah, heard they was pretty fierce. Men like that, well, that's another stone you don't want to be turnin' over. Got a whole nest of vipers underneath. Pilgrim, I'd get on that stage pronto."

Calamity was cackling with mean laughter. "Yeah? Well, what about that one haired-over hardcase used to ramrod them boys? Outlaw Torn Slater? He as bad as they claim?"

"Him?" Hickok cut in with a sly grin. "Maybe once. No more. I hear he was heifer-branded down in Yuma Prison. Heard some hard-assed warden busted him down to suckin' eggs. Last I heard, he was swishin', lispin', puttin' out head for half the guards. Hear he turned punk for some sergeant named Stryker."

Calamity roared with laughter.

"Some say," Hickok continued, "he was a punk before he even went in. Him, Bill Anderson, Quantrill, they was all punks."

Slater's eyes flashed. He poured water into his morral and soaked his face in it, then said, "Say, anybody hear 'bout that limp-dick mother, *Mild* Bill Hickok? And his bull-dyke whore-lady, Calamity?"

"If you mean *the* Wild Bill and Calamity, my researchers informed me on unimpeachable authority that they are up in Deadwood, in the Dakota Territory. I've written extensively about them, but never met either one. I'd wanted so much to get there and interview them. I hope I can still find them. Especially Miss Calamity. She's quite beautiful, I hear."

Calamity smiled widely.

"You wouldn't know how to locate her, would you?" the Professor asked Slater.

"She's easy enough to find, Professor. Just borrow two bits, then lay down in any Deadwood gutter."

The Professor looked shocked. "I find that hard to believe. I hear she's a real lady."

Hickok snorted, then stood and walked to the remuda. He began saddling his buckskin. The others followed.

"I agree with you, Professor," Calamity said as she threw her McClellan over the roan. "These two wouldn't know a real lady if they tripped over one."

Calamity walked to the Professor's horse. He was having trouble cinching up his saddle over the heavily distended belly of the dun. Calamity put a boot into the nag's gut, kicked hard, pulled tight, and eventually worked the buckle up three more notches.

"You gotta stick boot leather to this bloat-gut, pilgrim. You want that cinch tighter'n a gnat's asshole. In all this heat and lather and poor footin', that there saddle'll turn."

The horses rested, they mounted up. They saw the Professor across the fork, and pointed him toward the Overland station.

Then they reined their mounts around toward the trail up Nueces Mountain.

PART ELEVEN

44

They rode.

North into the mountains, up into the hot, high country of the Nations. They followed a creekbed, a twisting switchback of stones and alkali and merciless heat. The bottom was gouged and rutted, and the horses stumbled over the holes. Tangled sage and thorny mesquite obscured the ruts. Each time a hock disappeared into a hole, Calamity silently prayed the horse would not break his leg. They slowly wound and angled up the grade, saddles creaking, cross-bucks groaning, hardware clinking.

Calamity mostly watched the mule. And occasionally Hickok. For the same reason. They were naturally at home in this terrain. The platter-footed jack was loaded to the ears with supplies, and the double-ring cinches and chest harnesses were digging deeply into flanks and chest as he picked his way around the holes. Hickok always looked for Mexican mules or, failing that, for crosses of Mexican and American. The purebred U.S. jacks were bigger and stronger, but the Mexican mules, after centuries of desert-breeding and traveling, had learned to feel their way over the rocks, grope their way around cactus. Hickok claimed they could *smell* a hole or a dropoff.

Calamity also watched the way Hickok and Slater handled their own horses. Damn, they could ride. They were balanced and agile. They absorbed the jolts without a blink. Long ago they'd learned the difference between riding a horse and riding with a horse, something Calamity was coming to appreciate.

By now she felt that her McClellan was growing teeth, eating its way up her back. As for Hickok and Slater, the short pommel and low cantle and lack of padding meant nothing to them. When they came to a deep rut and their mounts danced sideways, Calamity marveled at the way they continued to loll in the saddle with undisturbed ease. She noted the stiff-legged way they stayed deep in the fork, even as the horses lunged sideways at a buzzing, coiled rattler. The same twisting, jackrabbit jumps that had her grabbing the apple, Hickok and Slater ignored with no apparent effort, loose-reined and low in the kack.

When the sun reached its zenith, they found some shade under a granite overhang. They had climbed a thousand feet since leaving the Professor, five long hours ago. They tied the mule by the packline to some hardy mesquite, the horses by the *mecates*. They loosened cinches, unloaded the cross-buck packsaddles, and broke out the water bags and grain sacks and feedbags. After caring for their mounts, they could look to themselves.

They made a meal out of canned tomatoes, hardtack, and Arbuckle's. They had softened the hardtack in the coffee that morning. They ate it now. Then they speared the tomatoes with their barlow knives. They hauled out their tin cups and Hickok filled them from a canteen of Arbuckle's brewed that morning. The desert sun, beating down on the two-quart canteen, had kept it warm. Now, squatting like Yaquis, they sipped the bitter brew and rocked on their heels. They rolled their smokes and stared up the winding trail.

"Could've used some of that Jack Daniel's whiskey,"

Slater said slowly, letting the smoke curl out of his mouth. "Would've helped me choke down them biscuits."

"Too bad we ain't got the makin's for some real victuals," said Calamity. "I'm some kinda belly-cheater. Get me a little sourdough, hell, I'd make you biscuits so damn light, it'd take all three of us to hold them down."

"Could've gone for some sonofabitch stew," Hickok said.

"Cube the tongue, chop a little liver with some fat and sweetbreads, fry it all up with some onions, a little flour, salt, and cayenne," Calamity said, nodding. "I can taste it right now."

"Damn, Hickok," Slater said, staring at Clem, "you better marry that woman. She can cook too. Makes me hungry just listening to her."

"Oh, yeah. She can cook. I be your witness there."

Hickok stood and walked over to the pack mule. He unlashed the tarpaulin and pulled it off. From the top of one of the kyacks he pulled out three grain sacks. He lugged them to the shadow under the overhang, where Calamity and Slade were still hunkering on their heels. He dropped the plunder in front of them.

"What's this?" Slade said wearily, staring up through the heat.

"The edge." Hickok knelt on one knee.

He took out two parcels of oily rags. Inside were three .36-caliber Navy Colts of blue-black steel, with pearl grips. He wiped the neat's-foot oil off the guns, one at a time. Calamity noticed that one of the Colts was his slip-hammer vest job, the one with the cut-down barrel and the tied-back trigger.

"Why the hell you wanna use them ancient cap-and-ball pistols?"

"Better accuracy and stoppin' power. Hell, you can get more powder in them, for openers. And as to them single-action Army Colts you two are packin', the riflin' twists left. Them shots'll drift left a good foot at, say, a hundred yards."

"Why did we use them in the Needle?" Calamity asked.

"Oh, they're good enough for fightin' Injuns. You can also match the cartridges with your Winchester. They'll both take .44-40, which is what we got, not .45. You can carry one hell of a lot of bullets that way. You might even shoot them too, if the cylinder-stop spring, the pawl, the pawl spring, the mainspring, or the hammer notches don't bust on you. What I mean is, them guns ain't that reliable."

"Suppose they'd busted in the Needle? What then?" Clem asked.

"Oh, we could've done a lot of things," Hickok said with a small smile. "Rotate the cylinder by hand. Maybe thumb the shots home. If the mainspring'd broke, we could have hit the hammer with a rock. The thing is, with the Injuns we had extra guns and some time. Gunfighters like Jess and Cole don't give you no time."

"Them Army Colts is easier to load. Faster too," Clem said, still unconvinced.

"Yeah, but the actions in them ain't built for speed or accuracy. And with these extra loaded cylinders, I can punch in six more beans at a clip if I want." He unrolled some more oily rags and took out a half-dozen extra cylinders, then, from another sack, boxes of powder, caps and balls. He began cleaning and loading the cylinders.

"You worked on them pieces much?" Slater asked. "Bein' a big-time gunny and all?"

Hickok held out one of the Navy Colts. He spun the action lovingly. The cylinder whirred and clicked on its rachets. "Oh, sure. I altered the grips, honed the sear, lowered the hammer spur. I experimented with a lot of shoulder holsters." He removed a half-breed shoulder rig from another grain sack. "Nowadays I just keep two in my belt and this cut-down slip-hammer stashed in the half-breed."

Hickok tossed a Colt to Slater. Slater spun the cylinder. He whistled. "Quiet as a tomb."

"Bill," Calamity said, "you expectin' any special trouble from these nickel-plated pistoleros?"

"I locked up, pistol-whipped, shot, and killed some of their friends. That was when I lawed in Kansas. And if that ain't enough, I also bluebellied ten damn years. Torn, them

reb outlaw friends of yours ain't gonna forget that too quick.
Some of them Quantrill boys claim I red-legged. Some claim
I sniped Generals Price and McCulloch. And that was in
Missouri, the gang's home state.''

"Did you?"

"I sure tried. In fact, Torn, lookin' back on my life, I don't
think my gettin' you outta Yuma's gonna cut much shit, not
with them.''

"Speakin' of which," Slater said, "expect some problems
'tween me and Cole.''

"Yeah, he did leave you for dead back there in that Tucson
desert," said Hickok.

"A little more'n that. Cole's the jealous type. 'Specially
'bout Belle Starr. Twitches like a dog passin' peach pits
every time someone looks twice at her. Which, if you
know Belle, is kinda hard *not* to do. Well, I done more
than look.''

"You fucked Cole's wife?" Calamity asked, her eyes
narrowing.

"She weren't his wife then. Cole didn't even know her.
But Belle just couldn't leave it be. Couldn't stop tormentin'
Cole with it. How I'd done this to her, how I'd done
that.''

"Maybe you just got it done," Calamity said.

"Maybe. That's the way she laid it out for Cole. Got him
mad enough to kill a rock. It's why he left me in that
arroyo.''

"How was Belle, now you mention it?"

"Oh, she's a wild one, all right. Makes you wanna get
up and kick your grandma. Ain't nothin' she wouldn't
do.''

"And she told Cole every filthy thing you done to her,
huh?''

"Reckon so.''

"So we got a jealous husband. A man who wants your
balls," Calamity said. "As well as a whole band of Johnny
Reb outlaws who likewise want Bill's.''

Calamity glanced over at Hickok. He now had his three
Colts wiped clean and laid out on a grain sack. The pearl

handles gleamed against the blue-black steel. Hickok slowly stripped off his dirty striped shirt, reached into a second sack, and removed an Arkansas toothpick in a back-sheath rig. He slipped the steel out of its sheath. The straight-pointed blade glinted in the sun. The double edge was three inches wide at the base. The cross-guard was five inches. The entire blade was ten and a half inches.

"Used one of these to kill a grizzly," Hickok drawled.

"Yeah, I can see that," Calamity said, eyeing the livid claw scars along his naked left shoulder. "I suppose you also used one against the bullet that put the hole through your chest and against the Cheyenne lance that gouged out that volcanic crater in your hip."

"Can't win them all," Hickok said with a shrug. "That's why I brought these." He reached into a third grain sack and pulled out two bundles of clothes and a black felt sombrero with silver conchos around the red leather hatband. The low crown and two-foot brim were adorned with gold embroidery.

"That's right," Calamity said dryly. "You'll kill 'em with that Mex hat."

Hickok tossed his Stetson aside and put on the black sombrero. He unrolled another bundle. In it was a white linen shirt with ebony buttons. He put it on over the toothpick, now strapped behind the back of his neck. He took a string tie with a black obsidian clasp out of the shirt pocket and tied it. From the bottom of the grain sack he drew a red silk Mexican sash. He stood and wrapped it around his waist. From the sack that had held the guns he bent over and pulled out the half-breed shoulder holster. He strapped it on and tucked in the sawed-off Navy Colt. He opened the loading gates of the other two Navies and pushed the long-barreled pistols into the sash and held the pistols firm as holsters. From the other sack came a carefully folded black broadcloth frock coat. He shook it out and slipped it on.

"Damn," Hickok said. "I feel better already. Bet I look like a million dollars too."

"You look like a Mexican pimp or an out-of-work undertaker," Calamity said. "I can't figure out which."

"I've arranged a few cheap funerals," Hickok said agreeably.

"You may have to arrange a few more, Injun-slayer."

"Then I'm dressed for the occasion."

45

They headed higher into the mountain country of the Nations. The trail twisted steadily through the hard rock. It wound between the jumbled boulders till it became a draw, then a gorge, both sides looming above them.

As they continued their climb, the land came to life. First saltbushes, then cholla and creosote, then pinyon and greasewood. Coyotes and mule deer and javelinas were staring at them from dried-out stands of prickly pear and salt cedar. The sand kicked up, the dust thickened, and the gorge became a tangle of rough undergrowth—nettles with thorny branches and spiny leaves, impenetrable thickets of gray-green mesquite and twisted chaparral, gnarled clumps of cactus and catclaw.

The sun rose. They climbed higher and higher. The twisting gorge became an inferno. Dust devils danced crazily up and down the pass. The wind moaned, scalded their throats. They began to choke on the alkali dust. They soaked their bandannas and pulled them over noses and mouths, but still the dust filled their throats and nostrils and the corners of their eyes.

Their batwing chaps were torn and cut, and the bedrolls they strapped around the chests and flanks of the animals were getting ripped to shreds. Cholla and yucca and prickly pear and palo verde and mesquite. Their way up the mountain was a trail of thorns.

The sun burned hotter and hotter, turning the gorge into an oven. Again and again they stopped and loosened cinches.

They emptied water bags into their morrals and Stetsons and watered the stock. They washed their horses' noses and mouths with wet bandannas. They rubbed down the lathered flanks and withers with empty grain sacks.

And still the sun burned.

46

Late that afternoon they met the first lookout.

They spotted him a hundred yards up the pass: a tall, hawk-faced man, his skin as dark as an old boot. Waving an eight-gauge Greener high overhead, he was dressed *charro*-style in a white muslin shirt tucked into black pants tapered tightly around the middle of the legs and shoved into his boots. He wore a heavy straw sombrero with a steeple crown and a two-foot-wide, turned-up brim. His Colts were holstered with their butts forward, and across his chest were strapped crisscrossed bandoliers, the webbing filled with shiny brass cartridges. He shouted, *"Quién es?* Slater, *amigo?* We heard you was out. *Es verdad?"* He kneed his grulla and slashed the neck with the *romal*-end of the reins. He loped down the pass toward the three riders. When he pulled up in front of them, Calamity got a closer look at his outfit—the carved leather saddle with a dinner-plate horn and a low cantle. The heavy sombrero had a rattlesnake-skin band with a tail cluster of at least eight rattles.

"Es verdad," Slater nodded. "So put away the Greener, Cholo, before I shove it up your ass stock-first."

" *'Ey,* Chaky," the Mexican said, widening his grin. "Is no way to talk to an old compadre, *un amigo muy bueno.*"

"That's right, Cholo. *Amigo muy bueno.* Now how far's the camp?"

"Maybe a half hour, maybe less." He turned to Hickok, taking in the dude clothes, not liking what he saw. " 'Ey, the *yanqui pistolero. Hay-cock.* The big gringo gunman. You gonna take on the whole mountain? Maybe you ride for Parker now, huh?''

"Just ridin' another tired pony outta Texas," Hickok said, slapping the buckskin's neck.

"*Muy bien.* We need *dos hombres muy machos* like you."

He reined his mount around, and they headed up. As she kneed her horse, Calamity said to Hickok, "What's that dumb *mestizo* mean—*dos hombres muy machos*?"

"He means we're two stud horses—and we kill for fun. Or for nothin'.''

"He may be right," said Calamity.

"Just don't tell him otherwise," Hickok said.

"Yeah," Slater agreed. "He meant it as a compliment."

47

They rode through the village gate at dusk. Its adobe wall was fifteen feet high and half as thick. Guards manned corner gun towers.

The wall curved around the village, ending at the brink of a cliff. Along the scarp's perimeter stretched a small wall, beyond which a canyon dropped off into empty space.

In the village square, a Gatling gun was mounted on a flatbed wagon and ringed by sandbags. A *bandido* in a white muslin shirt leaned lazily over the sights of the machine gun and waved as the Mex led them through the village.

The place itself wasn't much. Long, twisting paths and alleys, winding rows of dirty adobe houses.

Here and there, women in black rebozos—maybe twenty in all—stood watching, their eyes flat. Each had a baby on her hip or slung on her back. The women who weren't on their feet were kneeling in the square, grinding corn on flat stone *metates* with hand stones called *manos*. Their men were in the fields or squatting in front of the buildings, drinking.

Nothing else. The droning of flies, the bawling of babies, vultures picking at garbage in the dusty streets.

At the edge of the square was a large adobe cantina. A half-dozen horses were tied to the hitch rack. In the doorway leaned a gringo in a black slouch hat, bullhide chaps, and a gingham shirt. He wore a tied-down gun on each hip and one in his belt. He had small, mean eyes, a hard, weathered face, and sandy hair.

"Know him?" Calamity asked Hickok.

"You mean Cole there? He passed through Abilene. All of them did once or twice."

"Did you arrest him?"

"We kept out of each other's way."

They rode up and swung off their mounts.

By now, two Indian boys in dirty cotton clothes were racing to the cantina. The Mex pointed to the stable. The boys led the stock there to be watered, curried, and grained.

Cole walked around the hitch rack. Ignoring Calamity and Hickok, he went straight up to Slater and stared at him fixedly. When Cole put out his hand, Slater took it, but his eyes were blank, expressionless.

"Hell, I knew you'd come back," Cole said. "Ain't no prison strong enough to hold Outlaw Torn Slater. Not Yuma, not no prison on earth. Come on in, Torn. Come on in," he said, waving them toward the cantina doorway. "The boys is waitin'. We got a lotta drinkin' to catch up on, a lotta hell to raise."

Calamity needed a moment to adjust to the darkness. She could see a half-dozen men leaning against the bar. Four of them were wearing wide-brimmed sombreros, the others black slouch hats with low, flat crowns. They each carried at least three guns. It occurred to Calamity that she'd never seen so many guns on so few people. Colts, Remingtons, Dancers, Smith & Wessons, Sharps pepperboxes, derringers. Each of the men looked up, and when they saw Torn come in behind Cole, they crowded around.

A tall, mustached man in a black slouch hat stepped forward.

"Jess," Slater said quietly.

Jesse James nodded. "Torn Slater. I figured you were boot-buried in that Yuma boneyard by now."

"You was worried about me?" Slater drawled.

"Gospel. But here you are—like some old painter or puma down from the high lonesome, fangs bared, snaky-tailed, talons arched. I'm seein' a ghost, I just keep sayin'. Just can't be Outlaw Torn Slater."

"Them days is gone, Jess. I'm a man of peace, here to repent my evil ways."

"If I'd killed and maimed and tortured as many as you, I'd repent too."

"Now don't get righteous on me, Jess. You sent a couple to glory yourself."

"Why, Brother Torn, that were mostly in the War. Which makes it all right." He glanced over at Hickok, his eyes cold. "At least for us Johnny Rebs. Not for no bluebellies, 'course."

Calamity strolled up alongside Slater. She curled the front brim of her Stetson with both hands and cleared her throat.

"Damn, Slater, you got some strange friends here. Not one of them thinks to buy a lady a drink."

Jesse James raked Calamity with a slow look, taking in her man's hat, man's shirt and pants, man's gun.

"Don't see no ladies here," Jess said quietly.

"Nor no women," Cole said from the side of the room.

Another man stepped forward from the bar. His mustache was streaked with gray, and his sombrero's hatband was studded with three-inch silver conchos. He carried his pistols shoved down in his belt, butts turned out, like Hickok's. And his smile was full of wide white teeth.

"Ease off, little brother," Frank James said. "Bill's just brung Torn back home. And as for the little lady, I'd purely admire to accommodate her. You need a drink, ma'am?"

"Do generals need wars?" said Calamity.

Frank James grinned. He walked back and picked up three shotglasses. He wiped them off with a bar rag and filled them to the brim.

"I'm recommending the mescal here," he said. "You're welcome to try the whiskey. You might even taste the alcohol in it—somewhere between the lye, gunpowder, cayenne, laundry soap, tobacco juice, coffin varnish, and tarantula piss. But I doubt it. This here oughta suit you better." He returned with the glasses and passed them out to Calamity, Hickok, and then Slater. Raising his glass, Frank James said, "*Salud y pesetas.*"

"Health and wealth," Slater translated, raising his glass.

"*Salud,*" Clem agreed. She tossed back a full tumbler of mescal. Her throat blazed like fire. A second later, bright lights exploded behind her eyes. "Hail Mary, full of grace," she rasped. And held out her glass in anticipation of another round.

Frank watched Calamity knock back her mescal, and giving Hickok a pleasant smile—which never quite reached the eyes—he nodded and tossed off his own. "Damn," he said with a wheeze, "that's good stuff. It's also good to have you back, Torn. Hell, this gang's yours as much as our'n. More, maybe. You gotta forgive my younger brother, though. While you was away, them Pinkertons got on us something fierce. Killed a lotta friends back home, just 'cause they tried to hide us out. Seems now every time Jess sees a tin star, he gets riled. Anyway, him and Cole, hell, they's nothin' but hair, teeth, and rattlesnake venom, louder'n a span of mules breakin' wind. Don't mean nothin', you know that. We're all proud of the way you busted out of Yuma, swimmin' that river and all."

"Didn't bust out, Frank, nor did I swim that river. Clem and Bill here busted me out. Bill carried me out of that river belly-down, over his shoulder."

"We respect 'em for it, too. Don't think we don't. Not one second. Jess? Cole?"

Jess shrugged. Cole looked away.

"Hell, yes, we 'preciate it," Frank continued. He grabbed the wicker-covered demijohn off the bar and refilled Calamity's glass, then Torn's, then Hickok's and his own.

Calamity tossed back another healthy shot.

"Ain't you never drunk mescal before?" Slater asked.

"No, but I still got time to learn." She held out her glass again.

"Yeah, this is good mescal," Frank said. "We brew it ourselves, right from the maguey plants. Just strip the leaves off, bake the head, then distill it like Missouri moonshine. Gets it done."

"That it do, sport, that it do," said Calamity.

Frank laid the demijohn on the bar. Cole and Jess helped themselves to glasses. Then Jess walked up to Slater. He stared at Slater for a long, hard moment, then offered his hand, which Slater shook.

"Sorry 'bout the cold reception, Torn. Them Pinks got me a little crazy. I'm so hot, I spend half my time anymore lookin' for a dog to kick. I know how Yuma was. And Hickok here"—he reached over and shook Hickok's hand—"I can't guess why you helped, but it sure took sand."

"Took sand to get through that Needle, too," Torn said.

"That's what the newspaper said. Claims Slater and his so far 'unidentified accomplices' killed more'n fifty 'Pache gettin' through that canyon. And closed up the Needle's mouth for good."

"That was all Hickok's show," said Slater.

"Hickok," Frank said, "them dime novels been callin' you 'the Slayer.' Guess ol' Buntline knows what he knows. That was some shootin' in the Needle."

"I'm a peaceful man," Hickok said with a shrug. "I always avoid violence."

"You cat-eyed bastard," Frank roared, slapping Hickok on the back. "You're more full of shit than a Christmas duck. And I like you. I don't care how many towns you lawed in."

"I do," Jess said softly.

"Jess," Frank said, "you got to be more open-minded. You just don't appreciate history. Hell, Bill *is* history. He tamed the rawest, wildest hurrah towns in the memory of man. Nossirree! We won't never see places like Hayes or Abilene again. Five thousand drovers and five hundred thousand longhorns hittin' town like rockslides, and nothin' but Wild-fuckin'-Bill here standin' between decent town-livin' law-abiders and hell's own hordes. Wild-fuckin'-Bill against the vultures of Prometheus. It's the stuff of legends, Jess. You got to respect that.''

"My older brother better quit readin' them books,'' said Jess in a slow Missouri drawl. "They be addlin' his brain. Frank keeps forgettin' that we was with the rockslides and the vultures. That was *us* Hickok was shootin' at.''

"Just like he fought us in Missouri. In the War,'' Cole put in. "Don't care what you say. He was with them red-legs. He fit agin the Cause. Generals McCulloch and Sterling Price, they sleep under the sod 'cause Bill-fuckin'-Hickok planted them there.''

Red-faced, Cole glared at Hickok.

Hickok's face was expressionless. "Maybe. I was in the War. I was wild and headstrong. And them big Sharps rifles carry quite a ways.''

"Little brother, them days of his are over, just like the War,'' said Frank. "Hickok ain't lawed since Abilene. Ain't that right?'' Hickok nodded. "So you gotta be more understandin' of him.'' Frank turned to Calamity. "See, dear, you gotta understand somethin'. My little cousin is still fightin' the War. Everythin' he does is still 'cause of the War.''

"That be so,'' said Cole evenly.

"It's the would-be preacher in him,'' Frank went on. "Cole still feels the call. Feels it somethin' fierce, somethin' righteous. Claims all them banks we robbed and men we shot was for Quantrill, Christ, and the Cause.''

"That be so.''

The sun was down. From the darkening courtyard, Calamity heard a whistling *hiss*, a *crack*, and a *clink-clink*, *clink-clink*. A woman strolled through the doors and into the cantina. Calamity sized up the competition with grudging respect. She was swinging a wrist quirt with a leaded stock, and two heavy lashes of plaited rawhide with three-inch poppers on the ends. Dressed in faded Levis, black blouse and Stetson, she slapped the *cuarta* across her knee-high riding boots, heeled with six-inch buzz-saw rowels. The spur leather arched across the instep, with conchos on the outside of the band. A couple of loose chains clanked behind the heels, and two bell-clappers, known as "janglers," clinked inside the rowels.

Calamity took in the woman's body with mounting dismay. Her Levi's were so tight against her legs and hips that they looked ready to burst. She wore a black leather gun belt and a holstered Navy Colt. Her black cotton blouse had mother-of-pearl buttons, the top three boldly open. Her Stetson was canted at a rakish angle. Under the tilted brim, Calamity caught a glimpse of the slanting black eyes, wayward, filled with wickedness.

Still slapping the heavy quirt against one boot leg, Belle Starr stared at Cole Younger and repeated, "You 'shot them for the Cause'? Christ on the Cross! You couldn't shoot a barn door from the inside with the door shut. You whimperin' limp-dicks couldn't say shit if your mouths were full of it. Damn it, I heard from my kid that Torn Slater was out of Yuma and had brought back Bill Hickok and his whore-lady. As prisoners, I'd assumed. And here I find you quiverin' and twitchin' 'round them. *You got the law here. And a former fuckin' Union spy to boot?* And you're treatin' him like royalty? Damn, you men must be blind, gelded, or both.''

"Jesus H. Christ!" Slater yelled hoarsely. "Belle Starr and her ugly fuckin' temper. Snake blood in her veins and buffalo bile in her mouth. Cole, if I was you, I'd whomp that filly with a knotted plowline.''

"I tried. It don't do no good.''

Belle fixed Slater with a contemptuous stare and snorted, "Watch me hurrah this short-horned stranger.''

She crossed the room toward Slater, the *cuarta* quirt rising and falling. Her rowels clanked on the hard-packed dirt floor and her left hand rested on the butt of her Colt. As she neared Slater, she was reaching back and whipping the quirt downward. Only at the last second did she deliberately overshoot the lash and fall into his arms, her open mouth pressing against his, her knee forcing its way between his legs.

Cole exploded across the room. Pulling her off Slater, he cracked her across the side of the head with an open palm as she simultaneously pivoted, bringing the quirt across his face with a whistling *crack!*

An ugly welt rose diagonally across Cole's cheek. His hand rose instinctively to the raw flesh, his eyes tearing over with pain.

"You sonofabitch!" Belle screamed, raising the quirt above her head. "You touch me again and I'll kill you. I swear before God I'll kill you."

Cole's face worked in rage, the welt livid on his cheek. When his hand snaked toward his gun, Frank James clamped his wrist.

"Bob, Jim," he said angrily, teeth clenched, "get your brother out of here. Stick his head in a water barrel. We're celebratin' Torn's return home, and I ain't lettin' this party get busted up, as usual, by his goddamn family squabbles. Cole," he said, staring at his cousin with calm, unreadable eyes, "go grease that cut on your cheek. Get that temper under control. And that bitch of yours, too. 'Cause if you can't control her, Jess and me will."

Belle was already storming toward the door. "You sonsofbitches!" she shouted. "So help me, you're all still pullin' on your mamas' tits. Torn, you were the only real man of the lot, and Yuma probably turned you queer. It sure as shit turned you dumb, what with bringin' Hickok and his whore-bitch in here, passin' 'em off on us as though they were long-lost kin. Stick with Hickok and he'll ride you boys straight under cottonwoods."

Belle fixed Calamity with an angry stare. "Hickok, you got one homely whore there. If I had a bitch dog that ugly, I'd shave her ass and make her walk backwards."

She spun around and marched out, the quirt still cracking against her boot, rowels still clanking.

Cole's brother eased him down on a stool. His eyes were glazed, unfocused. "Belle?" he was mumbling under his breath. "Belle? Where'd she go, Frank? Where'd she go?"

Frank shook his head slowly. "Jim, Bob, get him out, sober him up. Your brother's jug-bit. That's all. He'll come 'round. Maybe you oughta pour some Arbuckle's in him. Never saw a man yet who could hold his liquor like a bottle."

They grabbed Cole under the arms and lifted him to his feet. They half-walked, half-dragged him into the courtyard.

"Hey, Cholo," Frank said to the Mex leaning against the bar, "have your *señora* cook some grub. Our *compadres* had a long ride. We're roasting the fatted calf tonight."

"Bueno," Cholo said, and headed toward the door.

Frank and Jess were now alone with Calamity and her two friends. Slater uncorked the demijohn and filled their glasses.

"What's that shit with Cole and Belle?" he said. "She was always wild, but this is loco."

"What can I say? She always had him cunt-struck, but now it's like a disease."

"Is it always this bad?" Slater asked.

Frank James shrugged. "Hard to say. Two years ago she run off with an Injun, name of Henry Red Eye. Ol' Cole come down after her, faced Henry down Injun-style, and gutted him throat to balls with a bowie. Cole was crazy-mad, convinced Belle was fuckin' every Injun in the Nations."

"Maybe she was," Calamity said.

"She's capable of it. And Cole's capable of killin' every Injun. Had to drag him back to Missouri, kickin' and screamin'." Frank shook his head. "As you can see, we couldn't keep him there, neither. Six months ago he dragged us all back down here to hunt up Belle. And supposedly duck the law."

"And he just can't keep her in line?" Slater asked incredulously.

"I got to stand up for my brother on that score," Bob Younger said, returning to the cantina. "Cole's tried ever'thin'—hollerin', threatenin', punchin', kickin', even whip-breakin' her. Nothin' works. And it ain't for the want of him tryin'. She keeps right on fightin' back, raisin' hell, and fuckin' 'round."

"She's sleepin' 'round on Cole Younger?" Slater looked genuinely surprised. "Cole must have a hundred fuckin' scallops on his guns."

"Nothin' he *can* do, outside of carvin' *her* scallop on that big Sam Colt. Cole whips her ass every which way but loose, hell to fuckin' breakfast. It don't do no good. All Belle gets is older, meaner, and still around."

"Ain't *nothin'* he can do?" Calamity asked.

"What else is there?" Jim Younger added. "Winchester quarantine'd hold her. But only as long as he was willin' to shoot."

"She acts like she ain't got both feet in the stirrups," said Slater.

"Maybe not, but that don't slow Cole down none. Hell, Cole claims he wants to marry her again."

"Well, I guess marriage is okay," Calamity said, giving Hickok a terse smile. "Beats bein' flogged and castrated."

"That's Belle's feelin'," said Frank. " 'Course, Cole's convinced she just prefers Injuns over him. Can't stand gettin' turned down." Frank gave Slater a hard look. "Now that Torn's out of Yuma, Cole'll think he's standin' in the way."

Slater scowled. "She always did encourage that shit."

"Maybe Cole's got somethin' to be jealous about," Frank conjectured.

"She is awful pretty," said Calamity.

"What did she say 'bout Clem?" Hickok added, grinning. "I should shave her ass and make her walk backwards?"

"She advised that if'n you had an ugly dawg," Frank James said diplomatically.

Calamity raised her glass to Frank, and tossed off the shot, as Cholo's wife pushed the tables together and loaded them with food.

48

She served them dishes of tomatoes and scorching red chilis topped with poached eggs. That was the appetizer. For the main course she brought in several platters of enchiladas and beans, covered with melted cheese. There was a big pot of stewed meat in the middle of the table, seasoned hot as hellfire. Around the table were bottles of beer and pots of Arbuckle's. The beer had been chilled in a spring-fed well.

The conversation passed easily. Slater told how Calamity and Hickok had busted him out of Yuma. He told of their battle through the pass.

She was pleased when Frank James raised his glass and said, "Hear, hear."

Frank and Jess spoke of their own problems with the Pinkertons in Missouri. Frank told how Jess shot Agent John Whicher on the public road.

"Then my little brother went to Chicago and stalked Allan Pinkerton through the streets."

"No shit?" Slater was impressed.

"Didn't try to shoot him, though," Jess said, lifting a glass of beer. "Just looked him in the eye. Just wanted him to know I could do it to him too."

The talk moved to guns. As they ate, Slater told of Hickok's marksmanship in the Needle with the Sharps "Big Fifty."

"That's mighty fine shootin', mighty fine," said Frank James.

Hickok shrugged. "There's one hundred and seventy grains of powder behind a seven-hundred-grain slug. With that big a charge and that much lead, all you need is the range and a rifle scope. It's a trick shot, that's all."

"Hittin' a target's one thing," Slater said. "Hittin' that target with a 'Pache war party stormin' through the pass is another. That's the difference between gunfightin' and target shootin'. Bill here's a gunfighter. He could do it under pressure."

Then the talk got more personal. Jess pointed to the inside pocket of Hickok's black frock coat. He asked about the eyeglasses with the smoked lenses in the velvet-lined box.

"Eyes got sensitive. Light, dust, wind, everything. They need protection anymore."

"You seen a doc?" Frank asked.

"When I was back East with Bill Cody's Wild West Show, a New York sawbones looked me over. Said all them years in the high plains, the winter snows, and the summer dust could've left me moon-eyed. He also asked me if I ever had the clap. Only two or three times, I told him. Explained that after fifteen years in army posts and cowtowns and mining camps, it's kinda rare for a man not to have it. But I swore I took the cure. Even so, the croaker said that could've done it."

"Don't seem possible. All of us'd be stone blind by now if'n them colds-of-the-pants reached the eyes," said Jesse.

"Hell, yes," Frank nodded. "And anyway, your eyes was okay in the Needle. Killed yourself fifty fuckin' redskins. Woo-ee!"

"Woo-ee!" Jess echoed.

Frank laughed raucously. As he reached for another beer, he said, "Torn, remember when my little brother joined up with the Colonel? Quantrill didn't wanna take him 'cause he was so young-lookin' and fair-skinned."

"Frank, I was only fifteen."

"We know, little brother. It was Torn here who figured out how to let him earn his keep. Torn would dress him as a girl in crinoline and bonnets, then send Jess around to the whorehouses. Jess would pretend he was contemplatin' the whore-lady business. He'd find out in the meantime where the money was, then wait in the back of the parlor that night for us to kick in the front door. When we fought them Jayhawkers inside, Jess would bushwhack them from behind with his hideout piece. Afterward he'd show us where the loot was hid."

"It weren't my proudest moment."

"We was all proud of you, little brother. Oh, some of the boys thought it'd be fun to job you a little about them clothes and such. Cole liked to ride Jess special. Till Centralia. Jess killed eight men in Centralia. 'Fore then, Cole's nickname for Jess used to be Dingus. After Centralia, Cole didn't call him that no more."

Through the dim night, they heard the distant howls of a young child.

"Sounds like that kid bit the wrong wolf," said Calamity.

"That's Belle's kid. The one from that Injun, Jim Reed. She's whalin' on him with that quirt. Does it every night, 'bout this time."

"Any reason why?" Calamity asked.

"Belle don't need no reason, 'cept that maybe she likes doin' it. She's a mean one, all right," said Jess.

"Yeah," Frank agreed. "I never believed in sparin' the rod, but Belle goes hog-wild, stripes that half-breed boy of hers from horn to hocks."

Slowly they all pushed their plates away, their appetites for both food and talk finally satisfied.

49

They were finished with coffee and rolling quirlies when the others drifted into the cantina—the Mex first, then Jim and Bob Younger. They all converged around the bar.

"Sorry we missed dinner," Jim Younger said. "What was it?"

"Looked like yearling beef to me," Calamity said, "only I don't see no squeeze chutes 'round here, nor no drovers nor no brands. You ain't slow-brandin' cattle now? That'd be a come-down for such noble outlaws."

"Not likely. Who says that were beef anyway?" Jim Younger asked.

"What did it taste like to you? Slow elk?" Calamity responded.

"Come on, Clem," Frank said pleasantly, "you know I don't swing no wide loop nor run no maverick factories here."

"I know," Calamity nodded, grinning broadly. "Best slow elk I ever et."

Then Belle made her entrance, the buzz-saw rowels still clanking, the plaited quirt still punishing her boot.

"Hey, Belle," Jesse said coldly, pointing toward the sound of the child's sobs, "why don't you shoot that kid of yours, put him out of his misery?"

"May have to. Less'n I find me a man somewhere, one who can act as father to him. And husband to me. Probably have to get another Injun. Ain't a white man left alive can handle me."

She went around the bar and grabbed a jug of whiskey off the shelf. She poured herself a tumbler and had a snort.

"Hear that has rattler heads in it," Calamity said.

"Girl, I am part rattlesnake," said Belle as she drained the glass. She glared at the James brothers contemptuously. "Stopped by here earlier. Started to come in, then I heard your confab. Cole'll be glad to know how friendly you men are with this red-leg. After what the law done to his little brother John, and the way them red-legs murdered his pa and burned his home and stole his land. You're makin' your kin proud, Frank James. Your ma'd be right pleased after the way Hickok's kind done your'n."

"You best understand, Belle, I ain't lettin' you start nothin', not tonight. You get Cole riled and I'll hector you horn to hoof."

Cole Younger came through the door, red-eyed and disheveled. His hat was pulled down behind his neck, and his hair and gingham shirt were drenched. He shouted, "Fuck you, Frank. I don't need no James to hector my woman. Nor do I need your high-handin'. Torn has come bargin' into *our* camp, bringin' *his* lawman. And fuck it. I need me some answers."

Frank averted his eyes and stared out the cantina window. He said, "Cole, go ahead. Ask Torn for an explanation. He won't hurt you too bad." Frank turned his back on Cole, walked to the far end of the bar, and poured himself a drink.

"Torn," Cole said, "I want to know why Hickok's here. Him and his whore-lady went to a lot of trouble to bust you off that rockpile, then ride you clear over here."

"Bill's on the owlhoot. So's Clem," Slater said, his voice flat.

"Fuck that."

"Cole," Slater said, not unpleasantly. "I don't owe *you* explanations for nothin'. If explanations are due—"

Calamity stepped between the men. She put a finger into Cole's chest.

"We're here 'cause we're outside the law. If'n you had brains enough to pour piss out of a boot, you'd see that yourself."

Belle Starr howled with laughter and poured herself another slug of sidewinder whiskey.

"Now Hickok's whore-lady's takin' Cole down," Belle said gleefully. "Here, Clem, use my quirt. He responds real good if you flog his face."

"Lay off, Belle," Frank said. He turned to Hickok. "Bill, you really on the prowl?"

"Straight deal. Just can't make it marshalin' no more. When that Henry Stanley fella and Buntline wrote that stuff about me, started callin' me shit like 'Hickok the Slayer,' it ended my career as a marshal. I can't keep no peace. Every time I put on a badge, someone wants to shoot it off. I come into a town, just my bein' there starts trouble."

"Cody'd take you back in his Wild West Show."

"No, I tried that once. I tried my own show, too. I just ain't built that way. Cody can take the bullshit that goes with it. He just gets drunk. I start fights with the audience, get thrown into jail. I ain't at home back East. I don't fit in."

"And I still don't believe it," Cole said.

Torn Slater spoke up. "Hickok did do one thing. He freed me from Yuma. And, Cole, that took some doin'. Hickok and Calamity, you can ride the river with them. They proved that. We'd been caught, Warden Stark woulda had them right smack on the rockpile alongside me."

"I still don't like it," Belle cut in.

"I didn't see you nor Jess nor Frank nor anyone else gettin' me off no rockpile," Slater said bitterly, "nor any of my other friends here who may not like Bill and Calamity. Goes especially for you, Cole." He looked Cole Younger in the eye.

"Suppose they stay the night," Jess said pleasantly, "head out in the morning. And you stay. Torn, this is your gang as much as any of our'n. More, maybe. But Hickok's lawed too many years. And them lawman morals die hard."

Slater nodded. "I understand that. But Hickok's got a plan, and it sounds good. It's gonna take some brains and some sand to pull it off, but it's the best thing I heard of. If'n he's right, and we go for it, then I say him and Calamity are in."

"Okay. What's the plan?" said Frank. "Maybe we can settle this right now."

Hickok poured himself a drink. "Ran into Lonesome Charley Reynolds up in the Badlands. Claimed you men got a Gatling gun up here. Couple weeks later, General Crook tells me the bank in Fort Smith is holding two million dollars' worth of gold ingots. Plan to build a mint nearby for stampin' double eagles, and they need the bullion. And I know ol' General Crook ain't no liar."

"Fort Smith?" Cole said, spitting tobacco juice next to Hickok's boot. "You got to be out of your mind."

Hickok ignored him. "Now I been to Fort Smith, and it ain't really a fort. Just a town. A few marshals walkin' 'round. A few bluebellies. No heavy artillery to speak of. Certainly no Gatling guns. I figure ten good men—men that rode by the light of the moon with Bloody Bill and Colonel Quantrill—plus a Gatling gun, they could take that bank."

"Sounds like the tin star's settin' us up," Belle said angrily. "Fort-fuckin'-Smith. You gotta be loco."

"Maybe," Jess said. "But it sounds interestin' to me. That's a rich bank there. If it's holdin' gold bullion, I say it's worth a shot. I say we send Cholo to look it over. If it checks out, we oughta consider it."

"I agree," Frank added. "I can understand how a man might wanna jump the fence. All of us figured to try it straight one time or another. I felt that way a lot of years. You think all you gotta do is straighten your hand and the deal'll turn up square. A lot of hurt and scars and heartbreak cured me of that kinda thinkin'."

"That's very sad, Frank," Belle said with contempt.

"Well, it showed a profit. And that's something I also understand. That Fort Smith bank, it'd be profitable."

"I still don't like it none," Belle said, glaring at Frank James.

Frank grinned. "Belle don't trust anybody even looks sorta straight. Or who ain't done time." He kept smiling, but Calamity saw that the eyes remained cold. "Neither do I."

"Frank," Slater said, "you and I go back a long ways. I wouldn't want to see a little business transaction come between friends. It would purely pain me."

"Same here, Torn."

"But as for Hickok's plan, if'n we go for it, he's in. After what he did for me at Yuma, ain't no other way."

"Fuck what he did at Yuma," Cole said, stepping between Torn and Frank, his voice rising. "That still don't mean I got to like Hickok or the way he works. Hickok, you always rode alone, didn't you? Scout or spy or sniper. Even marshal. Never wanted backup, as I recall. You're like some lone part of nothin', and where I come from, that *makes* you nothin'. I don't understand you joinin' up."

Hickok nodded. "Maybe that was a mistake. And maybe I learned that too late. One thing I know. A man alone can't cut it no more. I'm forty. I spent twenty of them years, half my life, fightin' other men's wars, for other men's reasons, for other men's gain. Rate I'm goin', I'm dyin' broke and blind in a pauper's grave. Time I tried livin' a little. So this time it's gotta be for me."

"Just words," Cole said. "Sounds good, but it's just talk."

"He got me out of Yuma," Slater said. "That's more than just words. That's more than you did, Cole, even with all that horseshit about family and lone wolves and stickin' to your blood. That bank job we pulled in Tucson put me in Yuma. You killed them tellers I got sentenced for. I ain't cryin' about it, but I didn't see you riskin' your neck gettin' me off that rockpile."

Cole moved away from the bar, and Slater turned to face him. The others drifted away.

"Know what I think, Slater?" Cole said, his temper flaring. "I think you spent too much time on that rockpile. Sun softened your brain. I think you spent too many years in the hole, lopin' your mule."

"Cole," Frank said.

Cole slipped the hammer thong off his Colt. "Know what I think? I think Hickok's been pimpin' his whore-lady on you, Torn. You must have a drop-forged, case-hardened, blue-steel pecker, comin' off that pile. Maybe Clem softened it a little. What's pussy taste like after all them years? Vanilla ice cream?"

"Cole, that settles it." Slater took the split-leather thong off the hammer of his own Colt. "Hickok's comin' in. Anyone says no, anyone disagrees, anyone wants a piece of Hickok or Calamity, they're comin' through me."

Cole went for his gun, but Hickok had already moved across the room. He hit Cole Younger in the side of the neck with a hard left hook—just as Cole was reaching. Blindsided, Cole went down like a hammered steer.

Slater pushed Hickok aside. "I step on my own snakes."

But Hickok ignored Slater and stared fixedly at Bob and Jim Younger.

"He's your brother," Hickok said quietly. "You lookin' to interfere, I'll accommodate you."

"He may be our brother," Bob Younger said, "but he's also a stupid shit, throwin' down on Slater like that. Leave him be. He's my blood, but he spoke out of turn. You just kept him from gettin' hisself killed by a better man."

Belle Starr exploded. "You mean you gonna let the law come in here and cold-cock your brother, and you just stand there? What are you afraid of? You think Hickok's gonna take your guns away from you? Make you go home and cry to your ma? I know you got shit for brains, but what are you usin' for balls these days?"

"Belle, shut up," Frank James said, not taking his eyes off Hickok. "Slater's right. This settles it. I'm speakin' for my stupid, out-cold cousin, too. After a fool move like Cole just made, maybe he needs Hickok here to clean up his diapers after him, make him wash behind the ears. Calamity's in too.

Jess, you agree?'' Jesse James nodded. "Me too. Torn, that settles it.''

"I 'preciate that Frank,'' Slater said.

"Don't 'preciate it and don't get me wrong, neither of you. 'Specially Hickok. I been ridin' this trail twenty years. I've robbed banks and stages and trains. I massacred pretty near every livin' thing in Lawrence, Kansas, with Colonel Quantrill. Don't cross me, Hickok. I know you're snake-fast, that you're a hard and desperate man. I know you're Torn's friend. Just don't cross me.''

Suddenly there was a commotion in the doorway and a man was pushed into the cantina. He was wearing a black bowler, a brocade vest, and a frock coat. It was J. P. Paxton, poet and lecturer.

"Ah, my good people,'' he said to his former companions. "I ran into some gentlemen who were good enough to warn me that Frank and Jesse James, as well as those three wretched Younger brothers, were in the area. These kindly gentlemen also informed me that Outlaw Torn Slater had escaped from Yuma Territorial Prison, where he'd most cruelly and wickedly broken the pelvis and kneecaps of a poor unfortunate guard. They surmised that this scoundrel Slater would be headed this way. And since you three had been so kind to me, I felt it imperative that I catch up with you and warn you of your peril.''

"Who's he?'' Frank asked incredulously.

"Some sort of professor or somethin'. Talks a lot,'' Calamity answered.

"I write poetry, sir. Heroic epics of the glorious West. Nearly a dozen volumes in all. And don't make light of my learning. I've written exhaustively and extensively on the lives of the notorious James and Younger brothers, of brave scouts such as Bill Cody and Kit Carson. How well do I know the heroic exploits of that legendary marshal and scout, Wild Bill Hickok! Right now I am finishing a tableau of terror, a *magnum opus* entitled *The Life and Times of Outlaw Torn Slater*. In fact, his dastardly and despicable escape from Yuma Prison will be the penultimate chapter in this tome. Do not underestimate me, sirs and ladies,''

Paxton said, raising his voice emphatically, eyes blazing. "I am quite knowledgeable in the ways of these outlaws and gunfighters."

Astonished, Frank stared at Calamity, Slater, and Hickok. "Torn? Calamity? This man a friend of yours?"

"In a manner of speaking," said Calamity.

Now Cole was coming to. He was mumbling, "Frank, Bob, Jess, we gonna let Hickok get away with this? We're blood. He ain't got no right."

"Shut up, Cole," Frank said.

The Professor's jaw dropped to his chest. "Hickok? Torn Slater? Calamity Jane? Cole Younger? Frank and Jesse James? Ma'am," he addressed himself to Belle Starr. "You wouldn't be Belle Starr? I've written so much about you. About all of you."

She averted her eyes in disgust.

Frank said to Slater, "I suppose *you* want him along, too?"

Slater shrugged.

Jesse James grinned. "Why not? Long as we're in this thing together, we can at least see he gets to the fort. That little fart can't do us no harm. Just make sure he ain't around when we do our banking business. He won't be no bother. In the meantime, he and Frank here can recite Shakespeare to each other. Frank always liked that poetry shit."

Frank agreed wearily. "Yeah, this bird can't hurt us. And we been kinda low on entertainment 'round here. Professor, let me buy you a drink. 'Book of verses underneath the bough, a loaf of bread, a jug of wine,' and all that. The jug's on them planks spannin' the two hogsheads."

50

The bottles piled high.

And as the guitars whanged and strummed, as the Mexican and half-breed *señoritas* spun and shouted to the music, the crowd overflowed into the courtyard.

During the revelry, Frank James dug up a newspaper that reported Slater's escape from Yuma. Shouting for quiet, Frank handed it to the Professor and asked him to read it aloud to those assembled. In a deep, sonorous voice, the Professor obliged.

" 'Warden Stark, distinguished expert on prison reform, has announced his resignation today. It is reported that the recalcitrance and eventual escape of Outlaw Torn Slater was more than the renowned penologist could bear. In more than thirty years of prison work, Warden Stark was oftimes heard to declaim: "The man has not been born whom I cannot break." He had felt it his Christian duty personally to bring rebellious prisoners into line, and it is said he had come to view the reforming of Slater's incorrigibility as a personal crusade. When Slater did not break and then succeeded in escaping, Warden Stark said he had to accept the fact that he had personally failed in his God-given task, and that Evil had triumphed in Yuma Territorial Prison.

" 'Warden Stark says he plans to finish out the year at Yuma Prison, but afterward plans to enter politics. He wishes to campaign for a more vigorous application of the death penalty, particularly in non-capital offenses involving repeat offenders such as Slater now reportedly under indictment in thirteen states and territories. Warden Stark says that his experiences with Outlaw Torn Slater have driven home a most important lesson. As Warden Stark succinctly explained to this reporter: "Outlaw Torn Slater confirmed in my mind once and for all that for certain men, leg irons, chastisement, and solitary confinement are not only a waste of the taxpayers' dollars, they are indeed a very poor substitute for the dropping trap door, the taut noose, and may-God-have-mercy-on-your-soul. When dealing with misfits and miscreants as hard and recalcitrant as Slater, there is no alternative to meting out justice at the end of a rope."

The gang was howling with laughter until halfway through the last paragraph. They caught the look on Slater's face. The laughter stopped. J. P. Paxton backed up and reread the paragraph most of them had missed.

"'Held accountable for Slater's dastardly escape was one Thomas T. Harper, a fellow convict and medical doctor. During issuance of a stern flogging by Warden Stark—a mild reproof, given the severity of Harper's offense—the prisoner died of heart failure.

"'One of the guards was heard to remark later, "After what happened to Sergeant Stryker, the old man deserved to hang anyway."'"

The look on Slater's face was so terrible that, one by one, people left. Soon Belle and the Jameses and Youngers and their whores returned to the cantina to do their drinking.

Calamity and Hickok slipped away, thinking it best to leave Slater alone.

51

Calamity lay with Hickok on blankets and straw mattresses on the dirt floor of an old adobe hut. It was near dawn, and Hickok was tired.

But not Calamity.

"Bill," said Calamity, sounding hurt, "you ain't touched

me since we left the Arizona territory. If'n you don't want me no more, just say it.''

"That McClellan's a man-eater, Clem. It's already taken my ass and balls. Guess now it's startin' on my cock.''

"Maybe you'd prefer Belle. She is awful pretty.''

"She ain't my type,'' Bill said, yawning. "Let her use that quirt on Cole. Or maybe Slater. All them years in Yuma, Slater may like it.''

But then Hickok was leaning toward her. She could feel his thigh pushing her legs apart and the pressure of his rising cock growing against her crotch. He bent to kiss her, and the roughness of his mustache bristled against her upper lip. Then she had her left arm around his neck and was pulling his mouth down on her own, forcing his lips and teeth apart with her tongue. Her right hand reached down and under the pants for his hammer. Through the muslin shirt she could feel his muscles, hard and supple. She unbuttoned the front of his shirt and slipped her hand under the muslin. Slowly she rubbed and massaged the hardness of the knotted muscles under the smooth, soft skin, working her way over to the scars.

As her fingers roamed the dense knots of tissue, her mind wandered aimlessly. She'd known many men over the years—perhaps hundreds—but never any with such scars. None, that is, until Torn and Bill. For these two bore the marks of men, the wounds of warriors. What she touched were not the rope burns of drovers or the bumps and abrasions of miners. These were the scars of bullets and claws, of wars and the hunt.

All were entered in the front, none on the back.

First she fingered the coarse, weltlike slashes on the left shoulder where a grizzly had gouged flesh before Bill gutted him from breastbone to balls with his Arkansas toothpick. Gently she palpated the rakelike grooves, trying to imagine the glinting fangs and the cavernous jaws, the stomach-turning stench of the bear's panting breath.

Slowly her fingers brushed against one of the puckered bullet holes, the one exiting from the back, to the left of the twelfth vertebra, above the right-hand shoulder blade.

She wondered whether Bill had screamed when he was shot—as he was now shuddering and groaning to her touch.

Next, the belt buckle and the fly. She eased down the pants and his member was hot, alive, erect. She slipped out of her drawers and slid down his body.

She was staring at his cock now, but what really held her attention was something else—another scar! She stared in awe at the great, gaping hole in his hard left hip. She imagined the thrust of the Cheyenne lance driving through the bone and cartilage.

And when she groped the gaping pit, his breath came out of him in a rushing *whoosh!* followed by an almost death-rattling groan. She took his bursting member into her mouth.

She bobbed her head up and down, squeezing the underside of his cock tightly with her tongue. Hickok was groaning ecstatically now, and Calamity, balancing the base of his member with her left hand, resumed stroking the hip scar with her right. Small gouts of semen exploded into her mouth, and clutching a knee with her cunt, she pounded away while his small, bursting orgasms built into one powerful flood and her own crotch ached with spurts of fire.

Now he was done, but her own labia were swollen with lust. When Clem's cunt was engorged, the lips bulged like a clump of grapes, and the clitoris inside was as hard as a ball bearing. So Bill would not be let off. Reversing the positions, she eased his head into her lap. And as his mouth opened to her cunt, she moaned.

Hickok's tongue rimmed the swollen lips, taunting her, avoiding the rock-hard, oily button. Teasing, teasing, till with each circle she groaned for release. And when he finally touched her clit, it was so hot and swollen, it was like a Navy Colt with a hair-trigger pull. When he licked it with conviction, the dam broke.

Only now she wanted more. His tongue was not enough. She had to have his cock.

Pulling away from him, she slid down till she was lying by his legs.

It lay there, flaccid. She took it in her mouth and sucked on it. Grow, grow, she silently pleaded. Then, gripping it tightly, she massaged the head with her tongue.

He sighed, his member rose, and it made her so hot she ground on his leg with her cunt. Hickok's head was rolling back and forth, caught in the ecstasy of her red-hot touch. He was frantic with desire. And Calamity knew, now it was time.

She rolled onto her back, and he was instantly on top. The enormity of his hammerhead was nuzzling her folds.

"Like that," she whispered while he massaged her labia with his cock.

Then he was in her, up to the hilt. And as she felt him tilt her hips forward, he began to pump up and down, hard but slow, keeping the friction firm and steady, angled forward, stroking her clit, till her need was rising out of her in one wide spin.

She was coming so hard she was barely aware of it. It was like pounding through the Needle with the walls blowing up. Lights were exploding behind her eyes, thunder rumbling in her ears. Her body erupted in a great breaking loose, a terrible coming apart, taking her on a journey she was not prepared to make. She'd had many men before, she would have many men again, but she knew no one else could make her feel like this, ever. Hickok was hers. Hers alone! Her soul was breaking free, cut adrift. She was cast to the winds, her moorings slipped, a rudderless ship in a nether sea. She could feel Hickok's come, pumping into her over and over in great, long gouts. God only knew what tomorrow would bring— pain, hardship, Parker's noose. So be it! If she was hanged tonight, she would not care. All she wanted, all she would ever want, she had now, for all time.

52

The evening went on. The men got drunker, the music and dancing wilder. Toward dawn, Frank James and the Professor rejoined Slater. The three squatted on their haunches by the fire.

Before them was a pile of mesquite that they occasionally fed into the flames. The dry night air had a tinge of chill, and they opened another jug. They sipped mescal from mess cups. Frank James cracked jokes and Paxton seemed thoroughly amused. But in the cool gray of the desert dawn, Slater was silent, withdrawn.

"You know, Torn," Frank said, "you got kinda quiet when the Professor first finished that newspaper article. I can understand that. I can understand a man not wantin' to hear 'bout that hellhole. Must've been a pisser. I can't picture you adjustin' to jail."

"Seems like I spent half them three years in that hotbox or down in the bedrock hole for bad behavior."

"Why was that?" asked J. P. Paxton.

"Couldn't take it. Doin' life in Yuma's worse'n dyin'. And after Cole shot them tellers, that's what I got."

"Torn, I hope you still ain't pissed at Cole," Frank said. "That'd grieve me sorely. We been through some rough times together."

"He was only the best friend I had. And he left me to rot in that Arizona desert."

"He thought you was dyin'."

"He were wrong, Frank."

"Yes, it hurts him as bad as it does you. He's got pride, too much pride. You hurt that pride. You was always the strong one, Torn, always plannin' the jobs, goin' back after them that was wounded, always holdin' the gang together. And the one time you needed Cole, he weren't there. That pains him awful.''

"It weren't only that.''

"Something in Yuma?'' Paxton asked.

"Yeah, Professor, you got it. See, there was this eddicated man, like you. He looked after me, from the first time I got throwed down in that hole in Yuma. See, I was bullwhipped pretty bad. That Durado blacksnake has a two-foot rawhide popper on it, and this here Warden Stark, if he was after you, he'd make that popper cut you clear to the bone, then let you die in the hole, slow and hard. So while I was down there in the bedrock, this old convict, who was also a doc, would come and vist me. He'd stanch the cuts, stick hot metal to them that needed it, and put some carbolic dressings on my back. Stitch them up some, if need be. And since I was down there so much, I got to know the old coot real well.''

"He wasn't the man that Warden Stark . . . ?''

"You got it again, Professor. Yeah, Stark killed him during that flogging. Plumb beat him to death. Couldn't've been too pretty. The ol' doc made a mistake in bein' friends with me. Maybe he felt some sympathy, both of us bein' convicts and all.'' Slater looked at Paxton. "You know, he had these two books. Only two books I ever read all the way through. Got to know them real well.''

"My collected works, I hope,'' Paxton said gently.

"Almost,'' Slater said with a smile. "The *Iliad* and the *Odyssey* by Homer. Havin' a year and a half or so to kill in that hole, I read them works backwards and forwards. You got some light from the cracks in the ceiling grid, and for half my stay in Yuma I sort of lived in ancient Greece, fightin' at Troy, driftin' in the Aegean. Then that old man'd come visit me, and we'd talk about them books. To listen to him, you'd think it weren't books at all, but life itself on them pages. He used to say my life was an *Iliad*, what with them 'Paches and Shiloh, then you boys and Quantrill. That old man claimed that Yuma hellhole was the end of my *Iliad*. 'War's end, odyssey's beginning' was the way he put it.''

"You believe that?'' Frank asked.

"Beats me, Frank. Outside of the Professor there and that old man, you're the only one I ever knew who read books. And he claimed my real journey was just beginnin'. So far he's been right."

"Where'd he claim you was goin'?"

"Didn't say any special place. Claimed I'd find somethin' in the end. 'My Penelope,' he'd call it. I'd tell him, 'Yeah, I could use some of that action right now.' Then he'd say he meant somethin' intangible, a 'secret sharer,' he said. 'A dream.'"

"Or the end of dreams," said Paxton.

Slater gave the Professor a look. "Say, you're pretty smart. That's what I told him. I said 'the end of dreams, you mean. Sell my fuckin' saddle.' And then you know what he said? Told me that a man had a destiny. And he said my destiny weren't to die in Yuma. Sure, he thought I'd face death many times, but he told me not to fear. Death, he said, was my wisest advisor. Death was a gift."

"That's one way of lookin' at it," Frank James said skeptically.

"He sounds like he was a very learned man," said Paxton.

"He sure could talk, I'll give him that. Got so that half the time I used to almost believe him. Once when I was real low he told me it were all my own fault. He said if I would only stop hatin' Stark and Stryker, if I could cleanse my blood of lust and lies, then sins and yearnings would never torture me again, 'cause my soul would be stainless."

"Jesus, Torn," Frank said, "you believe that shit? Nobody ever accused you of havin' a soul before."

"Can't say that I do believe it. I sure as hell can't get it out of my head, though. I do know that old man was my friend. He gave me hope. He kept me goin'. Now that bastard Stark took his life."

"You want to kill Stark, don't you?" said J. P. Paxton.

Slater nodded, gazing into the fire. "Seems like somehow I have to. It's like I ain't got no choice."

"Don't, Torn," said Frank James. "That's back in Yuma. That's a thousand miles behind. And it's too hard a hand. Stark's holdin' all the cards back there."

Slater shook his head sadly.

"Torn," the Professor said, "isn't that exactly the sort of thing the doctor advised you against? How will killing Stark make things better for anyone?"

"It'll make me feel better. Anyway, if it's true what that old man said about me havin' a soul and a destiny, and beginning a long journey, I know one thing: that journey ain't beginning till I kill Stark. He gave me back my life, that old man. And when Stark killed him, it's like he took it away again. If that odyssey's ever gonna begin, I have to go back down to Yuma and kill Stark."

PART TWELVE

53

The morning sky was cloudless. For three days Calamity and the rest of them stood around the square, or tipped back against the adobe buildings on rickety chairs. They stared indolently at the bright sky and listened to Cholo's wife strum her guitar.

Other than that, there was food. Lamb, goat, and sides of "slow elk" turned on spits over deep charcoal fires. The fragrant odor of the barbecue mixed with that of Arbuckle's brewing in two-gallon pots. Endless cauldrons of beans seasoned with chilis, onions, cayenne, tomatoes, and goat's meat added to the redolence. Extra jugs of mescal and bottles of beer were chilled in the spring well.

A month on the trail had melted the tallow off them. Now the three lolled around and put some back on. They listened lazily to the guitar, ate when hungry, and drank.

For female diversion, Calamity noted that the gang had attracted the usual run of loose women, army- and cow-camp followers picked up here and there—half of them blanket Indians or hard-looking Mexican *mestizas,* the other half the usual *escapadas* from the back-alley brothels of Denver and Abilene, Deadwood and K.C. At night these women hung around the fire, carousing. Or else they plied their trade in the huts. By day they drank and slept it off in the dirty adobe hovels.

Everyone saw Slater spend inordinate amounts of time with these daughters of joy. Jesse James observed, "Damn, Torn, three years in Yuma must've left you with a mule dick. Ain't nothin' seems to wear it down."

Other than these diversions, there was horse breaking.

Early that spring the farmers had caught a wild mustang and turned him over to the gang to break. Not cowboys either, they hadn't gotten further than one gut-twisting ride per man in the makeshift breaking corral.

The rest of the stock was staked and tethered outside the village.

The bronc was a black stud mustang, so mean the outlaws were almost afraid to bridle him.

Only Cole put up a brave front.

He had spent two full weeks trying to break him. But all that horse got, as Jesse put it, was "meaner and still around."

Much of the gang's conversation centered on Cole's bronc-busting. If someone speculated on how soon the gang would return to Missouri, the reply would be, "Oh, we'll get back one day, 'bout the same time Cole breaks that snaky mustang."

They also had target practice. It was their life. Every day they were down in the meadow, trying their hands. Hickok, because of his fame as a marksman, took a lot of kidding, especially from Frank, Jess, and Cole. They were all dead shots and were convinced no one was better.

So when they invited Bill to a friendly wager over some competition shooting, Hickok, Calamity, and Slater instantly took them up.

Cole split off three pine blazes from a fresh-cut stump. He drove them into the ground, then braced them with large rocks. Each man paced off a hundred yards from his own blaze.

Then Cole began. His right arm extended, he slowly sighted and squeezed off five rounds into the first blaze. Then he switched guns and squeezed off five more from his second Colt. Frank and Jesse then followed in the same way, slowly, carefully.

Frank turned to Hickok and said, "Your play, gunman."

Hickok stared at his target intently. The sun was bright and hot, and he wore his sombrero pulled down over his eyes, already shielded by his gray-tinted goggles. His Navy Colts were stuck, butts forward, in the red Mexican sash. They were held in place by the open loading gates. Clem thought the red sash and the ivory grips of his blue-black Colts looked striking against the dark blue shirt. Clem even liked the string tie and arrowhead clasp.

" 'Scuse me," Slater said, taking Hickok's arm. "Just one second. Anyone here trust me for my marker? I'd take a few hundred more of that there James-Younger family fortune, if'n I had someone here to finance me."

"Me too," Clem said, looking at Hickok. "If the banker can put up another two hundred."

Hickok nodded.

The hammers rested on empty cylinders, so he also had five beans in each wheel. As he turned toward the distant pine blaze, he was already drawing his Colts and simultaneously jerking the loading gates shut.

He emptied his guns in less than ten seconds.

"It was fast, I give you that," Cole said.

Then they walked to the targets. Before fifty yards had passed, Clem was elbowing Hickok, knowing that he still would not see the pattern through the smoked lenses.

Jess had hit the blaze with six, and so had Cole. Frank had punched eight rounds home, though his pattern was scattered.

Hickok had put all ten into a tight diamond three inches on a side.

"Tougher when the target shoots back," Cole grumbled. But he stared uneasily at the ten tightly grouped holes.

54

But it did not end there.

The black stud mustang in the breaking corral circled the pen hour after hour, day in, day out. And his presence was a constant goad to Cole.

Belle especially would not let it rest. "That damn horse's got more balls than the men here. That's the real story. The man masters the horse, not the other way around. You climb on intendin' to pile off, you will. That's the plain truth."

The plain truth was that Cole was scared of the horse. He wouldn't admit it and swore he'd stomp that bronc yet. Clem had seen Cole try, seen the results, seen the fear.

And not only was Cole scared, the others were too.

For them, one ride was enough.

Clem learned why, the morning Cole got thrown. It took three men to hold the horse down long enough for Cole to saddle and mount him. Jess dallied the *mecate* twice around the center snubbing post while Jim and Bob stood on opposite sides of the stallion's head, each twisting an ear in one hand, a fistful of mane in the other. When Jess unclamped the snubbing *mecate* from the headstall and they let the mustang loose, his back went up like a rocket.

The black stallion broke from the post, pile-driving, humping his back with each buck. He put his head between his legs, then came down on all four, stiff as ax handles. With each crash, Clem could see the downward jolt reverse directions and shoot straight up the stallion's legs into Cole's ass and then up his back and neck. The horse was almost taking Cole's head off. Each crash whiplashed Cole so hard that it almost cracked his neck, and Clem feared he'd shatter his teeth as well.

But still Cole hung on.

The black mustang hammered his back and kidneys and twisted his guts, and instantly Clem knew what Cole was made of, that he could take it and that the ribbing men gave him was not out of disrespect.

The straight pile-driving wasn't working, so the horse changed styles. Dipping one shoulder with each buck, the mustang began to sunfish, to twist his body into a crescent, first one shoulder down, then the other, always rearing back high, sunning his belly with each kick.

But still Cole rode him. It seemed he rode him forever. Twice he came loose in the saddle, twice he fought his way back on. Once he had to grab the apple, and his brothers and cousins hissed.

"Shake hands with grandma!" Frank yelled.

"Spur him on the hairy side!" Jess was shouting.

And brother Jim screamed, "Waltz with the lady!"

Cole fought the reins, and the black stallion came down with such a crash that Clem saw Cole's head snap back, watched the teeth slam together, and was sure Cole had broken his jaw.

Shortly after that, Cole bucked loose a third time, stayed loose, bounced twice off the cantle, and piled off. Bob Younger diverted the horse long enough for Jesse and Jim to pull Cole out of the corral.

Frank jumped off the six-foot-high fence. He was staring at his American Horologe watch. He yelled, "Cousin Cole, by my gold, key-wound railroad watch, forcibly donated by a kindly conductor on the Kansas-Pacific line, that was a nine-second ride. Not bad, shorthorn. Not bad at all."

Not bad at all? Well, if they wanted riding, she'd show them riding. She'd give them a man who'd ride that horse forever.

"Not bad at all?" Clem yelled out. "That ride weren't shit. Hickok'll ride that nag till he starves to death."

"Do you ride?" Slater said, staring at Hickok skeptically.

"Bill's a double-distilled, triple-tough, case-hardened bronc-buster from way back," Calamity yelled across the corral. She glanced at Hickok and saw that he looked ready to crawl into a hole. She wasn't sure why. She'd seen him stomp broncs right into the hard ground.

"You think he can beat Cole's ride?" Bob Younger yelled back.

"Hickok will ride that ringtailed swayback to a standstill." She looked at Hickok, who was staring gloomily at the stallion. The big, deep-chested stud was now starting to slam sideways into the rough adobe corral, as if trying to scrape off the saddle.

"How 'bout you, Frank?" Clem called.

"I like my women wild and my horses gentle," Frank hollered.

"You think you can beat Cole's time?" Jess asked Hickok directly.

Hickok shrugged, but to no avail.

Belle was in it now.

"That sissy sonofabitch?" Belle said as she moved up by the corral. "My little boy, Ed, could beat that ride."

Suddenly Clem wasn't sure this was such a great idea. But it was too late to back down.

"Bill can ride anything with hair on it," Clem shouted, "fair and square and *not* pull leather." She deliberately referred to Cole's grabbing the apple and the hisses he'd drawn. "He can ride that snaky bastard now! He can ride him an hour from now! He can ride him next year!"

She glanced over at Bill. He was still leaning up against the corral, watching the mustang. The horse was rolling around on his back, still trying to scrape the saddle off.

Cole strode arrogantly around the corral. He walked up to Hickok and said, "I'll ride anything you can ride, lawman. *Anything*. You wanna put up that four hundred dollars you and your friends took off'n us at 'target practice' "—he said the words with a sneer—"that's just fine. Just don't think I'm forgettin' the way you and Slater whipsawed me two nights ago. I'm forgettin' nothin'. 'Cause when we get done with this Fort Smith bullshit, I'm takin' you down, just you and me, lean and mean, hard and fast."

"Okay, Cole," Hickok said decisively. "That's the way

you want it, that's the way it's gonna be. This afternoon we start with the horse.''

55

That afternoon, Slater, Clem, and Hickok returned to the corral to study the bronc. Slater thought he had him figured.

"The problem is, he ain't *un*broke. These bastards made him mean when they tried to break him. After he bucked off every man here, and Cole ten or fifteen times more, they tried scarin' him. Belle says Cole tried jaw-breakin' him first. He tried bear-trappin' his mouth with a big spade bit, tried bustin' him with a grain sack over his head, tried starvin' him, thirstin' him, tried whip-breakin' him. So what you got now is an outlaw. All that Cole's taught that horse is that every time a man gets near him, he's in *mucho* trouble.''

"I was hopin' to slip a saddle on and off him ten or twelve times, sweet-talk him, gentle him a little, get him used to me.''

'No such luck. This horse ain't never gonna be fit for nothin'. He's been outlawed for good.''

"What kind of bucker is he?'' Calamity asked.

"He's no pattern bucker,'' Hickok said, "so it ain't a matter of givin' him a long rein and stayin' deep in the fork. I'm gonna have to power him.''

"And stay alert,'' Slater said. "He's a killer. And that money ain't worth dyin' for. He gets near that fence, starts tryin' to scrape you off, just jump. If he starts to roll, same thing. You ain't no good to no one with a busted leg or planted in a hole.''

"One thing I know. I need another saddle. That muley-horn Mexican'll do,'' Hickok said, pointing to the rig on the adobe fence. "Cole likes them deep-dish Texas slick-forks, so he can squeeze the biscuit if he starts comin' loose.

Someday he's gonna get that biscuit shoved through his balls, and that high cantle rammed up his kidneys.''

"Imagine a Texas slick-fork on a bronc," Calamity said, shaking her head.

"Oh, yeah. Cole's got *cojones*. I don't take that off him. But I'd let myself get dusted a hundred times 'fore I'd put that apple between my legs. It's too close to my pride and joy," Slater said.

"Your 'drop-forged, case-hardened, blue-steel' pride and joy, as Jess calls it?"

"You'd have to ask them scarlet sisters hereabouts."

56

Later in the day the rest of them came back to the corral. Hickok took the muley-horn bronc saddle, unbuckled the stirrup leathers, and measured them between his armpits and finger tips for the right length. Then he and Slater stationed themselves at opposite ends of the corral, and each sent wide maguey loops snaking out at the horse's neck. As the ropes dropped over the stallion's head, Hickok and Slater dallied them tight on the outside bucking posts. With the horse snubbed off, they entered the corral.

Slater clamped a *mecate* to the snaffle rings on the head-stall, then dallied it around the center snubbing post. Hickok uncinched Cole's saddle and pulled it off. The horse was wide-eyed and snuffy. As Hickok rubbed him down with an old grain sack, the outlaw shied bites at Hickok's face and shoulders.

Finally Hickok threw a fresh blanket over the mustang's back and smoothed out the creases and wrinkles. He tossed the muley-horned bronc saddle high above the horse's back, and when it came down square, he quickly began to tighten the cinch. He put his boot into the horse's gut, pushed in hard, and pulled up tight. With each pull the horse shied more bites at his head, and each time Hickok rapidly pulled the cinch up two or three more notches before the mustang could get another breath. By the third pull, the saddle was strapped on to the mustang's belly so tight that the latigo was driving him spraddle-legged.

Hickok walked over to the corral water barrel and pulled his batwings out of the water. He'd kept them soaking there for two full hours.

"That ain't fair," Cole was saying. "He soaked his bullhides."

"'Bout as fair as a kick in the balls," Hickok agreed. "But it ain't against no rules."

He clamped them on, then returned to the horse, who had his wind back and was ready to stomp. Slater had the lass ropes off, and held the mustang rein-snubbed against the center post, his jaw jacked flush against his flank. Slater held him there till Hickok swung on. When Hickok had the reins, Slater unsnapped the *mecate* from the snaffle rings on the headstall, freeing the horse.

The bronc exploded.

Calamity had never seen Hickok bust a bronc this mean. She believed he could. She'd seen him before.

But nothing like this.

The mustang took one twisting sidestep away from the snubbing post, then went straight into the air. He came down foursquare, a thousand pounds of him, jolting Hickok almost out of his socks.

But Hickok not only didn't flinch, he deliberately spurred him. Over and over after each buck, Calamity watched in blank astonishment as Hickok raked him with the rowels, as if challenging him to buck again.

When the horse came down from the buck and got raked, he bucked even harder, but he was also confused. Hickok endured his own brutal battering, tight-lipped. He kicked the stallion repeatedly, great tearing kicks, gouging, infuriating him further, till the bronc was going off in consecutive twisting jumps, banging Hickok harder and harder, each time landing stiff-legged on all four hooves, sending tremendous jolts through Hickok's spine and neck. But Hickok was ready, and each time he kicked and gouged and yelled out for more.

The crowd was screaming, "Ride 'er, cowboy!"

"Waltz with her!"

The mustang continued to pile-drive, fighting to get his head all the way down between his legs, where he could hump Hickok off. But Hickok took the beating, powered the head up, and the black mustang, unable to swallow his head, made sideways jackrabbit jumps, left and right, right and left, zigzagging, spinning, pounding, kicking.

Frank James yelled, "Time!" But Hickok stayed on. Again he raked the black's gut till his spurs dripped crimson. Hickok sawed the reins, working the bear-trap bit around the tender mouth, and the horse blew blood instead of foam and bucked even harder, handing out more.

Now the mustang was bellowing with every buck, kicking, pawing, grunting out his rage. Hickok kept his rowels up front, driving them deep into his flanks, raking the withers, still sawing brutally at the reins with every lunge and jump.

The horse bucked right, and Hickok wrenched him left. The horse dodged right and Hickok raked his flanks. The black lunged again, tried to dodge, squealed, fought the pain. But Hickok yanked his head up and the black bucked and danced, cut to the right, and was whipsawed left. He hooked right and side-jumped and lunged toward the fence, but pulling his head away, Hickok drove the rowels harder.

The horse stopped pile-driving and went close to the ground. Bucking hard and quick, he kicked sideways with his hind legs, fantailing, then sunfishing, fighting to pile Hickok off.

But now the mustang was snorting blood. His tail was wringing, and he was careening off the fence. Again Hickok wrenched him around with the bear-trap bit, and again he drove the spurs into the flanks. The mustang's flanks and gut were covered with rakelike slashes, and he was snorting and choking on the bloody froth blowing out of his nose and mouth.

His strength was flagging. The black tottered, foundered. Still, he fought. Arching his back, he buried his head and went high one more time. He came down stiff-legged. Hickok eased the reins, challenging him to go on. The horse tried but faltered. He was now spraddle-legged, walleyed, blood flowing freely from his nostrils, mouth, and sides. He tried to buck once again, and again he foundered.

"Pile off!" Slater yelled. "He's fallin'. He'll land right on you!"

The mustang was blowing out blood in great clots. He was staggering and swaying, and Hickok swung free, vaulting away from the saddle. The mustang went down with a deep *thud*.

Hickok's legs were gone. He bent over against the corral, barely able to keep his feet, fighting to get his breath.

"He killed that horse," Jim Younger finally said. "The sonofabitch killed Cole's horse on purpose."

"He oughtn't to've done that," Bob Younger mumbled. Otherwise they were still.

Calamity stared at the bronc. The black mustang with the blaze face and three white stockings was on his side, beyond wind-broke. He'd busted his lungs. He lay there in a gathering pool of his own blood.

Slowly Hickok straightened and walked painfully over to Calamity's side of the corral. His guns and red sash were next to her on the fence. She handed them to him.

Hickok looked at her. The corners of the eyes were etched with sharp lines impacted with dust and sweat. She handed him his tinted eyeglasses, and he nodded his thanks. He turned around. Cole was on the opposite side of the corral, a good forty yards away. He was standing outside the corral's open gate. The sun was still high overhead. His black slouch hat was low over his eyes. He wore a gingham shirt. Under his armpit was a sawed-off .44 Remington in a shoulder rig. Alongside the outer thighs of his Levis were strapped two Colts, butts turned in. A quirly dangled from his lips.

Hickok leaned against the corral. Calamity noted that he was still swaying from the battering he'd taken.

"Cole," he shouted, moving away from the fence. She noted that simultaneously he was flexing both his hands and moving toward Cole. Instinctively, Clem moved away from behind him. "Cole, you and me got a bet," said Hickok, moving slowly toward him. "You said you could ride anything I could. And you bet four hundred dollars. Unless you figure on gettin' that horse up and ridin' him, that four hundred's mine." The fallen mustang was snorting out his agony, and Cole was shaking his head. "That mean you ain't gonna ride him or you ain't gonna pay?" Hickok asked.

"I ain't doin' neither," said Cole. "You killed my horse."

Calamity saw a flicker of movement. She glanced sideways just as Slater fanned his Colt. Three rapid shots slammed into the horse's head from across the corral. Two shots hit the horse directly between the eyes, the third was an inch high, but in the center of the forehead. Already, Slater had his loading gate open and was ejecting the spent shells and shoving three more bullets into the empty cylinders. Calamity pulled her Colt and thumbed two rounds through the heart of the settling pony.

"That's what's known as a 'coop of grass,'" she said easily. Like Slater, she quickly replaced the spent shells and kept the Colt in her fist, flush against her right thigh. "Like Slater, I hate to see a dumb animal suffer."

Hickok stopped ten yards from Cole, who was now easing behind the nearby gatepost for cover.

"Little cousin," Slater said gently, "that gatepost can't hide ever'thin'."

"Cole," Hickok said, "ever since I got here, you been insultin' people. I get your best friend out of prison, bring him home, and all you can do is abuse me, my woman, and the man you left to rot in that Arizona desert. This mornin' you insult my shootin'. This noon you insult my ridin'. You make a bet and insult me by refusin' to pay. Now, I may be dumb, and maybe I don't understand you smart Missouri cow thieves. But where I come from, that makes you a scumsuckin', one-way motherfucker."

As if to prove he was not drawing, Cole grabbed the top of the gatepost in front of him with both hands. Hickok stared at Younger in stunned disbelief and yelled, "I got no choice, boy. Now, you gonna haul that iron or sing 'Battle Hymn'?"

Hickok cross-drew a Navy Colt and pumped three rounds into the post, directly in front of Cole's crotch. He drew his second Colt, walked to within six yards of Cole, and, both guns blazing, shot off Cole's hat. Then he blew the two holstered sidearms off Cole's hips. By now he was directly in front of him.

"You still got a .44 Remington in that half-breed," Hickok said.

Cole Younger shook his head. His face was twitching, his chin trembling. Hickok shoved his left-hand Colt back into his belt. He grabbed Cole's shoulder gun and heaved it across the corral toward the dead horse. Grabbing Cole by his shirtfront, he tried to drag him loose from the post. When Cole refused to let go, he hammered Cole's fingers with the barrel of his Colt, then pistol-whipped him twice—backhand and forehand—across the sides of his jaw. The only thing keeping Cole on his feet was Hickok's grip on his shirt. Hickok let go, and Cole Younger collapsed in the dust.

"Anybody here wanna stand up for this man?" Hickok called out. He turned in a slow circle, the better to view the Youngers, the Jameses, and the Mex. And Belle.

"Not likely," Belle Starr said. She circled the corral, spat on Cole, and crossed the village square to the cantina.

"It ends here?" Hickok said, looking at Frank James. Frank nodded grudgingly. Frank then stared at Calamity and Slater, and they holstered their pistols.

"Jim, Bob, clean your brother up," he finally said. "Damn, if I don't get tired of this shit."

"I say we go on back to Missouri. This here Nations is more goddamn trouble than the Pinks," Jesse said bitterly.

"Little brother," Frank said, nodding, "I finally agree. You couldn't be more right. Just one more bank to rob, and we head back home." The James brothers drifted over to the cantina.

Three vultures had appeared overhead, circling the horse's remains.

57

It was early morning before Coleman Younger was sober enough to stand. In the faint light of predawn, he walked down a narrow alley. At the end of the dirt street near the cliff wall was Belle Starr's hut, where she lived with her boy, Ed.

Cole slipped in through the side door. Down a short, dark hall was the bedroom. He entered. A heavy wool blanket hung over the window.

Cole stood quietly a full minute, his eyes slowly adjusting to the light. He took in Belle's pallet. She was lying naked in her soogans, her slanted black eyes open, vivid in their cruelty.

Her small eight-year-old boy was lying next to her naked, whimpering.

Cole bent down and gently picked him up. He laid him on his own pallet on the other side of the room. He cringed at the welts and scars on the boy's back, buttocks, and legs. As he moved him, the child's whimpers turned to deep-throated sobs.

After putting the boy down and covering him, Cole slowly began unbuckling his belt. As he stripped off his shirt and eased down his pants, he heard Belle hiss, "What are you doin' here?"

"I need you," he whispered.

She raised herself and stared up at him. "I sure don't need no simperin' piece of shit like you."

"Please," he said softly.

His pants were pulled down below his knees. As he lay beside her, she got to her feet.

"Belle?" he whispered feverishly.

"Not tonight," she rasped, and turned, still naked, to the door.

"Belle, *please*!" he cried.

She spun around, the bloodied quirt strapped to her wrist. Swinging the full length of her arm straight over her head, she brought it down with both hands, the plaited double-lash whistling through the air, catching Cole flush across the back, cutting the flesh and muscle.

Frantically, Cole began shoving the rough wool bedroll into his mouth, fighting back screams.

"Not tonight, you sniveling bastard!"

The *cuarta* rose and fell, rose and fell. Cole swallowed more and more of the rough wool soogan, fighting back howls while the tears ran hot.

"Not tonight!" she hissed, the lashes swinging free, cutting welts across his back.

Finally she paused, bent over, panting.

"Please . . ." he murmured, his voice choking.

She spun around and stalked out of the room. Minutes later she returned with a pot of neat's-foot oil. She sat down on the pallet beside him and began rubbing the oil into his welts.

"Please . . ." he said with a sad throbbing moan.

Slowly she turned him over on his back. His buttocks burned with pain as they touched the rough wool soogans, but he endured it. She knelt between his legs and then lowered her face till her eyes hovered inches above his cock. She held her gaze there, immobile and intense. When the cock failed to rise, she carefully took it in her mouth.

Finally it came to life. She rose to her knees and, lifting her crotch above the stiff shaft, lowered her cunt onto the tip and eased herself over him. Now Cole was sobbing openly— the burning of his backside, the horrible pleasure in his crotch, overwhelmed him. He cried and cried, and Belle whispered to him gently, "There, there, baby. There, there."

Then, gradually, with incredible control, she squeezed the muscles of her vagina into a powerful fist. Grabbing his member, stroking it up and down, she jerked off his cock with savage strokes from her cunt, till his life force pumped out of him in great, shuddering sobs, wringing him dry.

Only when his cock shrank inside her, reduced to tiny impotence, did she release him. Then she got up and looked at the blanket-covered window. Daylight was filtering around the coarse brown blanket.

Finally she lowered her eyes and glanced at the boy and the man, groveling in their blankets on the floor. The man was moaning pathetically, and she turned her head in disgust.

Then she looked at the half-breed boy. He was staring at Cole, his eyes narrowed, his lips pulled taut against his teeth.

58

It was the next morning, and the sun was beginning its long, scorching ascent over the Nations. The gang was on its way to the Fort Smith bank.

Calamity and Hickok led the way. They were to be a half-days' ride ahead of the others, both to scout the trail and to reconnoiter the fort. As they eased their mounts down the hill, Frank James rode up between them.

"Didn't get a chance to speak to you yesterday, either at the shootin' or at the corral. You was real impressive, Bill."

Hickok shrugged absently.

Calamity just lolled in the saddle.

Mostly she thought about Hickok's present to her. Hickok had gotten her a horse, a wonderful horse. He'd bought an Appaloosa from Frank James's remuda. Bred by the Nez Percé Indians for warfare and the buffalo hunt, these spotted ponies were considered the smartest and most agile on earth. And among the most beautiful. When he and Frank dickered over the price, Frank had said, "Money don't buy what this horse will do. He'll turn on a dime and give you change."

Frank had been right. Hickok traded the Jameses' debts and Cole Younger's markers for the Appaloosa.

Clem thought him the most magnificent horse she'd ever seen.

As they continued down the slope, hooves clattered behind them. When Clem glanced over her shoulder, she saw the Mex coming up on their rear. He was drunk on mescal and shouting to them crazily.

"*Eh, amigos,* I just want you to know, when we get to Fort Smith, I want Judge Parker in my sights. Just one time. A lot of my *compadres* danced on the end of his rope."

"I don't care about Parker. Just no women or children," Hickok said. "This is a bank job, not a war. We ain't Colonel Quantrill nor Chivington. This ain't Lawrence, Kansas or Sand Creek."

Frank James smiled as the horses carefully picked their way down the slope. "Hickok, you sure you ain't still part lawman?"

"I just don't want your kill-crazy cousin shootin' every livin' thing in the bank."

"He won't be in the bank. He'll be with the Mex. They'll both be outside with the Gatling gun. You're gonna be inside with Slater. Me and Jess'll be in there too. 'Cause, you see, we don't trust you any more than Cole does. So when you receive that forced donation from Judge Parker's bank, we're gonna be right there too—covering you and Slater. So set your mind at rest. You'll be real safe. You got Frank and Jesse James on your back porch."

Frank and the Mex wheeled their horses around and headed up the slope without saying goodbye.

Clem and Hickok continued on, threading their way among the salt cedars and smoke trees, the prickly pear and spring ocotillo. A wind began to rise, blowing the dust and grit and sand off the desert floor and up the mountain. Calamity and Hickok pulled their bandannas up over their noses.

Hickok removed the velvet-lined eyeglass box from the inside pocket of his frock coat. He took out the circular eyeglasses with the smoked lenses and put them on.

PART THIRTEEN

59

Custer had been right.

When Calamity and Hickok entered Fort Smith after a two-day ride, it proved to be a town, not a fort. In fact, the army post had been closed years ago. The only soldiers were frequenting the fifty saloons and the half-dozen sporting houses. They were also there for the afternoon's entertainment—a twelve-man hanging.

Calamity and Hickok rode slowly through town. Hickok's long blond hair was knotted in back and folded up into his hat. With the tinted glasses hiding his eyes, he passed unrecognized.

From the courthouse square, high up on a bluff, visitors could enjoy a stunning view of the river. But the square's main attraction was its twelve-man gallows. George Maledon, the notorious "prince of hangmen"—as he was flamboyantly heralded in the Fort Smith *Gazette*—had personally supervised the building of the massive scaffold. He was on it today, preparing for the afternoon executions.

Hickok pointed him out to Calamity as they trotted up the

street. Calamity saw a small, wiry man with a long black beard. He was dressed appropriately for his trade in a black three-piece suit and tie, a fresh, boiled white shirt, and—as befit an officer of the court—a brace of Remingtons in cross-draw holsters, strapped to his hips.

Clem stared at him as she and Hickok passed by. It was not Maledon's owlish solemnity or ministerial dignity that fascinated Calamity. It was the scaffold that got to her. Not that she hadn't seen gallows before. Hell, she'd watched men hang any number of times. But those grisly occasions had been nothing like Parker's infamous gallows, designed and constructed by his "prince of hangmen."

The scaffold was a good forty feet high and thirty feet across. The base was concealed by black curtains, but when a breeze briefly blew the fluttering drapes aside, she caught a glimpse of the underpinnings.

The gallows was supported by a great jungle of posts and beams, and the trap itself was braced by hinges on one edge and secured by a system of deadbolts on the other. A half-dozen hundred-pound sandbags dangled from ring bolts along the bottom of the trap. Once the deadbolts released, the sandbags would accelerate the dropping of the greatly extended platform. Calamity could see the long lever, reaching up to the scaffold above, which Maledon later that day would pull, and which would, in one motion, withdraw all the trap bolts and release the long trapdoor.

The grim spectacle filled her with disgust.

"The gates to hell," Hickok said quietly.

"Opened by the Prince of Hangmen."

Across Garrison Avenue from the great square, with its gathering crowd of onlookers, the Fort Smith Guarantee and Trust was located. Calamity and Hickok stopped by the bank's hitch rack and swung down off their horses. They tied up their mounts and the extra bay pony, which Hickok led by the halter.

He opened the door and they went in. There was a long row of tellers' windows, and a bullpen of loan officers' desks.

Hickok turned and walked out.

Standing by the hitch rack, he said to Calamity, "Banks always make me nervous."

"All that money?"

"Naw, them white shirts with black elbow garters. Always look like tourniquets to me."

"Them tellers look like faro dealers to me."

Hickok looked at her with amusement.

They drifted down the street to the nearest deadfall, a garishly decorated watering hole called the Bald Eagle. This saloon had a big spread-eagle painted above the batwing doors, and when Calamity shouldered her way through, she noted the long mahogany bar with its porcelain top and polished brass footrail. A dozen different whiskeys, rums, and gins were stacked on shelves behind the bar, and the room was crowded with hard-drinking men and gaudily made-up fancy women.

Clem glanced around. The ceiling was more than twenty-five feet high. The blue, yellow, and white floor tiles were spread out in a huge sunburst pattern. Massive paintings covered three walls. They were of Chinese concubines and princes on huge beds with fluffy pillows. Their dressing gowns fell open, exposing copious breasts and shapely limbs and loins.

Such paintings were invariably paid for by the local whorehouse proprietors.

Several score of round tables were surrounded by quartets of bentwood chairs. Faro, poker, and keno games were being dealt by men in white shirts with black elbow garters. These large, fancy tables were covered with green baize. Calamity guessed the Bald Eagle had a hundred and fifty customers. Not a bad crowd, considering the big show outside.

Clem and Hickok ordered whiskey.

"You got some time to kill, while I'm reportin' back to Frank and Jess. At least four hours," Calamity said.

"Reckon so," he agreed.

Hickok was already eying a six-hand stud game at a corner table.

Calamity flagged down the bartender. "Seems like we

always end up the same. In a bar, gettin' drunk, then gettin' shot."

"And likely shootin' back," Hickok said.

Calamity groaned, then tossed back her drink.

"We do play some cards," Hickok continued.

Calamity shook her head. "Cards and guns ain't no life for a grown man."

"I figure maybe that's why I'm settlin' down this time."

"Really?" she asked, her face a mask of disbelief.

"Well, maybe. If I can get a stake. I figure to mine a claim in the Black Hills."

"What for?"

"Maybe show come color, make enough to get some real land, a few head of cattle."

"Don't sound likely, knowin' you."

"Don't seem so now. But I plan to change."

"You'll change. 'Bout the time shit loses its stink and buzzards stop eatin' carrion." Calamity threw back a second shot. She shuddered and groaned. "God, this is awful stuff." She stared painfully at the empty shotglass. "Long as I been drinkin' it, you think I'd get used to it. But I don't. Tastes like cat piss."

"Like coffin varnish."

She poured herself one more and stared at it. "That's real apt, given our future situation and all."

"Guess so."

Hickok poured himself a healthy slug. "Clem, reckon I don't know how to say this to you, but if I ever did straighten my hand and settle down, get married, have kids, I'd want you to be there too. I kinda come to like havin' you around. I never knew man nor beast nor woman could do for me like you. Never told you that, I guess."

"How 'bout that circus woman you're married to?"

"Fuck her."

"You actually serious? 'Bout gettin' married, raisin' kids, settlin' down, and all?"

"Been thinkin' on it some," Hickok said with a shrug.

"But then you have a few drinks, a few hands of cards, it goes away?"

Hickok nodded. " 'Spect so. You wouldn't like me anyway. All I do is keep you miserable and almost get you killed. You got better'n that comin' to you."

"Bullshit. I know what I am and what I were. For a time, with you, I been somebody. I rode with the best. Not too many people can say that."

Hickok threw back another shot. Then he lifted his empty shotglass and the neck of the bourbon bottle in the left hand, keeping his gun hand free.

"Well, the best is about to face that six-handed stud game. Long as I got time to kill."

"Let's hope that's all you kill. 'Least for the time being."

"That's a thought."

Calamity stared at him as he started for the game. "By the way," she asked, "where's Custer?"

"He's around. When you and I telegraphed him again, comin' out of the Nations, he said he'd be here by express troop again."

"I don't see no troops."

"Must be out of town, hidin' his men. He knows Frank and Jesse ain't gonna walk into no possible ambush without checkin' it. Neither of them is fools."

"I still don't like it."

"Just bring them boys. After I get you safe, Custer'll move in. He'll be here."

"*You* just be here."

"I'll be by the bank when you ride up." Hickok glanced at the stud table and grinned. "Unless I'm winnin'."

"That's what I figured you'd say." Calamity was nervous now. "Custer sure better be here, is all."

"I'm more concerned about drawin' that diamond queen. Bad enough takin' on Frank and Jess, three Youngers and Torn and Belle. All I need is that red bitch. Enough to make you give up poker."

"But not quite."

"Not yet."

Calamity headed for the door. Hickok walked her up to the batwings, and as she rounded the hitch rack and swung up onto her Appaloosa, Hickok smiled.

"Damn, Calamity, you're pretty enough to marry."

"No," Calamity said softly, slouching low in her McClellan, shoving her boots deep in the oxbows, right up to the heels. "You're married already. And not to no damn circus lady. To that diamond queen. Till death do you part. You just don't know it yet."

She wheeled the big Appaloosa away from the hitch rack and booted him up the street.

60

Fort Smith was known as "Hell in the Nations." For if the Nations swarmed with every kind of murderer, road agent, and fugitive, then Fort Smith was its capital, the place where the outlaws flocked.

At the same time it drew the pilgrims. On hanging day, especially. That was when they descended on the town in droves. Lawyers, newsmen, doctors, farmers, city slickers, and drifters of all shapes and sizes.

The Bald Eagle in particular filed up with these shorthorns. It was across the street from the scaffold, so that's where they went.

To watch the hanging.

And to play some cards.

So Hickok knew this game would be tough. On hanging day, the card games had an extra edge. The hardcases were out in force. And they didn't like other men getting in their way.

At Hickok's table they were already running out of marks. Mostly he saw sharpers, men on the make, stone-cold professionals in wide-brimmed hats, black frock coats, and brocaded vests.

The gamblers' vests drew most of Hickok's attention. They concealed a world of woes—cheating devices, reflectors of every size and shape, daggers, bowies, Arkansas toothpicks.

And guns. Hickok watched mostly for the guns. Sharps pepperboxes, .45-caliber, double-barreled derringers, stingy guns, short guns, and tied-back slip-hammers like the one in Hickok's shoulder rig.

You had to watch for the guns. In games like these, the action was fast, the rules bent. These were hard-eyed professionals who challenged the odds. Anything went.

And if they were caught?

They went for their guns.

Like the elegant Southerner in the white planter's suit. He looked aristocratic but played like a cheat. And Hickok had also seen his piece. Sutler made sure that everyone saw it. It was the fastest hideout made, a stingy in a spring-holster, the muzzle pointing up the sleeve. Not even Hickok could beat it for speed.

And Hickok found that men who wore them suspected they would be caught.

The game was fast, and the whiskey flowed freely. The piano man played "Streets of Laredo" while a ballad-thrush belted out the sad refrain. The talk was loose, the play lively.

And most important, the money clinked loud and clear. In fact, the green baize was awash with shiny coins: double eagles, cartwheels, Imperio Pesos—which Sutler fumed against as "them fuckin' 'dobe dollars"—eight-sided goldpieces from California, and all kinds of "bits," as well as Carson City silver.

When a player ran out of coins, then crisp paper money flicked across the table—shinplasters, specie, greenbacks, and scrip. The dollars stacked high, and the cards slapped the baize. Ante up. Fold 'em or call. Raise and cross-raise. No help here. No help to the lady. Read 'em and weep. The cards slapped the table or spun from the deck.

The elegant Southerner sported a gray goatee and had a penchant for cigars. He also talked a lot. Not the usual banter of women and guns. He had other topics. The town's hangman, the Lost Confederate Cause, and Hickok's miraculous luck.

For, once again, Hickok was taking pot after pot.

Which meant that once again, Hickok was in trouble.

That sleeve gun ain't no watch charm, he reminded himself.

Throughout the game, Sutler baited Hickok. "Suh, your luck is phenomenal. I can beat any man at this table in this heah game of skill. But I cannot beat dumb luck. No, suh! Why, you could beat the hangman with this heah luck. If Lee had had your luck, suh, we'd've won the War."

"A queen of hearts to two black ladies," Hickok said casually. And raked in the pot.

"Suh, I bet you could even beat that hangman, that little man called Maledon. Put you on the trap, noose up your neck, why, the trap wouldn't drop. I'd bet my life."

"You're betting mine."

"So I am. So I am."

The pasteboards flicked across the baize, and the dollars stacked high. By midafternoon, when it was close to hanging time, a pilgrim suggested they take a break.

"What do you think? Twelve men at once? Should we break the game to see it? In about ten minutes? It's a record, I believe."

"Hell, no," said Hickok. "For one thing, that ain't no record. They hanged thirty-six up in the Dakotas that time."

"But suh, them was Injuns," Sutler countered. "And that was in the War. Surely that don't count."

Hickok nodded. "Guess that's so."

"But what of this Maledon?" Sutler said quizzically. "I hear his darlin' daughta run off with this heah gambler man. Parker brought him back and sentenced him to hang. Imagine that! Hanged him 'cause a woman whip some pussy in his face. Judge'd be hangin' every boy back home, if that was a legal law."

"Call of the blood," Hickok said as he turned his hole card. He filled a flush and raked in the pot. "That's all it is."

"That's what I say," the gambler said, staring in dismay at Hickok's hand.

The pasteboards slid like bullets from Sutler's fingers, and the game went on.

"What good can you say about a man like Maledon?" Hickok mused. "Line up twelve nooses and twelve livin' men, then drop that trap. What kind of man would choose a trade like that?"

"Know what they call that droppin' trap?" Sutler said. "'Parker's gates to hell.' Maledon pulls that greased noose tight around your neck, the preacher says his words, and it's ten feet down. Off into the void."

"Like a stone droppin' down a well," a pilgrim offered.

Hickok raised on a double pair. "But you never hear it hit bottom. If you're the one on the trap."

"Like the end of the Rebellion," Sutler observed, studying Hickok's raise with a perplexed face. "It never seemed to end. Lilacs on gravestones, band music and oratory. It still goes on in a thousand village churches. Shiloh, Antietam, Manassas, Fayetteville, Cold Harbor, Harper's Ferry, Vicksburg, the Surrender. We never forget. Never."

"Our friend is a romantic," Hickok said dryly. His hole card, a king, filled out a full house—three kings, two tens. He stared at Sutler's sleeve gun a brief moment, smiled absently, then turned over the card. He raked in the pot.

"What do you mean, suh?" Sutler said angrily.

"What do I mean by what?"

"By 'romantic'?"

"Like others I know. Livin' out your life in the gray shadow of that Cause, that Lost Cause."

"No, suh," Sutler said, lighting a panatela. "I live for today. The Cause is just like one of Parker's victims falling through that trap on that ten-foot drop."

"I hear that drop ain't bad," the pilgrim said, trying to lighten the mood. "Leastways not that first nine feet."

"It's that final foot that wears you out," Hickok agreed.

"Not for Maledon," Sutler continued, still eying Hickok. "The black bag over the head, the thick rope 'round the neck, the thirteen turns to the noose, the knot up tight behind the ear, the droppin' trap—all that stuff's the hard part for him. That last foot ain't nothin' to him. That's where he gets his."

Hickok stared at his hand. Queen on a case queen, one a club, one a spade. And two jacks up. A good hand, Hickok thought to himself. Good enough to die for? In a short while, Calamity and the James-Younger gang would pull up in front of the bank, armed with a Gatling gun. And he would have to face them. All of them.

Of course, there was Custer. That was a point he had not really broached with Clem. When he wired the day before with his portable transmitter, he had gotten no response. He had hoped that the lines were merely down. But suppose Custer did not show? The negative consequences of *that* were too vast to ponder. And anyway, he still had Sutler to live through.

"Three double eagles," Hickok said tersely, and pushed the big coins to the middle of the pot.

Sutler was staring at Hickok's hands. His eyes were insolently skeptical. He called the three double eagles and held.

Hickok examined his hand again. It hadn't changed. Queen on a case queen, one a club, one a spade. And two jacks up. But it was the queens that bothered him. He stared at the fifth card with trepidation. He could not bring himself to look at it.

"Two more double eagles," Hickok said evenly, still not looking at the card.

"I got to call," Sutler said, as the others dropped out.

Hickok simply stared at his fifth card, facedown on the baize. He sat there frozen, still afraid to turn it.

He finally looked up, and Sutler was glaring at him.

"Sir, I simply do not believe your impudence. You place your bet without even lookin' at your hole card. When called, you still do not look. Do you know the card already? Is it bad enough you cheat us? Must you insult the players too? Rub our noses in your thievery?"

Anger flickered across Sutler's face, and three pilgrims backed up their chairs.

The professionals simply left the table.

Hickok also knew it was now. He knew that Sutler would go for the sleeve gun. And would beat him to the draw with that snake-fast hideout. Not able to beat Hickok with cards, he would beat him with the gun.

"It's bad luck to look at the hole card. Sometimes I feel that," Hickok said truthfully.

"It's worse luck to cheat."

"Maybe I don't need that hole card."

"Maybe you're a lyin', thievin' Yankee sonofabitch."

Sutler went for it. And the draw was fast, as fast as Hickok had ever seen. The Sharps pepperbox snaked from the sleeve in one fluid motion, a lightning draw Hickok could never have matched. To reach his gun, Hickok's right hand would have to cross his body, then draw the Navy Colt from either his red sash or his half-breed shoulder rig. Then he'd have to pull the gun, clear the table, and fire. Sutler needed only one quick move.

But the Arkansas toothpick came out of Hickok's back sheath in a blur. Throwing it by the handle, he had the ten-and-a-half-inch blade in the air before Sutler could even cock his piece.

Sutler's eyes were huge with horror, and his last conscious act was to turn his neck.

Which was where the knife struck.

Sutler's freshly laundered white linen shirt, white planter's hat, and matching coat were soaked by a deluge of blood as he crashed to the floor, upending his chair. His features, to Hickok's grim satisfaction, twisted into a grotesque death mask.

Blood had sprayed the cards, the money on the table, the green baize, the tile floor, and Hickok's frock coat.

Hickok stood and drew a Navy Colt.

"Any more complaints?" He surveyed the room. There were no takers.

Hickok then turned over his bloodied hand.

A full house.

The fifth card, the diamond queen.

"No more complaints?" Hickok asked again as he raked the pot into a saddlebag and threw it over his shoulder.

Only one. The staccato hammering of a hundred-caliber gun, a turreted Gatling, cranking for all it was worth, the reports plus a half-dozen pistols.

Hickok was up and across the room and through the batwing doors.

61

When Calamity hit town with the gang, she knew they'd be impressive. For fifteen years she'd heard tales of Frank, Jess, Cole—of their years with Quantrill and on their own. She'd heard how they'd hurrah towns—charging up the streets in white dusters and black slouch hats, pistols blazing, townsfolk cowering. She'd expected action.

But nothing like this.

The streets were empty in ten seconds flat. When they roared into the square, the crowd of a thousand onlookers swept in a wave toward the river. Eager for action, even Jess and Frank were caught up in the excitement. They swung off their mounts and went straight for the bank. Calamity waited outside, holding the horses.

But most amazing of all was the crazy Mex. From three blocks away she could hear his yells. Cholo came into town on the box of a freightwagon, blacksnaking a ten-span mule team, cursing like all the furies of hell. The mules, all fifty yards of them, were decked out in full regalia—bridles, collars, spreaders, and belly bands.

The Mex mastered them with that blacksnake whip, a jerk-line string, a sackful of stones, and a torrent of obscenities that would embarrass a buff hunter.

The mules were now a block away, and Clem turned around in her saddle to gape. The wagon's white canvas tarpaulin was stretched tight on its frame. Cholo was standing on the wagon box, the jerk-line clenched in his teeth, the whip in both his hands. He was giving the blacksnake a whistling swing, and with a snap of the wrist, the popper exploded like a pistol shot. Now all twenty mules were hitting their collars. Cholo swung again and again as the wagon thundered up the street. The chains wrenched tight, the bells clanging, the mules at a dead run.

Cholo hit the square, hauling the brake. The rig slid into a sharp turn. As the brakes and wheels screamed and groaned, the mules skidded on their hocks, braying and snorting.

Then Cholo cut the ropes and the tarpaulin fell off.

The Gatling gun stood uncovered in all its naked splendor.

When a handful of marshals went for their guns, the Gatling spoke.

She'd never seen it in action. The turreted gun was bolted to the wagon bed with Cole Younger behind it. Its cannonlike muzzle had ten long barrels, each an inch wide. All ten were spewing fire. The ammunition drum, which was locked above the breech, fed the inch-wide bullets into the chamber.

And did that drum feed! It loaded, cocked, fired, extracted, ejected, and reloaded as fast as Cole could crank. More than two thousand rounds per minute, Clem had been told, and now she believed it. The massive bullets were four times the size of the slugs in Hickok's "Big Fifty."

The crowd scattered like blown sand. Even the marshals fled. There was no way to fight back. Any kind of cover—rainbarrels, water troughs, wagons—the Gatling gun ripped to shreds in one burst.

After scaring off the marshals, Cole shot up the scaffold. The inch-wide rounds pulverized the platform, riddled the tops of the black curtains, shattered the frame beneath.

And with the curtains shot away, the gallows was exposed.

Twelve sentenced men were standing on the platform, awaiting their deaths. Black bags on heads, greased ropes noosed around their necks, hands and feet bound. Frightened half to death by the cranking gun, their legs trembling, their cries muted by the black bags, they screamed out for mercy even as Maledon raced for cover.

And still the Gatling cranked.

At first the big gun favored the victims. It fired high, and the first man's rope was shot in two. When it fell and draped itself around his shoulders, he dropped to his knees, praising God for this heaven-sent reprieve.

Then Cole lowered his sights, and one of the rounds caught

a victim in the chest. Third from the end, he was lifted from his feet, then dropped on the trap. Limp as a rag doll, the slack rope still tightly noosed around his neck, he lay inert in a widening pool of his own blood.

Cole paused for better aim. He replaced the drum, cut loose on the gallows base, and cranked with a vengeance. When he hit the deadbolt, the trap door dropped.

And the sentenced men were hanged by the neck.

All save two. One was the man whom Cole had shot. And the other, whose rope Cole had severed, fell with the rest. Stunned, he sat on the earth beneath.

But Cole's gun hand could not be stayed. Now he went for the underpinnings. He cranked round after round into the bottom frame. Listing to its side as, one by one, its supports were shot away, the scaffold broke in two. The eleven dangling men and the one on the ground were crushed to bloody pulp beneath the massive weight of the ruined scaffold.

The crowd was now a panic-stricken mob. They pounded over one another in their race to the river. Off the big bluff, over the river's edge, they leaped by the score. Mothers in bonnets, holding children. Bankers and lawyers in frock coats and bowler hats. Painted whores and drunken drovers.

Calamity rode up alongside the Gatling, pulled her Colt, and shot Cole off the gun, the bullet's impact knocking him over the side of the box-bodied freight wagon.

Now Frank and Jess and the two other Youngers were charging out of the bank. In black slouch hats and white dusters, they were vaulting their horses and shouting at the Mex, "Haul the gun around. The bank's got a time vault. You should have seen it, you stupid motherfucker!"

Cholo, his sombrero back against his neck, jumped from the wagon box into the wagon. Swinging the Gatling gun around, aiming it at the crowd, he grabbed the crank and commenced to turn.

Calamity's jaw dropped in astonishment.

Slater's first round caught Cholo in the right eyeball.

Slater's second shot got him in the left shoulder. It spun him around and would have dropped him in a heap, but Hickok was in the street and firing rapidly at Cholo. Hickok's first two rounds struck the spinning Mexican in the right and left shoulders in turn, causing him to spin even more rapidly until Calamity's round struck him below the scapula and hurled the spinning Cholo bodily out of the wagon and onto the ground.

Then Slater vaulted into the wagon. He threw the coiled blacksnake over his shoulder and tilted the Gatling straight at the gang. Hickok and Clem were both behind a horse trough, their guns blazing.

The odds had changed.

Jesse rode past the horseless Cole and swung him up behind him. Then the six of them kicked their horses on up the street.

"You're dead men!" Frank screamed at Hickok and Slater, as he covered the gang's retreat. "You're dead fuckin' meat! Calamity too!"

PART FOURTEEN

62

With Hickok in the lead, they were riding out of the Nations. J. P. Paxton was in bad shape, saddle-galled and slowing them down. Calamity tried to talk him into returning to Fort Smith. But he insisted on staying. He still intended "to face the frontier, confront the country."

Whenever Calamity glanced back, she nodded sympathetically. She suspected he'd lost his mind.

Slater and Hickok led extra horses, the ones they had taken from the James-Younger remuda after the Fort Smith shootup. Twenty in all. Pintos, duns, sorrels, grays, mustangs, buckskins, and paints. Those horses would determine who won this race.

Clem was pleased. A string like this took months to build. Beating the gang back to the pony herd and grabbing Belle had been a major coup. Parker's deps had diverted the gang just long enough. And Hickok had stolen the initiative.

Now the gang would follow, but with inferior mounts. And Hickok kept saying, "If we can just stay in front, George Armstrong Custer will do the rest."

Clem, of course, had her doubts, but never Hickok. If need be, he would take them clear to the Dakotas.

It was a rough ride. Paxton was hurt. Belle, whom they'd kidnapped along with the horses, rode awkwardly, strapped to her kack. Her hands were cross-tied to her saddlehorn, hips lashed to the cantle. As for Slater and Hickok, they were slowed, pulling the jerk-line string.

It was a hard ride, as hard as the journey through the Yuma Desert and the trek across the Staked Plains. They rode from Fort Smith to Kansas City across a land as dry and barren as ashes. The terrain held nothing—save buzzards, mesquite and wind-bent sagebrush. Not a tree nor a hill nor rimrock nor breeze. It was flat. The horizon stretched before them till the earth dropped away.

They were on the prairie, remote and empty as time itself, scorching plains that Calamity called "the very edge of hell." They crawled on its surface like infinitesimal insects. No guideposts, no landmarks, no mountains to fix on.

Other things might change, but not this land.

63

Nor had life changed for Custer. He was still in trouble with the brass, still under the gun.

His present situation was an example. He faced Philip Henry Sheridan—the second-ranking general in the United States Army—in his office. Sheridan's uniform was rumpled, in contrast to Custer's carefully tailored blues. The two top buttons of Sheridan's tunic were undone. His brass was tarnished.

And he was furious.

The man's upper lip was drawn back tight against his teeth. His knuckles were white on the mahogany arms of his leather desk chair. His eyes blazed.

"George," the general said, "I can't help you. Grant wants you flogged and castrated, your head on a stake."

Custer nodded bleakly.

"You're in a corner," said Sheridan, "and you can't get out of it."

Custer looked grim. "There must be a way. Maybe Pope or Hooker could say something on my behalf."

"Not likely. They're bad friends, but worse enemies. Betrayal is second nature to them."

Custer let his breath out slowly. He crossed the room to the louvered side window facing the main gate.

"Tell me, Phil, is it better to be a potent killer or an impotent priest?"

"I don't know. We don't get much practice at the religious life, impotent or otherwise. We see men die, we hear confessions, but we grant no absolution."

"And we receive none," said Custer. He turned to face Sheridan. "They say the evil that we do lives after us, but the good is interred with our bones. Do you believe that? God, it's a dreary thought."

"Men achieve some good along the way. Even soldiers."

"We turned Lee's flank at Appomattox, didn't we? Right in front of that goddamned depot. Remember?" Custer's face brightened.

"You turned it, George. It was you. Lee gave you the white flag."

"But you set it up, Phil. And when Lee signed the terms of surrender, he gave you the desk he signed them on." Custer smiled. "Then your wife gave that desk to my Libbie."

"We all loved Libbie."

"God, Phil, is this how it ends? We, who stood in blood up to our ankles while men screamed and died? Is this the way it ends? The money-changers drive us from the temple?"

"They're braiding the whip, George, even as we speak. It's over. Make a deal. Find some cover. It's gone too far this time, and it's too late."

"Just give me back the Seventh Cavalry for one more engagement. I'll make my own deal."

"Not likely. Not after that Fort Smith fiasco. God, if Grant learned you were behind that, he'd have us all by the balls."

"Just one last fight. Let me lead my men at the Rosebud. General Terry wants me there. He wired you about it."

"And what of Fort Smith?"

"It was Grant's fault I didn't show. He relieved me of command, not you. I would have stopped those men."

"But they got away."

"Hickok's taking care of that. He's kidnapped Belle Starr, and those longriders are following him right now straight to the Rosebud. He wired Captain Keogh at Fort Lincoln. My men will be waiting."

Sheridan stared at him, uncomprehending.

"Phil, he's leading those murdering outlaws right into our arms. All we have to do is be there to catch them. It can still work."

Sheridan stood. Facing the window behind his desk, he watched a squad at close-order drill in the courtyard.

"Ah, hell. George, you're going to be the death of me."

"I'm begging, Phil. A last chance."

Sheridan turned and faced Custer, his eyes narrowed shrewdly. "All right. I don't know anything about this James-Younger lunacy. Neither do you. Whatever happens, happens. General Terry wants you on the Rosebud. I can stick my neck out one more time, based on his request."

"Phil—"

"Just get it done, George. Come back empty and I'll punch your ticket myself."

"Phil—"

"Don't say anything. Fail and you're through, boxed and tagged."

"I'll keep my head screwed on."

"If you don't," Sheridan said coldly, "your ass will follow."

64

For the second time in two days, Hickok stopped by a telegraph line. Calamity climbed the pole and hooked up the lead, and Hickok hammered out a message on his handset:

HAVE BELLE STOP GANG STILL IN PURSUIT STOP PLEASE ADVISE STOP END OF MESSAGE

Finally he got an answer. The rapid clicking of the response chattered briskly:

READY TO CLOSE TRAP STOP WILL MEET YOU BY THE ROSEBUD STOP FOLLOW TROOPSHIP THE FAR WEST STOP END OF MESSAGE

As he repacked the gear, Hickok explained his plan. "It's still on. We're leadin' them to Custer. Up on the Rosebud."

Calamity groaned. Slater looked stunned.

And Belle was outraged. "Lead them ol' boys clear to the fuckin' Rosebud? You just better get under something or behind something. Them boys catch up with you, they're gonna tear out your intestines and wrap them around these here telegraph poles."

"If we can hold this lead, we'll make it."

"And if pigs had wings, they'd be fuckin' angels."

"Your plan does call for extreme measures," the Professor remarked.

"This trip sure ain't gonna be for the weak," Hickok acknowledged.

"This trip ain't even for the *strong*!" Belle shouted in angry disbelief. "Does anyone really think they can keep this shit on the rails, from here to fuckin' Montana?"

Slater turned his head and coughed.

Calamity looked at her boots.

"Well," the Professor said, "perhaps we can somehow scare them off."

"How?" Belle yelled. "Jump at them out of a dark corner? Them boys are gonna be chewin' at your ankles like bloodhounds, from here to the Medicine Line. They'll catch you, too, 'cause they want it more. And 'cause they got more balls."

"They ain't got *no* balls," Calamity said. "They ain't got the fuckin' muscle."

"Them boys got muscles in their shit," Belle shouted.

"Professor," Hickok said, "for whatever it's worth, I still think you in particular oughta back out. This ain't your kind of game."

The Professor's voice was indignant. "I'm not sure I know what you mean."

"It means Hickok's givin' you a chance to get out of this shitstorm while you're still breathin'," Belle said.

"Do it, pilgrim," said Calamity.

"Then I would not be true to myself, Miss Calamity."

"Professor, Bill's givin' you a chance to get out with your hide, and if that ain't God's own no-bullshit truth, I don't know what is."

"No," the Professor said quietly, "truth is what we mean with our whole being, what we live every moment of our lives. I know that now. If I don't find my truth here, I never will."

"Well, you still got some time to back out," Hickok said. "Meantime, let's mount up. We still got some daylight."

"Ain't gonna do you no good," Belle said as she swung onto her horse. "This is the fuckin' deathwatch. I just hope they spell your names right in the papers. 'Cause you're goin' down inch by inch, slow and hard. You're dead in the water, and you don't even know it."

They were all mounted. Belle continued shouting and swearing, and Calamity loped ahead, trying to get away from Belle's taunts.

"You're dead meat, Calamity," she heard Belle shout. "Deader than Abe Lincoln's nuts."

65

They were on the Kansas prairie now—Cole, Jim and Bob Younger, Frank and Jesse James. They'd lost three days eluding Parker's posse and two more getting another remuda.

But now they were back in business; six Texas drovers with a string of wiry cutting-ponies bore mute witness to that. Their vulture-picked remains lay gaunt and bare in the sunburnt chaparral, five of them shot through the head, a fact not overlooked by Parker's men when they "lost" the gang at the border.

Three days and nights in the saddle, and they were one day's ride behind Hickok. By then their mounts were blowing and stove in, so on the fourth night they rested.

While Jim and Bob tended the stock, Jess and Frank stayed by the campfire, brewing up coffee.

"Damn, Cole is hot," Frank said to his brother. "Ain't seen him this hot since Lawrence."

"Guess we know why he left Slater in that arroyo."

Frank shook his head. "Slater was a good man once."

Cole squatted beside them. "He's a dead one as soon as we catch him."

"That's a fact, little cousin. I promise you that. Sure as the turnin' of the earth."

Cole nodded his agreement. "You plan on goin' back to Clay County with them three walkin' free? After gettin' buffaloed like that? Every tin star in Missouri'd be on our back porch. They'd be thinkin' we all grew paper assholes."

"'Fraid you're right. This here's one hand we gotta play out to the end," Jess said.

"It's more'n that," Cole said, staring into the fire. "Some things you don't let be. Like when them red-legs killed my

245

daddy and burned our farm. Things like that you don't forget.''

"Count on it, little cousin," Frank said coldly. "Them three's buzzard bait—dead as dead can be."

66

They reached Kansas City in six days. Their horses, except for the Appaloosa, were hipshot, wind-broke, ridden half to death. Hickok sold the crowbait to a local stable for five dollars a head. Then he looked for a train bound for Fort Lincoln.

Railroad travel was governed by more than seventy kinds of time, all in use, all at once. Stations tried to advise their passengers. They printed schedules and ran them in the papers. They blew whistles and fired guns at dusk, dawn, and noon. But when you reached the platform, no one really knew which trains were departing. Or which had arrived.

And when Hickok wired Parker, the judge confirmed what he had guessed. The gang was spotted riding hellbent through the Nations, through Kansas, straight for K.C. They had run off a herd of wiry cowponies, and they were making time. If they arrived before their train pulled out, the gang would shoot them on sight.

Hickok pinned an old marshal's badge to his shirt, then handcuffed Belle to his wrist.

Belle thought it hilarious. "Impersonatin' a peace officer. That's worth at least ten years in jail. And all this for me? Damn, this one ought to be great. Just get me a good seat, you four-flushin' sonofabitch. I ain't missin' this show for nothin'."

Hickok dragged them through a score of platforms before he found the right one. A big black locomotive with a spark-spreading crown-piece.

The string of cars was already moving when they climbed aboard.

"If they ain't on this train, we should beat them out of here," Clem said as they walked up the aisle.

"Beat them where?" Belle asked. "To hell?"

"If it's in the Dakotas," Hickok agreed.

They were on a hotel train, so they went first class. They sat in parlor cars on plush seats with thick Turkish carpets at their feet. Wall mirrors surrounded them. Hung between the mirrors were exotic paintings of far places: the rolling deserts of the Middle East, oases shaded with palm trees, the pyramids, harems, sultans, concubines with opulent breasts.

In the club car the tables were covered with snowy linen, the settings immaculate. The menu had prices that made Calamity groan.

"Is Custer payin'?" Calamity finally asked.

"He better," said Hickok.

"Yeah," Clem agreed, "but that don't mean he *will*."

At night they slept on the thick plush seats in the parlor car. One of them stood guard. This was usually Hickok, who couldn't seem to sleep. He'd now grown distant, opaque. Calamity couldn't imagine what had driven him this far.

67

On and on they rolled. K.C., Wichita, Denver. There they changed trains and it set them back five hours. Now Hickok was sure the gang was close behind.

From Denver on, the land changed. They chugged through steep valleys with mile-high slopes. They roared around great hills and through precipitous gorges, over towering trestles of crisscrossed braces.

Then came the granite face of the Rockies. Now the great mountains loomed all around them, sheer, snow-capped.

The train pounded north, carrying them into a land of rolling, tree-lined hills and great sprawling valleys. This was God's country, a land touched by grace and natural grandeur, a land breathtaking in its beauty.

But they knew the stories of the people who settled here, they knew the reality behind the façade. Half the settlers died within the first year. The forty-below winters froze them out, the rampaging Sioux took their hair, or the short growing seasons starved them out. They seldom survived the Black Hills, a land as harsh and spare and desolate as the Staked Plains.

Into the Badlands the train pounded on. Through vast oceans of eroded hills, steep, barren buttes, dried-up washes, and great, futile wastes. Here the winds moaned day after day, months on end, down from the distant north. The sound alone could drive people mad, and as these northers swept endlessly, they scoured everything in their path. Mountains were reduced to hills, hills to buttes. The few lone trees— greasewood, juniper, cottonwood—and the little undergrowth— the sagebrush, pinyon, stunted mesquite—was bent endlessly by these groaning winds. Otherwise, nothing. A land of shale, granite, and black lava outcroppings. A land where they hoped to track down General Custer. A land where they hoped to pay off Hickok's debt.

68

In Bismarck, Hickok got word from friends in Denver.

Yes, the gang was on the way, gaining on them fast.

"Just a little too fast," Hickok explained as they stood beside the track. "They're on an express train packed with army supplies needed in Fort Lincoln when Custer returns."

"But we still got a lead," Calamity pointed out. "A damn good lead."

"I ain't sure," Hickok said slowly. "The army's cleared the track and them brothers are pushin' straight through. They're highballin' all the way. They can still catch up. And if they catch us by that sidewheeler on the Rosebud, we fight them on the pier."

"Then fuck Custer," Calamity said angrily. "We give them brothers up. Let the marshals grab them in Fort Lincoln."

"Ain't no marshals in Lincoln," said Hickok drily. "Ain't no marshals nowhere. This ain't the U.S. of A. This here's a foreign fuckin' country. We're in the Great Sioux Nation. And that nation's makin' war."

"Then let the army have them outlaws."

"They don't want them. Not up here, not with ten thousand redskins huntin' hair."

Slater asked the vital question. "Will Custer still want them?"

"He asked for them. It was his deal."

"But he don't need them now, does he?"

"It was his deal. He'll want them."

"I hope you're right," Calamity said bitterly. "I sure hope you are."

69

When their train pulled into Fort Lincoln, they unloaded their gear and bought new horses. They led their stock to the pier, and watched as the dock workers loaded stock, packs, and saddles into steerage. By that time their ship was about to pull out. They had to hurry to make it, but they all got aboard.

The *Key West* was a beautiful ship. A flat-bottomed packet with a big sidewheel. She had three huge decks and lots of entertainment.

As they stood by the rail, the Professor stared at the river.

"Sorry you come along, 'stead of gettin' off in K.C. like we suggested?" asked Calamity.

"Oh, no, my dear," the Professor said. "Why, at last I'm seeing the West, I mean the real West. I've had a marvelous time. Really." He shook his head. "Only I'm truly baffled by this water. It doesn't somehow look like water. More like yellow clay."

"More like horse piss," Slater observed.

"Too thick for piss," Hickok thought.

When Calamity added, "Too thick for piss and too thin to plow," Hickok cringed painfully.

After a pause, Slater said, "Well, if the whiskey ain't too thick, I'm havin' a snort."

When no one argued with that one, they headed below.

"Just no more cards, Bill," Calamity pleaded. "You start them cards and I end up bleeding."

"No cards this trip," Hickok agreed.

Calamity sighed. "It's too much damn fun, them card games of yours. My heart can't take the pace."

70

As Hickok led the group, Calamity's eyes darted back and forth. She was in a setting she'd never imagined existed. The salons were packed with stunning people in the most gorgeous attire. The women were all in laces, Basque jackets, paletots, balmoral skirts with muslin waists, high-necked traveling dresses of dark serge.

The men were decked out in bowlers and stovepipe hats, Prince Albert coats and brocade vests. She saw waist-length jackets of slate-gray flannel, with brass buttons and yellow-gold piping. There were Southern gentlemen with white planter's hats, smoking thin cigars and looking rich, wearing tropical suits of creamy white. They kept their pistols in their high black boots.

The decor was dazzling. Hand-carved teak trim, scarlet and gold molding, the ceilings glistening with gilt as candlelight flickered from the crystal chandeliers. Persian prayer rugs hung on the walls. The high-backed divans were of deep crimson plush. Waiters in livery with trays full of drinks swept back and forth through the ship.

On they walked, past the pilothouse, the hurricane deck, and even steerage. Far down below, Clem peeked in the hold at the barrels, bales, wagons and horses, sacks, boxes, cordwood for the ship's boilers, the endless store of cargo.

Hickok found a bar on the top deck. It had an elaborate buffet with scores of entrees and dozens of desserts. Somehow they managed to avoid the gambling tables.

With drinks in hand, the five of them spent the night walking the deck.

71

Toward midnight they drifted down into steerage. Clem, Hickok, and Paxton climbed up onto a huge bale of army blankets, six feet high and eight feet across. After laying out their bedrolls, they were soon asleep.

Slater preferred softer accommodations. In an empty horse stall at the other end of the hold, he broke open a bale of hay and threw down his bedroll. He pulled off his boots and stretched out. Yawning, he rolled onto his side and drifted off into sleep.

But it was not to be.

A hard-pointed boot toe slammed into the sole of his bare foot. And when he glared up angrily at his attacker—over the sights of his cocked .45—he grunted his disgust.

Belle Starr laughed derisively at him. She cracked her wrist quirt against the high black boot that had just kicked him. She raised her left hand, which held her spurs, and shook the six-inch buzz-saw rowels at him.

"Had to take these off to sneak up on you. But I did it. Sneaked up on the famous desperado, Outlaw Torn Slater! The big bad gunny! What a joke! Outlaw, if I'd had me a .45, I could've blown you a second asshole, big enough to drive a span of mules through. Could've collected that twenty thousand dollar *re*-ward they have out on your ass. Twenty thousand dollars! Woo-ee! Must be nice bein' worth that much *dinero*. Must be good for strengthenin' friendships, knowin' that if a *compadre* turns you in—or better yet, backshoots you,—he's rich for life."

"Belle, fuck off." Slater uncocked his pistol and rolled over on his side.

"I'm talkin' to you, cowboy!" She raised her right foot up behind her and drove a boot toe into the bottom of Slater's other foot just as hard as she knew how. "Don't you ever turn your back on me when I'm talkin', you slimy jailbird bastard!" She leaned back, raising her right boot, and prepared to deliver another smashing kick.

His move was so swift and precise she barely felt it. The instep of Slater's foot snaked behind the left knee while the other foot shot out, kicking her on the ankle. Balanced as she was on her left leg, it collapsed beneath her, and she fell onto Slater like a thrashing painter scratching, biting, growling with rage.

In a crazed frenzy she struck out, five fingernails clawing a shoulder. Her teeth sank into a bicep, and her knee was aiming for a crotch, when he almost took her head off with a short hard right.

She'd been hit before, but never like this. Slaps she'd known, and she could shake them off, then come back kicking, daring the man to try it again.

But the other men—men like Cole Younger—had never struck her with a closed right fist alongside the temple. Cole had never hit her so hard that her eyes blurred and went vague, her knees sagged, her ears chimed like bells, and the entire left side of her body went numb. Cole had never hit her so hard that she could only collapse limply onto the floor like a loose-jointed marionette, the strings cut.

When her vision cleared, she found herself lying on Slater's blankets, her ears still ringing, her eyes tearing over. Audible above the blood drumming in her temples, she could hear a tearing, wrenching *c-r-r-ack!* She turned over onto her side, and Torn Slater was standing over her. In his hand he held a pine slat, ripped off the side of a nearby shipping crate. Grabbing her by the left elbow, he dragged her to her feet and, twisting the elbow up behind her back, held her there with a hammerlock.

Belle Starr was hot.

"Lemme go, you scum-suckin' sonofabitch!" she yelled.

But when she aimed a kick at his shin, he only cranked the twisted arm higher up her back, all but separating it from the socket, the horrendous agony of the hammerlock almost dropping her to her knees.

Her teeth clenched abruptly as she choked back her howls and bit off her groans. Slowly, almost gently, she felt herself being led to the back of the stall. There, Slater sat down on one of the bales of hay, and to Belle's utter astonishment, he took her over his knee.

"You rotten piece of pigshit! Don't you dare!"

But now he was holding her nose. Her jaw opened so she could breathe, and as she lay there gasping for air, Slater stuffed the entire wad of his big red bandanna between her teeth. She tried to pull it out, but her arms were caught. Her left was still hammerlocked, and her right was trapped between her stomach and Slater's left knee. She tried to kick, but he quickly swung his right leg over the backs of her knees, instantly canceling that action.

Choking on the gag, her arms and legs pinned, Belle was consumed with rage. She could not believe this was happening to *her!* To Belle Starr! Belle-fucking-Starr, trussed up like a hogtied heifer, and now helplessly waiting for the red-hot branding iron.

Slater was speaking in flat, emotionless tones. "Belle, you've been askin' for this a long time. You've been askin' Cole for it. And you've been askin' me for it."

She glanced up over her shoulder at Slater. The pine slat was poised over her arched bottom. It looked hard. She shuddered reflexively. Against her will, she felt her anger melt into fear.

"Belle, honey, now you're gonna get it."

Slater began to whale on her bottom, and of course, her initial impression was one of pain. It hurt. Every ounce of Belle's being was instantly focused and transfixed on that inescapable fact. Her eyes and nose were flooded with tears. Her throat was choking on sobs and groans. Only the bandanna locked between her teeth stopped her from screaming. There was no denying it—an out-of-control firestorm was raging over her bottom.

There were other reactions as well. She felt genuine humiliation at being dominated—doubled up and paddled like an obnoxious child. Yet even amid her stifled howls, she also had pride. She found herself praying fervently that Hickok, Clem, and Paxton would not wake up. It was bad enough as it was. If she also had to endure their inevitable chorus of horse-laughs—*that* would be truly unbearable.

In the beginning she counted the cracks, and when, on the ninth one, she felt the board shatter against her rear end, even at that, she felt relief.

Still twisting her arm behind her back, Slater brought Belle to her feet. He stood over her and glared down into her eyes. She met his gaze fearlessly, her spirit unbroken.

"Girl, you're gonna remember this night all the way to the Black Hills."

He unbuckled her belt with his free right hand and then began pulling her Levi's down around her knees.

My God, he's going to rape me! Belle thought. Her crotch tingled with anticipation, but at the same time she vowed to show him only disdain. She silently swore not even to fight him but to lie there limp, like a rag, not giving him the satisfaction of witnessing her fear, her discomfort—or her need.

She felt her body sag, grow limp at his touch, but still she continued to glare up at him with cold, unwavering eyes.

Suddenly Slater was back down on the bale of hay, and she was tumbling over his knees.

To her horror, the eerie cracks were once again echoing up and down the steerage, only this time Slater's callused right hand was playing the loud, painful refrain on her bottom. Even more distressing was the strength of that hand. And the hardness. If anything, those years on the Yuma rockpile had toughened his palms beyond even the harsh rigidity of the pine plank. Instantly her eyes and nose were flooding with salty tears, and she was redoubling her muted sobs. The fireball dancing over her derriere smoked, popped, and crackled. Her blazing behind hurt so badly, her pride no longer cared whether Hickok and the others showed. She hoped they would show. She prayed they would come and drag this bastard off her. They could laugh all they wanted, just so long as they stopped Slater. The horrible hellfire scorching her backside transcended any considerations of paltry pride. If the rag had not stopped her mouth, she would have cried to them for help.

How long he spanked her, she could not even guess. If she'd known that he hit her till his hand and arm went numb, it would have come as no surprise. By the time Slater stopped, Belle was hardly in any shape to question or doubt anything. She was barely conscious. In fact, when he dragged her out of the stall, her Levi's still rolled down around her knees, and threw her half-naked into the passageway, it was all Belle could do to lie there and whimper.

She lay in the passageway for a seeming eternity, and it took her forever to pry the big bandanna out of her mouth. Her choking sobs had sucked it halfway down her throat, and she considered it a minor miracle that she got it out at all.

As for pulling up her pants, the thought never crossed her mind. It hurt too much. Her crimson buttocks burned so furiously, she feared she would never get her pants back on again.

She lay in the passageway and cried. Nobody had used and abused her like this since childhood. If she'd had the strength, she'd have gone after Slater with a two-by-four. If she'd had a gun, she would have killed him. But she had neither. She was too wrung out. And worse, she even lacked the will.

Lying there in a heap, Belle peered timorously at Slater's body, now asleep in the empty horse stall. Belle glared at him, wrapped up in his empty bedroll, not so much in anger but with something akin to awe. For Belle, subduing Slater was no longer a viable possibility. Her buttocks blazed too ferociously for such high-risk ventures. What she felt, studying Slater's peacefully sleeping body, was more akin to a fatal acceptance of their relative positions. She could not defeat him. She accepted that now. He was too strong, too cunning, and too remorseless.

Belle Starr—the Bandit Queen, the Outlaw Lady—had met her match.

For the first time in her roistering, hellbent life, Belle Starr knew respect.

Worse, deep inside, she knew that what she felt was fear.

Carefully, quietly, Belle crept toward Slater's stall. She did not want to startle or anger him. Instead, she inched toward him surreptitiously on hands and knees.

Once, when he yawned and rolled over onto his side, she froze in mid-crawl, terrified that he might look up and misconstrue her creeping approach. Only after he recommenced snoring did she continue her advance.

She wormed her way up to him till she was inches from his feet, then pulled softly on a pantleg.

"Torn? Torn, honey?"

"Huh?"

"I got to talk to you, honey."

"No way."

"Please? Torn, baby?" She was working her way alongside him. When she was directly even with his face, she placed a hand on his cheek and tried to kiss him.

"You make me sick," he said, pushing her away. He turned his back to her.

"Torn," she pleaded, "I was wrong, real wrong. It was always you. When you left me high and dry, and I had no place else to go, it was only then I turned to Cole. But it was you, Torn, all the way."

He was snoring again.

"Aw, please, honey. Don't be like that." She was now unbuttoning his fly, openly groping his crotch, stroking the immensity of his member.

It rose rapidly.

"See, I knew you liked me. You always did, baby. You always said you did." She began dexterously unbuttoning his shirt. "It's just that when you left me, sugar, I was pregnant. There was no father, and when Cole offered—"

Suddenly Belle's voice cracked. Her chin was trembling. She pressed her hands to her face. Hoarse, rasping sobs tore out of her throat. Slater turned over and stared at her. When her weeping subsided, she said sadly, "You'll never know how bad it was. Cole's so awful. Oh, Torn, if he'd only been like you. He always let me yell at him, humiliate him, push him around. If he'd treated me like you always done . . . Aw, Torn, honey, I always wanted to be good. I didn't want to be mean and spiteful. It was men like Cole done it to me. Whimperin', snivelin', weak-kneed, wimps like Cole. They made me bad, Torn."

Slater slowly stroked her hair and wiped the tears from her eyes. She began kissing the wet tears from his knuckles.

"Oh, Torn, baby, if you hadn't left me, it would have been different. I swear before God, it would have been a whole 'nother story."

Belle was kissing him now, kissing his hands, arms, forehead, cheeks, mouth, neck.

"I swear it would have been just us, babe, just you and me."

She was kissing his throat, shoulders, chest, stomach.

"I swear it would have been better. It will be better. Oh, God, I'll make it better."

She was kissing the lower part of his belly, luxuriating in his navel, coyly massaging his balls with her cupped hands as she tongued the inside of his thighs.

"I swear it'll be like before. It'll be good like you never had it before."

She was kissing the underside of his dick, working her way down, licking his balls. She went beyond the balls, pausing daintily over the taint, then continuing on to the tingling edge of his rectum.

"Oh, God, Torn, you'll want me again. I'll make you want me."

She had the length of his tremendous member fully in her mouth. She was sucking it rapidly, her head frantically bobbing up and down, her tongue half-in, half-out of her mouth, the enormous cock sometimes slipping out, covering her cheeks and mouth and hair with its drizzling semen.

"You'll love me, Torn. I'll make you love me."

He was coming now, and she sucked his cock with renewed fury. The massive flood tide of boiling come thundered out of his dick and down her scorching throat. She swallowed endless gouts of his white-hot sperm. Over and over his lust pumped into the voracious vulva of her osculating mouth, and when she could no longer swallow fast enough, it inundated her lips and spilled over her cheeks and down her neck. Unable to contain the mounting torrent, she struggled to appease his pounding member by licking and sucking its sensitive underside.

"Care . . . you'll . . . care . . ."

His orgasms stopped their insatiable pumping. The alabaster pearls of his come glistened in stark contrast against her darkly tanned face and throat and against the long, coarse shock of her thick waist-length hair, black as a raven's wing. Tear tracks and smeared seed commingled on her cheeks.

"Want . . . again . . . me . . . fuck . . ."

He turned Belle over on her stomach. Crawling down the length of her legs, he pushed a bare foot into her crotch, grabbed a boot, and pushing off against her cunt, roughly pulled it off. Her body convulsed with multiple spasms.

"Fuck . . . want . . . care . . . me . . ."

He turned around between her spread legs. She was still on her stomach. Her half-conscious body was writhing on the stall floor. Her face and hair were covered with dirt, straw, and come. She was clenching handfuls of hay in her fists and mumbling incoherent obscenities.

"Fuck . . . love . . . me . . ."

Slater pulled his pants down to his knees. His massive member was still fully erect and lubricated with lust.

He gently cupped the hot red buttocks. Her body recoiled at his touch, but when he eased a probing finger into her anus, her resistance ceased. Now her body began to spasm repeatedly, and in her half-waking dream state, she was sobbing again.

"No . . . more . . . hit . . ."

He spread the crimson cheeks apart.

"Belle . . . good . . . girl . . . no . . . .
spank . . . good . . . fuck . . . Belle . . . . fuck . . . good . . ."

He bent forward and kissed the side of her neck, breathing into her ear. At the same time he lubricated the cleavage of her ass with his spitting cock.

Her back was arched, and she was rolling back and forth, to and fro on her belly.

"Care . . . make . . . care . . ."

Slater reached under her legs. Roughly he palpated her hard clitoris, and Belle's whole body was rocking with orgasms.

He quickly sank the full shaft of his member into her ass. He plunged into her again and again, slowly at first, then faster and faster, harder and harder, till his balls were slapping violently against the glowing globes of her crimson behind. Rudely he rubbed the flaming clitoral button. Now grating groans were wrenching out of her lungs, and he instantly stifled them with his left hand. But at the same time she was pumping her butt rapidly, uncontrollably. His only response to that was to increase the length and velocity of his own pounding piston till both of them were rocketing away on a flashfire of white-hot phosphorus, trailing off over a nether sea, detonating high above the furthest reaches of darkest hell, lost, alone, doomed, disconsolate.

"Fuck . . . kill . . . you . . . me . . ."

It was done. Slowly he pulled out of her. He could hear Clem and his friends down along the far end of the hold, stirring. It was time to get up. Time. The hatch above them was glimmering with dawn's first light. The steam whistle screeched and shrilled. The ship was slowing, reversing its sidewheel, docking. In his stomach, hunger grumbled. Belle groaned in her sleep, writhed on the stall floor, and sleepily rubbed her crotch. Time. He stood up, pulled on his pants and boots.

Time to pack up, move it on out.

Time.

He woke Belle with a sharp kick to the ankle, then crossed the hold to his friends.

Time.

Where it would end, God only knew.

PART FIFTEEN

72

On down the Rosebud, the sidewheeler churned. The next day the ship docked. The *Key West* found a berth where Rosebud Creek flowed into the Yellowstone River.

In the adjoining slip lay its sister ship, the *Far West*.

As they walked onto the jetty, Hickok nodded to it and said, "Custer's troopship."

"But it's empty," Calamity observed.

Paxton winced. "And it reeks of manure."

"They haven't shoveled out the hold," Hickok explained. "Which means the horses and troopers debarked today. Late today." Hickok grinned. "We're almost home. Day after tomorrow we catch up to Custer."

"If those heathen Injuns don't catch us first. If we still have our hair," Slater said.

But Calamity was relieved. "We could start tonight," she said.

"No, not at dusk. They might mistake us for Injuns in the dark." We'll start at first light."

They collected their gear from the lower deck. Their stock

consisted of the nine saddlehorses and three pack mules most of which Hickok had bought in Fort Lincoln.

They set up camp downstream.

They grained and staked out their animals, then cooked the last good meal they expected to have for some time. Bully beef, canned tomatoes, fried bread, Arbuckle's, and canned peaches for dessert. And a quart of Double Stamp bourbon that Hickok had bought on the boat.

They sat by the fire, rolling smokes and sipping the whiskey.

"Bill," Calamity asked, "why do you believe them Missouri outlaws are gonna follow us up here to the Dakotas?"

" 'Cause it ain't out of their way. Hell, by river packet we're only three days from Missouri. If this were someplace down in Mexico, they might not go to the trouble. But we're on their back porch. And of course we hurt their pride."

"Any chance they won't find us?"

"None. I left a well-marked trail. Every stationmaster, every telegraph operator from the Rosebud to Bismarck knows Bill and Calamity are headin' this way."

"They must really want us bad after what we done," Calamity said.

"They live by their ability to intimidate. And we made them look foolish. They can't let somethin' like that pass. People might stop bein' afraid to hand over their money, or to hide them out. They have to make an example of us."

They lolled around the fire, half-reclined on their bedrolls and McClellans. Belle looked especially tired, and was snoring softly. J. P. Paxton was drinking Arbuckle's. Slater and Clem and Hickok were finishing the bourbon.

Clem put down her cup. The Rosebud River was murmuring along its banks. She leaned back. Overhead, a carpet of stars shone with unwinking fixity, blocked only here and there by the stands of pine and cottonwood strung out along the riverbank. She pulled the muslin pouch of Bull Durham from her shirt pocket and began building a smoke.

"Bill," she said quietly, "why are we here?"

"To serve God and grow rich."

"We got a right to know. You understand that, of course. Even the Professor here. What we done in the Nations, we all signed up for. None of us asked for a bloody Cheyenne nightcap. Nor a Sioux haircut, neither. That's somethin' extra. And that could come tomorrow. Them Cheyenne Dog Soldiers and Sioux warriors is huntin' hair. If they find ours, we got a right to know why we been scalped."

Hickok stared into the fire. He poured another slug of whiskey into his mess cup.

"Custer and me, we went through some times that ain't worth talkin' 'bout. Scoutin' Injuns and the like. I seen and done a lot of things that'd drive another man to drink or Jesus or worse. If'n it'd been anyone other than Custer I was servin' under, hell, I'd've quit years before."

Hickok took off the tinted glasses. His gray-green eyes were opaque. He was staring sightlessly into the fire.

Calamity thought to herself, He's forty now, a long, hard forty. And Christ, he looks it. Sad, pale eyes dulled by the dust, scarred by the wind and glare of the high plains. They looked old to her, indescribably old. "The eyes," Paxton once called them, "of a man who's diced at the foot of the Cross, who's ridden with Ghengis Khan, who's been broken on the rack, and who knows in his heart there is nothing left to fear and nothing left to love." His words had made Calamity shudder.

"Was it in the Rebellion?" she asked.

"Yes, it was in the Rebellion," Hickok said, his voice muted. "It was when I was still a young man, wild and headstrong. I guess I'd made a name for myself with the snipin' of Generals Price and McCullough. And there'd been them other shootouts and killings as well as the War. I'd fought under Custer while he was just a boy. When he got me over to Virginia. The War, he said, was being decided in a forest called the Wilderness. Or so he thought.

HELLBREAK COUNTRY

"My job at the Wilderness was some of that there 'advance reconnaissance.' I was to cross no-man's-land, reconnoiter the enemy, avoid personal contact at all cost, and return with intelligence on his strengths, weaknesses, and the terrain.

"We were preparin' for the major offensive. Part of it was through a patch of forest ten miles across. We had to know what was happenin' in there. Two days before, another division had fought there, and the action had been fierce. Some said it was still goin' on. Custer wanted a report on that too, whether there were enemy in the woods, could we move our cavalry through all them trees and undergrowth.

"My report was important. Sheridan had ordered us to take them woods, and if I didn't return with contradictory evidence, Custer would assume the Wilderness could be taken. And at dusk of the following day, Custer and Sheridan would move through."

"Was it safe to cross?" Calamity asked.

"No. In fact, the fightin' in the Wilderness had never really ended. As I passed through the woods, I found whole divisions on both sides still at it. The forest was so huge, the undergrowth so dense, the thing just got lost. No one knew who was there or how many were fightin'. No one on the inside knew how big the battle was, let alone us bluebellies in the rear. I heard later that men fought in there for a year.

"As I moved toward the forest's middle, I got this scary feelin'. It was like I shouldn't be there and should get out. The men retreatin' told me that. But I was wild and headstrong, and I wanted a fight. And I was even goin' against orders too, for I'd been told not to engage the enemy. I was there to observe and report back. Nothin' more. But nothin' could stop me.

"So that night I climbed a pine tree and slept in the branches. I came down at midnight and continued. I wanted to reach the enemy lines under cover of night, reconnoiter them at dawn, kill a few with my Sharps, and get out."

"You crossed through no-man's-Land without gettin' spotted?" Slater asked with a puzzled look.

"Yes, but it was unreal, like nothin' I'd seen. A battle had gone on, might still be goin' on. But I couldn't see nothin'."

"You walked through a battle without seein' it?" Calamity asked. "How?"

Hickok poured himself another slug of Double Stamp bourbon.

"I couldn't see nothin'," Hickok said. "No corpses, no livin' men, no weapons. I couldn't even see trees. Four days the forest burned, and the woodsmoke was as thick as the hand before your face—parched your throat, burned your eyes. And anyways, there weren't no battle nohow. Just fightin'. And, God, there were that. Twenty, thirty thousand men fightin' in that wood. But never really a battle. Just these skirmishes, seldom more'n one against one. With all that smoke, the men retreatin' said they'd gotten busted up, disbanded. They said they fought the enemy all right, they just couldn't *see* him. Pretty soon they just fought anything. If a rifle flashed, they shot at it. If a man moved, made a noise, they shot at it. Thousands of bullets were whinin', singin' head-high, so they all just crouched.

"The rifle fire sounded pretty bad and the men looked awful scared. But I was young. I figured, I been there before. And anyway, the battle was over. I kept on goin'.

"Dawn came, and I was in the middle of that woods. Smoke so thick the sun glared into the haze. But now I could see a little better. The bodies were strewn everywhere, over everything. I couldn't even walk without trippin' on them. The dead—reb and Yankee alike—was bent over saplings, sprawled on the ground, twisted, blowed open over the brush. Come to a fence, and every rail'd be littered with corpses. They hung upside down in the trees. One man I come to, I still see in my sleep—his back down across the rail fence, his face up, his eyes red from the smoke. His mouth was grinnin', but his face was contorted in pain. Lots of men lay there like that, mouths crooked with wolfish grins, eyes red and swollen from the smoke, faces gruesome in their fear.

"And they was all over, wherever you walked, turned, or stepped. I'd seen dead men before, but not everywhere. You couldn't pass a bush, a bent sapling, a forked tree limb, a gully—nothin' in that wood was without a man dead, lyin' there with that awful grin, made more awful by the rifle fire and the smoke. Many of them was still groanin' and dyin' or just wounded or crazy with the fightin'. They groaned through the night, beggin' for help, howlin' with the pain, sobbin' from the horror.

"And by now there was the smell, too. It were warm, and some of them bodies was ripe, molderin' three or four days and turnin' maggoty. This were wild country too, and there was wolves and buzzards. Them buzzards was the worst. Buzzard don't care what he eats, not man nor beast nor each other. These turkey buzzards with snaky necks and bloody, crusted beaks and black feathers was perched on the branches and fenceposts and was flappin' and feedin' on the dead, some of them birds too full to fly and only able to roost there. Thousands of them and their half-gutted meals. And me walkin' through that terrible dawn on the way to the enemy lines.

"By now I weren't so young no more, nor so headstrong nor so brave. I was covered with the blood and maggot-stink from stumblin' and fallin' over the dead, and I was bone-tired and scared and sick and all empty inside.

"Then, sometime after dawn, I come to the camp, and the smoke'd thinned enough to see their fires. I found the enemy there. Ten thousand of Lee's men. They was just arrived that night. They was also up and mounted and rarin' to attack. They was all gathered for a breakthrough where us Yanks was weak, what with only Custer and Sheridan and their cavalry, which could not cross, that woods bein' too dense and dangerous and smoke-filled and all.

"Our Generals—ol' Pope and Hooker—had been foxed again by Lee. Lee was gonna hit them where there weren't nothin'. Nothin' 'cept Custer and his five hundred horse soldiers who would be stuck and stranded in that wood.

"Hell, I'd planned on tellin' Custer to keep out of that wood anyhow. It were too thick with smoke and undergrowth for no cavalry. As he soon would see. There was too much confusion, too many rebs shootin' rebs, bluebellies shootin' bluebellies. Only now there were this too, maybe ten thousand rebs, all startin' through that wood to shoot them some Yankees.

"I turned and started back, crouched at a half-run, when some rebel scout spots me and yells and opens fire. Then I was runnin' through this wood afoot, with six or eight rebs on horseback poundin' after me hell-for-leather, shoutin', 'Spy! Spy!'

"I was down a gully, into a stream, over a fence. The saplings and thorn bushes and pine branches tearin' my face every step. Then they was shootin' from everywhere, reb and bluebelly alike, screamin' 'Spy!' and openin' fire. The smoke was so thick they all thought I were agin them.

"I finally ended up in a gully, facedown in a pile of dead. Bullets whinin' everywhere in that wood. I'd try and stick a rifle butt up out of that hole, and minie balls'd shatter it before it got up a foot. From either direction. People was just shootin' at anything, at nothin'.

"I lay there all day in the stink, with the buzzards. Some of Bobby Lee's men slogged through that ravine, and I just lay facedown in the mud and let them tromp on me whilst I played dead. And after they tromped, I still lay there for hours.

"Now it were safe, but I still could not raise my head. I was paralyzed with the fear. It took me hours to crawl out of that pit of buzzards and maggots and gutted remains. And when I went after Custer I was no more a man, but somethin' that crawled through the muck and mud.

"How long I crawled I dasn't guess. Bullets sang and whined overhead and I knew my regiment had been slaughtered to a man, 'cause I had not got back to warn them.

"Hell, I knew if I got back, I would be shot. My job had been to avoid conflict with the enemy, observe and report back. I'd advanced too far.

"I guess I was near that old camp. I was half-mad with

fear, guilty for havin' lost all them men. Figurin' to desert, head out West, anything, anywhere, just get away.

"When there he were. I looked up, and there were Custer. All spick an' span, that saber in his hand, ramrod-straight in the saddle, out reconnoitering the results of some action. I tried to put my face down, play dead or hide, when he seen me.

"He charged straight for me, that saber cuttin' the smoke and mist. I just got up and ran through the brush, crazy with fear.

"Custer's a horseman. Good as there be. He'd cut me off, then chouse me out, then cut me out, and ride me down. Them hooves on his gelding were iron-hard, and I was crazy with fright as he ran me down.

"I ducked as he went by and his horse banged me down. When I got up, he was over me, astride that horse.

"'You're comin' back,' he says.

"'Not likely, sir', says I.

"Then he brains me with the flat of that saber, and that was that. And when I came to, we was ridin' into camp. Sheridan's there, and Grant. They're wavin' to Custer, not to me. I'm belly-down over his pommel like a skinned-out buck, ripe for the smokehouse.

"We get near the cooktent, and he throws me off. When I look up at him from the ground, he's still looking at me.

"'We're movin' out at four o'clock this mornin'. That gives you fifteen minutes to get some chow. You're scoutin' ahead, and I want you *ready*.'' He reins his mount around and starts for his tent. But he turns in his saddle, looks down at me, and says softly, 'Try to desert again, I'll have you shot.' ''

Hickok leaned back against his bedroll and laid his head on his McClellan. He stared up at the night sky.

"That all?'' Calamity asked. "You didn't desert or nothin'?''

"Hell, yes, that's all. Custer had me dead to rights, full fuckin' desertion. He lost hundreds of men, 'cause of me. God knows how many troops the Union lost, all told. Could've had me shot for cowardice in the face of the enemy as well.

Or put in Leavenworth for life. He could've killed me himself right there in that wood. But he didn't.''

"He gave you a second chance?" the Professor said.

"Wrong, pilgrim. He saved my life, then gimme a second chance. And I don't know why. It were Custer who gimme everything I later had, or might've had, or done. He gimme it. Not me. And I owed him. Just like that. And you know, I never figured out why he done it.''

"Lotta men call Custer a fool," Slater observed.

"Yeah, and I killed a lotta them for the sayin' of it.'' Hickok shut his eyes and said quietly, "You know, there's some things in this world you just never forget. The smoke and the stink and fear so thick in your throat you could choke on it. Then Custer comin' out of that haze, astride that black gelding, swingin' that saber. Then knockin' me out with it. Me—Wild Bill Hickok—slingin' me over his mount belly-down and carryin' me out of that infernal wood where at best I'd've died, was meant to have died. Some men call him crazy, but he's a great man. And if he thinks bringin' in Belle Starr and Frank and Jesse and Cole'll make him greater, he can have them too. Without Custer, I'd have died back there in the Wilderness.''

"The Wilderness? Is that all that give you them terror dreams?" Calamity asked. "I figured it was that diamond queen.''

"That, the diamond queen and that wood too. All them soldiers and the buzzards and Custer and the smoke. As long as I live, I'll never forget it, none of it.''

73

At first light they broke camp and began their bitter ride along the west bank of the Rosebud River. The Rosebud was not much of a stream—three or four feet deep, barely a hundred feet across, cutting through the Badlands. The trip was grim, nothing but buttes and bluffs, gullies and dry washes. The ground was as hard as brick. What little grama and bluestem and buffalo grass had twisted up through the hardpan had been eaten off at the roots by Custer's stock. If they had not brought their own feed from Fort Lincoln, their animals would have starved.

The trail was clear, and they traveled all day and most of the night. Toward noon the next day, they reached the end of the Rosebud and turned off onto an old Indian trail.

They followed Custer's troops. The tracks of unshod Indian ponies and iron-hoofed cavalry mounts mixed in the inch-thick alkali dust. The land around them, with its endless ridges and swells, its gorges and ravines, was now not only treeless bur virtually denuded of grass as far as the eye could see.

"Where's the graze?" Calamity said, coming up between Hickok and Slater, who were riding point, studying the trail.

"It's been et up."

"Custer's stock ate up the whole fuckin' country? His few hundred lousy horses? Not likely, pilgrim." When they were silent, Calamity continued, "Our mounts is gonna get mighty sick of oats if a few fuckin' horses need that much forage."

"Them Injun ponies they're followin' ate it up," said Slater.

Calamity's face was expressionless. "That means there's one hell of a lot of Injuns."

"Yep."

"Thinkin' 'bout headin' back?"

"To where? The closest cavalry I know of is 'bout half a day's ride. Pull tight, push hard, and keep six beans in your wheel. Keep that Winchester full, sixteen fuckin' rounds. Them Injuns are up ahead."

"Just looks like a lotta little camps," Calamity said, pointing to the abandoned remains of skins and lodgepoles, scattered here and there. "Every few miles we come by one of these here camps. I think there's lots of little huntin' parties travelin' this trail."

"It's all one party," Slater said evenly.

"You mean all them lodges these last ten miles is all one party?"

"Yep."

Calamity whistled. "Some party."

They went on that day, and the weather was scorching. When they stopped to grain and water the stock, they had to unsaddle the horses and unpack the mules. The animals were lathering badly and had to be rubbed down and dried off with whatever rags or clumps of weeds they could scavenge.

They rode that night. At dawn they came to a deep, wooded ravine where they grazed and rested the stock. Then they pushed on.

By noon they had reached another wooded divide, and by late afternoon, in the far distance they could see a trail leading to a steep bluff. South of the bluff curved and twisted the snaky tail of a wide river.

"You know that river?" Calamity asked Hickok.

"Yeah, the Sioux call it the Greasy Grass. Don't know our name for it."

"Probably Grant or Sherman or something," Slater said drily. "Some egg-suckin' Yankee general."

They followed the trail up the long slope to the distant bluff. The footing was dry, and the air was filled with dust. They pulled wet bandannas over their noses and mouths.

The air began to stink. Dismounting, they dog-trotted up the rise and peered over.

The Greasy Grass River meandered downstream; Custer's trail turned north along the river's bluff. They mounted and went on.

Two miles upstream they came to a creek. As they forded it, they smelled the stench of offal. Over the horizon a dark funnel-cloud was forming. Calamity joined Hickok and Slater up front, while Belle stayed behind, where she watched over J. P. Paxton, who was rubbing neat's-foot oil into his saddle galls.

Slater was saying, "I thought them big buff herds was gone."

"They are," Hickok agreed.

"Then what's that there buzzard cloud floating over the rise?"

"I don't know, but one of us better go on ahead and find out."

The three of them were halfway through the creek when Hickok kneed his horse, threashing through the water, up the bank and out of the shallow draw.

Calamity started to follow, but Slater said, "No, it's better one person goes up front. And this one here is Bill's show."

They climbed out of the creek. Belle trotted up behind, and J. P. Paxton took up the rear. Both, Calamity noted, bounced gingerly on their saddles. Calamity also observed that Belle kept glancing over her shoulder at the Professor. She was touched that Belle had kept an eye on him throughout the trip.

They strung out four abreast, with Belle and the Professor pulling the jerk-line strings. Calamity could see the tornado-cloud of vultures, growing larger as more and more birds entered it, darker, more ominous, hundreds of them now in a whirling vortex above the valley.

Hickok was well ahead, and the going was rough. Everything was coulees, arroyos, cutbanks. Those they could not ride through, they went around, and by the time they rode out of the last ravine, Slater pointed to Belle and the Professor and motioned them back toward a clump of trees they had just ridden past.

The funnel-cloud of carrion birds was now several hundred feet high.

"You better get back," Slater said to Calamity.

"Why? You gonna slap me again? Like in the Needle?"

He grimaced tightly. "Naw, it's them buzzards. I hear that when the buff died, buzzards and wolves bred like wildfire. Now they attack anything, alive or dead. With no more buff to eat, them birds and wolves is crazy-mad with hunger. And they've increased maybe tenfold. Wouldn't want you eaten whole by no buzzard nor wolf.''

"Fuck you."

She lashed at the gray with the *romal*-ends of her reins and pounded up the rise at a hard lope. At the top she found herself on the perimeter of the whirling cloud. Overhead, a flaring spiral, hundreds of feet across at the summit, wheeled endlessly on spread wings. At the funnel's top they drifted on thermal drafts, floating in patient vigil. But as they dipped their wings and swooped, the bottom spiral tightened, the birds' speed accelerated, their landings became loud and violent, with shrieking cries, flapping wings, and arched talons. And down below on the battleground, a second field of death piled high, as the ravenous vultures fought and killed each other over the remains of Custer's dead.

Calamity dismounted at the top of the hill and gripped her mount by the cheek strap. His eyes were walled, and he was shying at the smell of blood and the sight of tearing, slashing buzzards and the gathering packs of wolves surrounding the killing ground. Calamity was a good rider, but she did not trust her mount. Horses spooked at death and sudden movements.

And down that hill, all the way to the river, were the remains of hundreds of bluebellies. Rotting in the sun.

Hickok had made it down the slope. Spurring his mount, whipping the birds away with the big black sombrero, he'd forced his roan into the center of the vortex. At least that was how he was now leaving the funnel-cloud, charging back up the hill, still flailing at the buzzards with his hat, his horse wild-eyed with fright. Calamity and Slater vaulted onto their mounts and rode down to meet him.

A man was slung over Hickok's pommel, belly-down, his long blond bloody hair waving in the wind, a bullet through his temple, another in his heart.

Now Slater was kicking his mount hard, beating back the flapping birds with his own hat. Calamity flogged them with her quirt, spurred her mount, and closed the gap between herself and Hickok. She reached him halfway down the slope, and he passed her, kicking his mount over and over up the ridge. She wheeled the gray and followed him, covering his flank, only now she was starting to cry. For she'd seen the man belly-down over the roan. It was Custer.

When she caught up with Hickok, Slater was already alongside him.

"Put him down, Hickok. I said put him down."

Hickok pulled away toward the top of the hill, and then Slater closed in on him, grabbed his horse's headstall, jerked him up shirt, and said, "Leave him here, please. He'd want to be with his men."

Hickok reined in his blowing roan. He let Slater take the general under an arm and lift him off. Slater dropped him there on the slope and lashed Hickok's horse with his own *mecate*. Both of their mounts shot up out of the basin. Calamity put her head down, and holding her Stetson over her horse's eyes, she booted him up the steep bank away from the Greasy Grass—known to whites as the Little Bighorn.

74

When they reached the stand of pine up on the knoll, Belle had watered, grained, and staked out the stock. Calamity dismounted quickly and uncinched and unsaddled the remaining mounts. Silently she and Slater pulled up clumps of dried-out grama grass and began rubbing them down. Belle strapped morrals full of oats over the horses' noses.

"How'd it go?" the Professor finally asked, staring at the darkening spiral of birds.

"Not good," said Slater. "They got Custer." He glanced up at Clem. "Reynolds too. I saw him with the rest."

Otherwise they said nothing. Belle knelt at the fire and poured herself a cup of Arbuckle's. Hickok slowly rooted through the cross-buck packsaddles lying on the ground. Out of the kyacks he eventually dug his crampons, sniper scope, and rawhide reata. He walked over to the tallest of the pines and clamped the spikes on the soles of his boots. He shoved the sniper scope in his pants, looped the trunk, and began walking up the side of the eight-foot-thick pine, flipping the reata up the tree every couple of steps.

"What's he doing?" the Professor asked Clem.

"Lookin' for Injuns. Tryin' to find a way out of here."

Hickok had an unobstructed view of the entire Little Bighorn Valley. And with the twelve-power scope, he could see almost to the Rosebud.

When he climbed down a half hour later, Hickok said, "There's a string of Injuns, maybe ten thousand or so, plus twice that many ponies, movin' west of here. Them that done Custer in. They ain't botherin' us, though. We're headin' north. Belle here's headin' east."

"Why east?" Belle asked.

"Thirty miles down our backtrail, your men are poundin' hard. They got fresh mounts and blood in their eyes. You'll meet them in a few hours if you ride hard. You won't wanna be with us if'n they catch up."

"You ain't keepin' me for no hostage?"

Hickok shook his head. "We got nothin' against you. Hell, I almost even like you, though you sure take some gettin' used to. We don't need you for bait anymore. Cut out a good mount and get back to your friends. There ain't no Injuns to trouble you in that direction."

"You don't have to ask me twice." Belle stood up, untied a lass rope from a saddlestring, and walked over to the remuda. She roped out a big bay gelding. Nuzzling and gentling him, she said to the others, "For whatever it's worth, you ain't gonna have no trouble from them James-Younger boys. Leastways not here."

"Why not?" Calamity asked.

"They can read a trail as well as anybody. And better'n Custer. They know there's Injuns 'round here. They start slingin' lead, them ten thousand redskins'll be all over them. The boys may be crazy, but they ain't stupid."

She threw a McClellan onto the bay's back. She buckled the cinch, slipped a bridle on and swung into the saddle.

Clem noted that she slipped into the fork with apparent discomfort. Belle looked at Hickok and grinned. "You know, back East they call this the Heartland?"

Hickok shook his head. He turned and waved at the tornado cloud of vultures. "Heartbreak country's more like it," he said. "It broke Custer's heart and Charley Reynolds's. It's broken mine."

Belle sat there on the big bay. She was a striking figure in her black shirt, black twill *charro* pants, and leather vest. She removed her black Stetson, and her long, coal-black hair tumbled down her back.

"Hellbreak's more like it."

Belle threw her head back and laughed. "Bullshit. Hickok, you're goin' on to Deadwood. To whiskey, cards, and sweet Calamity Jane. All you gotta fear is them diamond queens."

Belle smiled widely, and Clem thought with real jealousy that Belle was a handsome woman.

Turning gingerly in her McClellan, Belle looked down over her shoulder and yelled, "You don't have to worry none 'bout them ol' boys anyway."

"Why's that?"

"They're goin' back on the owlhoot. They're too broke to waste any more time searchin' you out. They needed that bank money like generals need wars."

"Yeah, but you got a reason to get them sore at us," Calamity said. "We kidnapped you, threatened you, dragged you all over creation." Calamity waved toward the vulture cloud spiraling above the Little Bighorn. "We coulda cost you that long black hair. It could be hangin' on Crazy Horse's war lance right now."

"You cost me shit. You ain't left me nothin' 'cept wiser and still alive." She was staring now at Slater.

"Then you take care," Calamity said. "I'm gettin' right fond of you."

"Same here." She whirled her horse around till she faced Hickok directly. She raked him up and down with a hard stare. "You know, Hickok, I wish I'd met you under other circumstances. You must be some kinda man, the way people—even fuckin' generals—depend on you. Only kind of men I seem to meet are murderin' outlaws like them Jameses and''—Belle sneered—''whimperin' limp-dicks like Cole Younger.''

"Give our best to them boys," Hickok replied.

"Hell, they ask me, you four died here with Custer—with your scalps off and your boots on."

She waved her hat to them, whirled the bay around, and headed down the slope at a dead run.

Slater stood. He walked over to his saddle and untied his own lass-rope.

"Ladies, gents," he said hoarsely, "I got to be leavin'."

"But the party ain't started," Calamity said.

"For me it has. In a little while this river country's gonna be crawlin' with bluebellies. I best be gone."

"So?" Calamity said. "Them federals got no jurisdiction over you. And the four of us got some hell to raise in Deadwood."

"Not likely. Them federals got *mucho* jurisdiction all over me. Them bluebellies catch me, I'm goin' back to Yuma. It's a federal jail, you know."

"Would they really send you there?" the Professor asked.

"Pronto, pilgrim."

Slater started toward the remuda, but Calamity stopped him.

"Torn, take the Appaloosa, then."

Slater turned, shaking his head. "No way. Bill bought him for you special. That's your own pet pony."

"He wanted me to have him, 'cause of this hard travelin' we done. You got the hard miles now," she said.

Slater disagreed. "All I got's whiskey, Sweet Rosemary, and one more train to rob."

"I doubt that," Calamity said.

Slater roped the Appaloosa out of the remuda. The white pony with the high, strong cannons and the big spotted rump was snorting at his new rider, glancing sideways at Clem. But finally he trotted up to Slater, obedient if wary.

"Where you really headin'?" Calamity asked.

"The high lines, the owlhoot trail," Slater said with a terse smile. He swung his McClellan onto the spotted pony and cinched up.

" 'War's end, odyssey's beginning'?" the Professor reminded him.

"Okay, pilgrim," said Slater. "Suppose I do drift down to Yuma? Suppose I do have a score to settle?"

Hickok stood up. He walked over to Slater and borrowed his reata, then roped out a second horse, a line-backed sorrel with strong flanks and heavy hocks.

"That's a hard-rock jail you figure on breakin' into. Stark catches you again, he's gonna make them last three years look like Sunday-go-to-meetin'."

Slater put his left hand on the horn. He started to swing into the saddle, then stopped. He turned and gave all three of them a long look.

"Yeah," he said. "I'd like to pass on that part, too. 'Cept there's one thing I just can't stop thinkin' on—that old doctor back in Yuma. 'Least he gimme somethin', somethin' special. All that talk 'bout souls and odysseys and such, I'm thinkin' maybe that old man with all that crazy talk did somethin' besides keepin' me alive them three years. Now it's like Stark took it away."

"Leave it be, Torn," said Calamity.

"There's some things you don't leave undone."

"Killin' Stark ain't gonna do that old man no good."

"It'll do *me* some good." Slater swung onto the Appaloosa.

The horse was confused by the new master on his back. Calamity walked over to him and rubbed the horse's nose.

"You sure that's part of your odyssey?" the Professor asked.

" 'War's end, odyssey's beginning.' That's what the old man said. And my war ain't ending till I kill Stark." Slater patted the Appaloosa's neck.

Calamity let go of her pet. Slater swung him around and loped down the hill, south, leading the strong-hocked sorrel by the *mecate*. He waved farewell with his Stetson.

Hickok and Calamity began roping mounts out of the remuda. Tossing a loop on her gray, Calamity said, "Professor, you best be comin' with us for a while. This Hellbreak Country's full of Injuns and outlaws.'' Nodding to the vultures, she continued, ''And other hungry types. So cinch up tight.''

Hickok added, '' 'Cause them saddles will turn.''

They swung onto their mounts, and the three of them headed on into the Dakotas.

AFTERWORD

Battle of the Little Bighorn

Fought June 25, 1876, the Battle of the Little Bighorn murdered more than Custer's army career and political ambitions, and the men of the Seventh Cavalry. It also portended disaster for the Sioux Nation. In a medicine dream, one hour before the battle, their famous war shaman, Sitting Bull, foresaw this doom. An Indian massacre, he believed, would occur not at the Little Bighorn but might transpire years later. He prophesied that if the Sioux stole the horses and stripped the clothes of the Long Knives, the dead would wreak their revenge.

The Seventh Cavalry exacted this vengeance at the Massacre of Wounded Knee.

The James-Younger Gang

Fate did not deal kindly with the James-Younger gang.

For years Frank and Jesse James—the gang's leaders—had debated the wisdom of robbing Missouri banks. Jesse argued that no jury in Clay or Jackson counties would convict a member of the gang, and so they should stick to banks in those counties. In the minds of Missourians, the gang was seen not so much as outlaws, but as war heroes: men, brave and true, who'd ridden with Quantrill, fought Jim Lane's Jayhawkers and Charles Jennison's red-legs in a time when peaceful men feared to raise their voices.

But Frank held sway. He argued that if they continued to rob Missouri banks, they would provoke the politicians and power-brokers who owned and banked in those institutions. And no one, Frank argued, beat those boys for long.

Their next job was on September 7, 1876. It was a Minnesota bank, and the gang went there by train. Dressed in white dusters and low-crowned black slouch hats, and transporting a boxcar full of thoroughbred getaway horses, the gang was hardly inconspicuous.

So by the time the train pulled into Northfield, Minnesota, the townspeople and constabulary were amply warned. Not only were the citizens alert and waiting, but the bank's vault was now kept indefinitely on lock.

When the gang robbed the bank, they were in for a series of ugly surprises.

The vault was not only unopenable, but a reckless teller commenced firing at them with a .45. Jesse James killed him on the spot, but now the townspeople were ready.

When the men reached the street, flat broke and on the run, they were in for a fight.

In quick succession, Frank and Jesse were shot through the legs. Jesse was then also blasted with a shotgun. Jim Younger was shot through the shoulder, then had his jaw blown off. Bob Younger had his right elbow fragmented. Cole was shot eleven times.

They escaped somehow, nearly bleeding to death.

Two days later, Frank and Jesse abandoned their cousins in a secluded ravine. Shot to pieces, they took off riding double, and somehow made it—thirteen hundred miles—back to Missouri.

As for the Youngers, their subsequent years were grim. Jim committed suicide. Bob died in prison. Cole did twenty-five years, hard time, and, after his release, took up the calling of his youth—preaching sermons and testifying, using what he called "my misspent life as my text."

As for Jesse James, he died under a cloud. He was shot in the back, purportedly by a friend, Robert Ford.

Only Frank lived his life in peace. He surrendered to Missouri authorities after his brother's murder, and true to Jesse's prediction, no jury in Missouri would send a James to jail.

Acquitted on all counts, he quietly lived out his years.

Belle Starr

Belle's remaining life was shockingly controversial. She lived in the Nations with a succession of outlaws, each worse than the last. To be her lover meant almost certain death. The fates of these men bespeak her life.

—Cole Younger twenty-five years in prison.

—Jim Reed (one of the Jess James-Younger gang) shot to death, 1874.

—Sam Starr killed, 1886.

—John Middleton shot by Sam Starr. Motive: Jealousy.

—Blue Duck, Belle's lover, killed 1886.

—Jack Spaniard hanged in 1889.

—Jim July killed by lawman Heck Thomas in 1890.

—Jim French shot in 1895.

Her brothers and children succumbed in other ways: Her brother, Bud, was killed by federals. Her other brother slain mysteriously in 1867. Her daughter by Cole, Pearl Younger, turned daughter of joy.

As to Belle's own fate, she died as she lived. For years she was reputed by friends and neighbors to have engaged in an incestuous, sado-masochistic relationship with her son, Jim Reed. One night when he took her pet black stallion out for a ride without her permission, she surprised her eighteen-year-old son asleep in bed and quirted him viciously.

He left home. And two weeks later, finding her alone on a country road, riding the horse over which she had flogged him, he cut her in two with a double-barreled shotgun.

He was later killed in a barroom brawl.

James Butler "Wild Bill" Hickok

As for James Butler Hickok, he and Calamity materialized in Deadwood that summer.

But Hickok's character would be his fate.

Deadwood was a wide-open town. Scores of saloons and brothels and gambling houses flourished, even though they had no legal right to exist. This was Sioux Territory, and sacred land at that. And since there was no official law to protect the decent citizens, a criminal underground ran Deadwood and tyrannized the populace.

When Hickok, Calamity, and J.P. Paxton rode into Deadwood that fateful summer day, they were greeted with cheers. The citizenry looked to Hickok for salvation. They hoped he would deliver them from lawlessness as he had delivered the citizens of those legendary hurrah towns, Hayes and Abilene.

It was not to be.

Hickok had learned his lesson by now. He'd tamed towns before, only to be driven out of those same towns by the people he'd saved, an exile, an outcast, a pariah. From the lawman's point of view, town-taming was a thankless trade.

Then there were his eyes. After his return, they rapidly deteriorated. Beyond twenty-five feet he was virtually blind, and for prolonged periods he could not see anything. Hickok needed money, but marshaling was no longer possible.

Professional gambling seemed his best bet. Or so Hickok thought. And he gambled each night.

But fame made him visible, and hence vulnerable. Too many men harbored imagined slights, and too many gunpunks hoped to build a name on Hickok's corpse. It now seemed that the card tables were filled with such players. And these were the men who haunted his nights as the scarcity of gold dust plagued his days.

And still the rumors of his return to marshaling grew. The Deadwood criminals saw Hickok as a clear and present danger. His Navy Colts could wreck their rule, end their profitable reign.

And the rumors grew.

Hickok did nothing to quiet the furor. One night he stormed into a notorious outlaw saloon. He openly challenged the gunmen to throw down on him, promising them "cheap funerals" if they tried. Then he humiliated them by taking the guns away from every man in the bar.

Two local crime figures named Varney and Brady hired a gunman to terminate this threat. They promised him money and legal immunity if he would kill James Butler Hickok.

The money was raised and the murder contract accepted by a man named Jack McCall, whom Hickok had staked and befriended.

McCall's chance came one day in the Deadwood #10 Saloon. For the first time in his life, Hickok sat with his back to the door.

He was holding a good hand: two aces and two eights.

But the fifth card was the Diamond Queen.

McCall sneaked up behind him, placed the muzzle of his pistol under Hickok's right ear, and blew off his head.

The townspeople who'd started the rumors that cost Hickok his life were too frightened to follow.

Only Calamity went after McCall.

Her gun was Hickok's Sharps rifle.

When McCall saw that it was Clem with the heavy rifle, he ducked into a shop, looking to hide. But she flushed him out, disarmed him, and turned him over to the unofficial law.

Just as they promised, Brady and Varney hung McCall's jury and he went free.

But a wave of protest swept the Dakotas. McCall was recaptured in Yankton and was indicted, tried, and sentenced in a day.

On March 1, 1877, Hickok's killer was hanged.

But even in death, Hickok was not safe. Souvenir hunters by the thousands thronged his gravesite. Headstone after headstone, monument after monument was chipped to bits by fanatical relic-hunters who sought from the stone some tangible talisman of the strength and the courage that had marked Hickok's life.

Even worse, in 1879, when the cemetery was relocated, Hickok's body had to be disinterred. To Calamity's dismay, the grave had been robbed. The Navy Colts with the ivory handles, and the Sharps rifle, which had been laid beside him in his coffin, were gone.

In death, Hickok, protector of property, upholder of the law, had himself been set upon by thieves.

James Butler Hickok—the man who had killed a grizzly with a bowie knife, fought the Sioux, Cheyenne, and Kiowa, spied for the Union, and tamed Hayes and Abilene almost singlehandedly—why had he done it?

As the years went by, biographers pondered the meaning of Hickok's life. Was he, as some maintained, "in love with death"? Had he really been repaying "a debt of honor"? To some scholars it seemed that Hickok's death was more than a killing; it was the end of an epoch. Hickok was born in a time of trouble—the Civil War, the Indian campaigns, the lawless violence of cowtowns and mining camps. More than any man of that time, more than Lincoln, Custer, Billy Bonney, or Sitting Bull, Hickok came to personify his age. In the Civil War he was the sort of man who killed generals and to whom, in time of trouble, the generals turned. During the Indian campaigns he scouted for Custer. In civilian life he was the savior of cattle barons and the common citizen—and the bane of the outlaw's existence. He was extolled in books, dramatized on stage, rhapsodized in the press.

But all this time his sands were running out, for Hickok's era was coming to a close. A new world was being born, a world that had no use for a Lincoln or a Custer, a Billy Bonney or a Sitting Bull, and likewise had no further use for Hickok. He had to die. If Hickok's assassination was manifestly destined, his very life had cocked and fired McCall's gun. For if a man's life comes too closely to exemplify his age, when those times change, the man must die.

So in the end the trail was too tearful and bloody, the land too big—too big for all of them. It broke all their hearts.

James Butler Hickok, 1837–1876, *Requiescat in Pace*.

Martha "Calamity Jane" Cannary

Calamity spent the rest of her life pining for Hickok. When she died on August 2, 1902, the townspeople of Deadwood graciously interred her remains in the Deadwood Cemetery.

Alongside Hickok's grave.

While never joined in life, they were so joined in death. Side by side, their gravesites lie on Mount Moriah in Deadwood, South Dakota, and may be visited to this day.

Two men crouched behind boulders. They both wore Plainsman's hats, broadcloth shirts, and canvas pants. And a lot of pistols. They carried six apiece. The pistols were 45's and the lighter Navy Colts, rechambered to take the new .38-caliber cartridges. Their mounts, a sturdy Appaloosa and a big roan war pony, were staked out behind them. Each of these also packed a brace of revolvers, heavy Walker horse pistols, the most powerful and accurate handguns made.

The larger of the men, well over six feet, was studying a massive railroad trestle which spanned a huge, almost impossibly deep chasm. He studied the trestle with its network of X-shaped underpinnings, its endless array of criss-crossed planks and beams. It seemed impregnable, substantial enough to endure anything—freight trains, earthquakes, even outlaws like themselves.

Carpenter turned to the big man and said: "Here, let me have a look."

Torn Slater handed him the spyglass. "See where we put the charges?"

Carpenter nodded. Yes, he could see them. A hundred feet from the eastern wall of the chasm, fifty-two separate charges were packed, braced, and jammed into numerous junctures of heavy wood cross-beams. Fifty-two charges that were laid approximately fifteen to twenty-five feet below the track. These blocks of explosive each contained between five and fifty sticks of sweaty dynamite. The task of planting them at strategic intervals between those criss-crossed pine planks was something that Carpenter would like to forget—he and Slater with haversacks of wet dynamite, packed in sawdust and strapped to their backs. Climbing hand over hand amid that endless, labyrinthine maze of beams and crossbars, forming what seemed to be an intricate matrix of infinite X's, stretching from the top of the trestle to the bottom of the gorge some fifteen hundred feet below. He and Slater wedging the tightly wrapped dynamite bundles into the X-shaped cross-beams, lashing them to the underpinnings with wire, then twisting the ends tight with pliers. Periodically, they went up top and loaded their packs with more blocks of dynamite, more caps, more wire. Into the abyss they returned, set the charges, lashed them secure, hoping that the bridge did not blow up in their faces then and there.

Finally the last charge was laid. A whopper—fifty sticks of dynamite in all. A giant square of explosive three feet on the edge, wired a stick at a time, flush against the south face of the trestle. This was to be Slater's target and detonator. He would blast it with his Sharps "Big Fifty" rifle when the train was almost over the chasm, blowing to high hell the second half—the one with the two hundred blue-bellies on it. The other fifty-one wired-up charges were so placed that when the big sheet of dynamite went, it would set off a chain reaction.

Carpenter peered through the spyglass at their handiwork. He was able to make out the big three-foot square of explosive, but it wasn't easy. The other charges were virtually invisible.

"Goddamn, Slater, can't we get closer? How on God's good earth are you going to hit that postage stamp from here, six hundred yards away?"

Slater just grinned.

Cimarron Rose was up behind them. "Hell, Torn here can shoot the balls off a runnin' buck at six hundred yards. Ain't that right, baby?"

"Don't know about that, but Carpenter, you see that bend in the track where the train, after leavin' its back half in the chasm, takes almost a right-angle turn and comes barrelin' down the desert straight at us? Right where we be sittin' now?"

"I follow."

"Well, don't worry about me hittin' the charge. You just worry about that Gatling gun on the flatcar, the one they be pushin' out in front of the locomotive. 'Cause, boy, they got a one hundred-caliber Gatling *leadin'* that fuckin' train. You know the effective range on a Gatling?"

"Of course."

"A thousand yards. A thousand fuckin' yards. And don't say they'll be shootin' it off a movin' flatcar so it won't be that accurate. 'Cause what they'll be shootin' is one thousand rounds per minute. Hell, if this here 'Big Fifty' fired a thousand rounds per minute, I could get up alongside the bridge, blow the trestle, and still nail them Gatling-gunners even though the train was high-ballin' *away* from me at sixty miles per hour, that is, one mile per minute, that is, thirty fuckin' yards per second. No, this way they still be high-ballin', but they be high-ballin' right into my sights."

"Aren't you forgetting something?" Carpenter said.

Slater shrugged.

"You'll be starin' right into their sights, too. Into the sights of a hundred-caliber Gatling. That's one inch in diameter, in case you forgot. When they come high-ballin' up that track, they're gonna cut you down like they were choppin' cotton."

"That's why I have you." Slater was smiling. The smile wasn't pretty.

"To do what?"

"To draw their fire. See that long line of boulders on the other side of the track?" The southbound section of track was about fifty feet from them. On the other side was a string of wagon-sized boulders. "You're gonna set up ten or fifteen powder charges on top of them boulders. Get yourself a red-hot stogie, and when the action starts, run up and down them rocks, settin' off the diversion. Hell, you'll get so much smoke explodin', them Gatlin'-gunners'll think it's fuckin' Shiloh."

"I'm gonna draw their fire? Uh, they be firin' one-inch rounds, about a thousand per minute. Range on those rocks will quickly reach point-blank, or pretty close to."

Cimarron Rose was grinning widely. Slater merely nodded.

"I could get killed," Carpenter said. "I mean, have you ever seen one of those Gatling guns in action?" Slater nodded. "Each of those rounds is four times bigger than your Sharps 'Big Fifty' bullets. And those 'Big Fifties' are considered goddamn big. I don't like it. I don't like goin' head-to-head with Gatlings."

"Like fightin' a grain thresher with kid gloves."

"I don't like this. I don't like it at all."

"Yeah, but if I don't get two clean shots at them Gatling-gunners, we ain't never stoppin' that train. And I just don't shoot well dodgin' rapid-fire artillery."

"So it's my turn in the barrel?"

"We each get a turn."

"I don't like it."

"Well, I do," Rose blurted out. "I like you settin' off charges and dodgin' hundred-caliber, thousand-round-per-minute bullets. I like it just fine."

It was dawn the next day, and Carpenter stood by the boulders watching the red sun blaze over the rimrock, throwing off shafts of red and purple and bright orange. Overhead a buzzard wheeled, keeping his patient, solitary vigil. For personal company, a mosquito, left over from the night, keened, waiting for a chance to strike.

Carpenter was developing a strange identification with this desperate beast.

It was then that Slater whistled to him, and, turning toward the trestle, Carpenter saw a big eight-wheeler Baldwin locomotive materialize out of nowhere. It was grinding toward the trestle like a black, hulking monster, an endless explosion of embers, smoke, and sparks belching out of its diamond-shaped stack. Its profusion of bright, polished brass glinted and flashed in the early dawn. Steam rose from under the wheels like fumes floating up from the pit of hell. As it inched onto the trestle, its whistle shrilled and wailed, chilling Carpenter to his soul.

But if the Baldwin chilled Carpenter, it was nothing compared to the thing on the flatbed that the Baldwin was pushing. For the lead car carried the bolted-down Gatling, ringed by sandbags. The big gun's muzzle, sweeping back and forth across the rails, was capable of cutting down anything in its way.

The two soldiers manning the Gatling waved the engineer forward, and slowly the locomotive moved across the bridge. First the Gatling. Then the locomotive, with its firebox and stack. The tender, stacked with cords of wood, the mail car. And then a whole succession of freight cars loaded with Rodmans, Bottle Dahlgrens, Mountain Mortars, Hotchkiss Guns, crates of Winchesters, shells, shot, powder, carriages, and accessories.

One, two, three, four, five, six, the freight cars rolled. When the sixth reached the other side, Carpenter knew it would be time. Slater would attempt to set off the square-shaped charge. The charge which, from Carpenter's vantage point, wasn't even postage-stamp-size.

It couldn't be seen at all.

Shoot the balls off a running buck at six hundred yards? Bullshit! Six hundred yards was over a third of a mile, and at that distance, scope or no scope, it couldn't be done. They should have gotten closer, that was all. Carpenter should have insisted. That way, at least they would have blown the train. At least, they would have had a shot at the two Gatlings. This way Slater would take his shot, inevitably miss, and then—

The roar of the "Big Fifty" caught Carpenter by surprise. His first reaction was to stare at the source of the noise, the detonation of the hundred and seventy grains of black powder which had sent the seven hundred-grain cylindrical lead slug rocketing toward the trestle six hundred yards away. The next blast, a full second and a half later, startled Carpenter even more.

He was so stunned that he'd forgotten the plan to blow the trestle was based on chain detonation, not one big bang. So when the next fifty-one blasts followed, first singly, then merging into one horrendous, echoing, ear-cracking roar, his bowels almost released.

Carpenter had been to the wars, and had seen a lot of work with explosives. But nothing seemed to him so—so—beautifully, that was it, so beautifully executed as the way Slater had mined and charged and then set off that trestle.

First there had been the timing. Slater had done something here which Carpenter hadn't believed possible. He'd coordinated the explosion with a moving object—down to the last millimeter, down to the last second. And the bridge blew at the exact moment that the sixth freight car crossed over. Bang. Right on the button. Just like that. Then there were the fifty-two separate, then suddenly merging blasts, culminating into the most horrific, ear-shattering sound Carpenter had ever heard.

Then came the catastrophic results. Most explosions were routine. Due to problems in the timing of the detonation systems, these blasts had to be limited to stationary objects like buildings. Hence, half the burst was absorbed by the ground, or dramatically slowed down by walls and ceiling and floors.

Not so with the trestle. The thousand pounds of dynamite was packed near its top, so the only things above the explosive were criss-crossed beams and planks, train rails, and, above those, six or eight freight cars. The only thing below the explosive was a quarter mile of timbers and planks.

And, indeed, Carpenter had never seen or heard one like it. It didn't simply blow. It blew and blew and blew. It began with a *ka-ka-ka* which quickly merged into a steady protracted *kaaaaaaa* which then merged into a *kaaaa-whummmmp-kaaa-whummmmppp!* which then finally blew into a numbing, rumbling, deafening, gut-churning *KA!WHUMP!WHUMP!WHUMP!WHUMMPPP!*

Then the trestle began to move. If it seemed to move slowly, that may have been because Carpenter was so far away. The burst was also going in four directions at once—down into the gorge, which was visible from Carpenter's vantage point, to each side of the gorge, and high above the gorge.

First there was a lot of smoke, a great billowing ball of it which obscured much of the view. Nonetheless, it was possible to see through and around enough of the cover to realize that the freight cars were literally breaking into a myriad of fragments, and simultaneously levitating. At the same time, the trestle beneath and around the blast was dissolving.

Then the ball of smoke slowly metamorphosed into fire. The ball grew bigger and bigger, burning off the white smoke, bigger, bigger, till the top of the ball simply exploded with a deafening *KA-WHUMPPP!* and quickly outswelled the smaller fiery globe six to eight times, until the red-orange fire-cloud took on the shape of a mushroom.

The blast was no longer fragmenting the trestle and the cars. The hellish heat was so intense everything simply evaporated in its path. Only the fragments from the initial blow-up survived somewhat intact. Many were pelting and showering Carpenter in a sooty, smoke-blackened hail of charred splinters and dirt.

After a veritable eternity the fireball receded—slowly, ever so slowly, and as it did, a surprising quantity of debris came back down after it, debris that had been blown thousands of feet into the air. It almost seemed to Carpenter as if the bits and pieces of wood and steel were returning to what had once been the trestle to take their exact, same, rightful place, precisely where they'd been before, and once again to keep right on spanning the chasm. Only, when these bits and pieces returned they did not stop, but kept right on falling, because now that the fire and smoke had receded, Carpenter could clearly see that there was no more trestle. It was simply gone, dispersed, as if it had never been. It was almost as though it had vanished unseen, as in a dream. There were only shards and slivers, dust and ashes, falling back from the sky and into the canyon. Nothing remained of the-thing-that-was.

Except the first half of the train.

Miraculously, the train had survived. It stood there on the track in that blasted, voided silence, its engine still chugging, steam rising up from under the wheels, sparks and smoke pouring out of the diamond-shaped stack. Then the whistle wailed and the drive wheels turned, and the next thing Carpenter knew the train was hauling ass, peeling around the bend, barreling down the south-bound track toward him and Slater.

In case Carpenter had wondered when to start setting off the powder charges atop the row of boulders, the Gatling-gunners made up his mind. Obviously scared out of their wits by the explosion, they were simply spraying everything in front of and around the track with hundred-caliber bullets just as fast as they could crank.

And the gunners were good. One man loaded fresh drums into the gun's breech as soon as the previous drum ran out, and Carpenter doubted that they lost ten seconds in rearming.

So he began setting off the charges.

As soon as the gunners spotted his smoke, they began laying it on with everything they had. The boulders shook as if they'd been kicked by the gods, and rock shards were flying over him like shrapnel. With every charge he touched off, he risked an arm.

Then he heard Slater's gun, and the Gatling was still. Risking a look, he peered from behind a rock. The gunner was blown clean off the car, lying a dozen feet from the track. Then the feeder grabbed the Gatling and was on him once more.

The train was near, ominously near, when the Sharps spoke again. The racketing Gatling was abruptly stilled. This time he jumped straight up in time to see the gunner get one all to himself.

He turned to look at Slater. He was already mounted. The Appaloosa bolted from a jack-rabbit start, and in an instant Slater was galloping parallel to the track. He was going to board the train.

Carpenter was on his horse, following his fellow outlaws. Slater had stationed them all well in front, and they were in full gallop as the train came alongside them.

Carpenter scarcely believed anyone would have the guts to swing on.

It was then that he saw Slater, silhouetted atop the mountainous pile of cordwood, towering over the tender. Bigger than Beelzebub, he stood there with his sawed-off eight-gauge Greener braced on his hip. He was looking down into the locomotive. And when Carpenter saw the shotgun swing off his hip, point down into the engine car, when he saw the flash and the scattergun's kick, he slowed down the roan.

He knew this train was coming to a stop.

Cimarron Rose did not particularly like her job as firewoman. After they had successfully commandeered the Baldwin locomotive, Torn wisecracked that if "she couldn't turn a Gatling any better than her two-dollar tricks, she'd better stoke the firebox."

But while she didn't care for the tone, she recognized his point: Crashing through the border at El Paso-*Ciudad Juarez* would be hell with the hide off. She wouldn't want to handle the Gatling or the eight-gauge or try fighting hand to hand.

And if the border crossing was jammed with *touristas*, a lot of innocent people could get killed.

Also, her job was important. As important as any on the train. They all knew the El Paso-*Ciudad Juarez* set-up, and to get through those barricades they'd have to high-ball. Which meant someone would have to keep that boiler hot.

That was Cimarron. She was stoking the engine. Balk after balk of cordwood she threw into the firebox. Every half hour she raked the box, then fed in more fuel. When she wasn't doing that, she was back in the tender, moving more cordwood to the front so she could get at it faster. She had to check the pressure gauge constantly. The needle must split the blue and the red. If it fell back into the blue, they were losing compression. If it hit the red, she had to pull the steam release valve.

She looked over her shoulder. Hardy, Bass, and Langford were up on the stack of cordwood at the rear of the tender. Abbey and Logan were on the mail car behind them. All were armed with Winchesters and shotguns. When she motioned to them for more wood, they kicked balks of pine down. Otherwise, they just passed a bottle of Old Crow and waited for the border.

On the flatbed car, encircled by stacked-up sandbags, Slater and Carpenter manned the Gatling. Periodically, Slater looked back at Cimarron and raised his fist over his head and pumped it up and down. This meant he wanted more wood, more steam, more speed. He seemed oblivious to the guage's red line.

Rose threw in more balks of wood. Sweat streamed down her face and arms. She was filthy from the dirty cordwood, the smoke and soot. By the time they reached El Paso, she would be bone-tired and black as a navvy.

Still she grinned and threw on more wood. She began to whistle "Yellow Rose of Texas."

She could not remember ever having been so happy.

Now they were five miles from El Paso and the border, high-balling to beat hell. The track edged precipitously around long washes. Steep mountains rose abruptly to the south.

Mostly the land was hot, flat desert—yucca and creosote, sage and prickly pear. Balls of weed tumbled in the dust-laden wind, and a lone, perennial vulture wheeled overhead. Abandoned adobe shacks and unplastered *jacales* began dotting the sides of the roadbed. And then, in the distance, she could see the town.

They were barreling into the city, full-bore. She wanted to shrill the whistle, but Slater had warned her off, saying they needed all the surprise at the border they could get.

She glanced over her shoulder once to check the men behind her. They didn't look happy. The firebox was cooking just as hard as it knew how, and the diamond stack was ablaze with embers and ashes. The men on the woodpile and atop the freight cars were getting it bad. Soot and red-hot cinders were stinging them like angry hornets.

Worse, she didn't like the looks of the steam gauge. The needle had fallen hopelessly off the dial and lay in the red zone as though it were dead. Every time Slater glanced back at her, she gestured toward the needle, but he just shook his head, raised his fist in the air, and pumped it up and down, meaning more balks of cordwood, which she faithfully threw in the box.

Now they were in El Paso. Horses and wagons, adobe huts, and people were all just a high-speed blur. The telegraph poles whipped by like pickets in a fence. The noise in the cab was a constant, ear-shattering roar. And hot? In the El Paso shade it was a good hundred and eleven degrees, and in front of that hellacious firebox, Rose figured a hundred and forty.

When she first heard the howling inside the boiler, she imagined the bone-breaking labor, the desert sun, and the cab's hell-furnace had brought on hallucinations. Because the shrill, banshee shriek echoing through that engine car was like nothing she had ever heard before. The throbbing, wailing scream was now literally exploding out of the depths of the boiler, like the supernatural screeching of some infernal monster, raging dementedly from the farthest reaches of hell.

Then the rivets started to go. They were blowing out of the boiler at a rate of one every five seconds, and in Rose's mind, she thought she heard the popping accelerate. Then it did. Next, they were popping simultaneously, with an irregular, staccato beat, banging, whining, and richocheting around the cab like bullets. She cringed behind the tied-down throttle, her hand reaching instinctively for the steam-release valve, when Slater, as if anticipating her move, turned abruptly, raised his fist, pumped it up and down, and mouthed the words, *More steam! More steam!*

Frantically, almost involuntarily, she threw more balks into the firebox.

When the last balk was in, while the boiler screamed and rivets clanged, she looked down the line and saw it: the American border crossing.

It was empty.

Slater was looking back at her and motioning toward the screech whistle. She opened up. It shrilled and wailed and howled up and down the tracks, letting everyone know they were coming through. As a further warning, Slater cut loose with the Gatling, shattering telegraph transformers, conductors, and insulators as the big locomotive screamed through town.

Through the American border they hauled ass, without a sign of resistance. Over the Rio Grande train trestle they continued to race, and Rose was giddy with excitement. She forgot the red gauge, forgot the banging rivets. She looked instead at the water below, and laughed. The river was perhaps two hundred yards across, and from the looks of the waders, maybe three feet deep in the middle. Rose saluted it as they roared on by.

She turned her head back down the track toward the empty Mexican border crossing, which she had assumed they would just whip on through.

Then it happened.

With an infinite, torturous lassitude, a seeming inch at a time, a burro pulling a two-wheeled ox cart piled high with hay, which was obviously far too heavy for the puny creature, crept up over the train bed, turned, saw the screeching, smoking train, panicked, got twisted up in the harness, lost his temper, sat down obstinately, and brayed.

It was not the biggest ox cart in the world, but it was big enough to derail a Baldwin engine, hauling ass at eighty miles per.

Rose wanted to cry, scream, throw herself on the floor of the cab and beat it with her fists, when Torn Slater turned and froze her with a look. Pumping his fist up and down, he ordered her to pour on more wood.

Which she did.

Carpenter dived to the floor of the flatbed car, put his hands over his head, and, no doubt, prayed.

It was then that Slater went to work. Slamming a fresh drum into the Gatling, he started cranking hundred-caliber, high-speed rounds into the cart. Closer and closer, they moved toward the obstruction. Harder and harder he cranked. One hundred, two hundred, three hundred rounds. Three hundred and fifty. Three hundred sixty.

Smoke and fire poured out of the overheated muzzle. Slowly, with excruciating torpor, hay fluttering in all directions, the cart began to shake, break up, fall apart, shatter.

Then Slater was firing into the cart at point-black range. Rose dived to the bottom of the cab, even as she saw the first pieces of the cart slam into the flatcar, the muzzle of the Gatling nose to nose with the wreck. Slater, still bolt upright, still hammered away.

Now the interior of the cab was simply one deafening, protracted howl—shrieking boiler, popping, banging rivets, the remains of the cart crashing into the Baldwin, metal screaming against metal as the train fought to hold the rails. When she could stand it no longer, she stood up in the car full of whirling splinters, straw, and sawdust, and pulled the whistle cord. Now the screech whistle, shrilling and wailing up and down the track, merged with the rest of the roar, *YIP-YIP-YIPPPINGGG* the news that Outlaw Torn Slater had hijacked an arms train, killed all its two hundred troopers, barreled over the border, the Yankees be damned!

When the sawdust cleared and she looked into the flatcar, Torn was slumped over the Gatling, his head skewed grotesquely, bleeding from the ears and mouth.

The Best of Adventure
by RAMSEY THORNE

5 EXCITING ADVENTURE SERIES MEN OF ACTION BOOKS

Mystery & Suspense by GREGORY MCDONALD

__FLETCH AND THE MAN WHO

(B30-303, $2.95, U.S.A.)
(B30-868, $3.75, Canada)

America's favorite newshound has a bone to pick with a most elusive mass murderer! From the bestselling author of FLETCH'S MOXIE and FLETCH AND THE WIDOW BRADLEY.

__FLETCH AND THE WIDOW BRADLEY

by Gregory Mcdonald (B90-922, $2.95)

Fletch has got *some* trouble! Body trouble: with an executive dead in Switzerland. His ashes shipped home prove it. Or do they? Job trouble: When Fletch's career is ruined for the mistake no reporter should make. Woman trouble: with a wily widow and her suspect sister-in-law. From Alaska to Mexico, Fletch the laid-back muckraker covers it all!

__FLETCH'S MOXIE

by Gregory Mcdonald (B90-923, $2.95)

Fletch has got plenty of Moxie. And she's just beautiful. Moxie's a hot movie star. She's got a dad who's one of the roaring legends of Hollywood. She's dead center in a case that begins with a sensational on-camera murder and explodes in race riots and police raids. Most of all, she's got problems. Because she's the number one suspect!

Great Mysteries by MIGNON G. EBERHART

__ANOTHER MAN'S MURDER

(B31-180, $2.50, U.S.A.)
(B31-182, $3.25, Canada)

Dead man's bluff—the Judge had been the town's leading citizen. Now he was dead, and it was all too clear he had been murdered. The shadow of his death—and of his twisted life—fell heavily upon lovely Dodie Howard. She alone kept the secret which could erupt into scandal, destroying the man she loved. Then one night she woke to see the murderer's hands poised over her throat . . .

__POSTMARK MURDER

(B31-181, $2.50, U.S.A.)
(B31-183, $3.25, Canada)

A strange curse . . . some might have called her lucky. Unexpected and fabulous wealth had descended upon her. But that was only part of her inheritance. For now her life was haunted by the terrifying specter of murder, ready to strike and strike again.

__UNIDENTIFIED WOMAN

(B31-195, $2.50, U.S.A.)
(B31-198, $3.25, Canada)

Crazy quilt of terror . . . To a young and lovely Victoria Steane there seemed no pattern to the murders. Yet one by one they took place—a man found drowned, a girl floating in the river, a woman strangled in the undergrowth. And these were just the beginning. Just one thing was all too terrifyingly clear to Victoria. Step by step the savage murderer was moving closer and closer to her . . .

__HUNT WITH THE HOUNDS

(B31-199, $2.50, U.S.A.)
(B31-200, $3.25, Canada)

At dusk, murder rode with the bright-jacketed huntsmen through woods and fields. Among them was young and pretty Sue Poore, involved with an attractive man, whose wife had been mysteriously murdered. Already under suspicion, Sue was ripe for murder—either as victim or killer. Death, the grim hunter, closed in for the kill . . .

__WITNESS AT LARGE

(B31-205, $2.50, U.S.A.)
(B31-206, $3.25, Canada)

Terror walks the fog-shrouded island. The pretty young girl called Sister knows that violent murder has been done and will be done again. Who is the unseen killer? Can it possibly be Tom, the man she has loved in secret for so long? As she wonders, the long shadow of the murderer moves forward to strike once more . . .